# Top Men

Published by Phaze Books
Also by GA Hauser

Man to Man
Miller's Tale
Pirates
Teacher's Pet
Vampire Nights
Two In Two Out
Double Trouble

# Top Men

# GA Hauser

**Phaze**

EXCEPTIONAL EROTIC FICTION

Top Men Copyright © 2011 by GA Hauser

All rights reserved under the International and Pan-American Copyright Conventions. No part of this book may be reproduced or transmitted in any form or by any means, electronic or mechanical including photocopying, recording, or by any information storage and retrieval system, without permission in writing from the publisher.

The scanning, uploading and distribution of this book via the Internet or via any other means without the permission of the publisher is illegal, and punishable by law. Please purchase only authorized electronic editions, and do not participate in or encourage the electronic piracy of copyrighted materials. Your support of the author's rights is appreciated.

Warning: The unauthorized reproduction or distribution of this copyrighted work is illegal. Criminal copyright infringement, including infringement without monetary gain, is investigated by the FBI and is punishable by up to 5 years in federal prison and a fine of $250,000.

This is a work of fiction. Names, characters, places and incidents either are the product of the author's imagination or are used fictitiously, and any resemblance to any actual persons, living or dead, events, or locales is entirely coincidental.

A Phaze Books Production
Phaze Books
an imprint of Mundania Press LLC
6470A Glenway Avenue, #109
Cincinnati, Ohio 45211-5222

To order additional copies of this book, contact:
books@mundania.com
www.mundania.com

Cover Art © 2011 by Niki Browning
Edited by Stephanie Stephanie Balistreri

Trade Paperback ISBN: 978-1-60659-583-1

First Edition • January 2011

Production by Mundania Press LLC
Printed in the United States of America

10   9   8   7   6   5   4   3   2   1

# Chapter 1

"Ah! Mickey! Not here, you maniac!"

"Shut up and come." Mickey Stanton knelt down in the middle of a living room that was not either of theirs. Unbuckling Jeff's utility belt; the radio, the cuffs, mace, keys, flashlight, and his Glock and extra magazine clips, hung heavily from the leather holders clipping it to Jeff's pant's belt. He flipped Jeff's hard cock from his briefs and wrapped his lips around it.

"Oh, God!" Jeff panted in heaving gasps.

He loved it! Mickey got off on him and Jeff doing wild things on calls. It was such a rush. There they were, in the middle of checking an open premise for a residential burglary alarm in West LA, having oral sex. It just didn't get any better than that.

The scent of Jeff's body, his dark pubic hair brushing his face as Mickey drew him in deep, he felt Jeff on the verge, his cock going rigid and his hands. Mickey reached out to grip Jeff's dark blue uniform shirt.

He wanted to release his own cock and jack off, but he didn't think the residents would like finding spunk on their plush white rug.

"Ah! Oh, Christ!"

Mickey groaned in pleasure as Jeff's cum filled his mouth.

"Eight-Adam-One."

"Ah…Mickey…dispatch is calling…"

"My mouth is occupied." Mickey lapped at the head

of Jeff's cock.

After an audible nervous swallow, Jeff keyed his shoulder mike. "Eight-Adam-One."

"Checking your status on the open premise."

"Under control."

Mickey laughed wickedly.

"Under control, Eight-Adam-One," the dispatcher acknowledged.

Sitting back, he looked up at Jeff's gorgeous face. "You sounded like you just came."

"Shut up." Jeff stuffed his soft cock into his pants and hoisted the heavy gun belt back to his hips. "You are insane."

"Don't you love it?" Mickey stood, wiping his mouth with the back of his hand. "Two cops sucking dick in the middle of a residential alarm? It's so fucking hot."

"Jesus, Mick…" Jeff double checked his zipper and caught his breath. "What am I going to do with you?"

"Suck mine on the next one." He winked, walking out of the living room.

After securing the home, Mickey dropped into the passenger's seat of their patrol car and began writing up a ticket for a false alarm.

Jeff collapsed next to him behind the wheel, resting his head against headrest and the Plexiglas divider that separated the backseat from the front. "I can't believe we got paired up together. What fucking luck, Mick."

"Yes, Officer Chandler, we are fucking lucky." Mickey finished writing the citation and tore off one copy. "Be right back." He hopped out, stuffed the paperwork into the mailbox and returned to the car.

"Lunch?" Jeff waited for him to get buckled in and cram his citation book back into the full nylon briefcase at his feet.

"Just had mine," Mickey replied, licking his lips and giving Jeff a sensuous grin.

"Was it enough to hold you all afternoon?" Jeff put the car in drive and began cruising down the street.

"No. I'll want seconds. Sloppy seconds."

"Shut up." Jeff laughed and slapped Mickey in the chest, hitting his Kevlar vest.

"Christ, I love doing that." Mickey squirmed in the seat.

"Make a decision, Mick. Clear the call and ask for lunch, or just clear the call. We can't milk it much longer."

"I want to milk you." He grabbed Jeff's crotch.

"You already did! Sheesh! Sucked me like a Hoover." Jeff grinned at him. "Clear the damn call."

Mickey picked up the mike. "Eight-Adam-One."

"Eight-Adam-One."

"Clear. Code One-Two."

"Eight-Adam-One, clear Code One-Two."

Mickey hung up the mike and stretched his legs as much as he could in the tight space. "What are you hungry for?"

"My cock up your butt."

Mickey broke up with laughter. "And you say I'm bad!"

Jeff pulled into the parking lot of their usual Mexican restaurant.

"You realize that's the one thing we haven't done on duty yet." Mickey unhooked his seatbelt as Jeff parked.

"On duty? Come on, Mick. It isn't possible." Jeff picked up the mike and asked the dispatcher for a lunch break. She gave them one.

They exited the car and walked together to the entrance.

"I'm not so sure about that," Mickey said. "I bet on the next alarm we could do it. You sitting on my lap. What do ya say?"

"I say you're nuts."

"I've got a rubber and a small packet of lube in my pocket."

"You've got your brains and a horny dick in your pocket." Jeff opened the restaurant door, allowing Mickey to enter first.

"I will nail your ass on duty," Mickey whispered out

of the side of his mouth.

"I doubt that's gonna happen, babe. Too risky." Jeff straightened his expression for the woman who waited for them to approach.

"Hello, boys," the hostess greeted them. "Busy day?"

"Not too bad so far." Jeff smiled at her.

"Got a table up front by the window. I know you guys prefer it."

"Thanks, Conchita." Jeff winked.

Once they sat down she asked, "The usual, or would you like to look at menus?"

Mickey licked his lips wickedly at Jeff. "I know what I want."

"So do I." Jeff chided Mickey with an imploring look and said to Conchita, "The usual, please."

"Coming right up."

Mickey adjusted the volume on his radio so he could hear it but wasn't loud enough to annoy anyone else. "What are we doing tonight?"

Jeff waited as Conchita set down two glasses of water for them. After he thanked her, Jeff sipped his. "What do you want to do?"

"Fuck each other in uniform."

Choking on his water, Jeff cleared his throat. "Don't you get sick of always being in this thing?" Jeff tugged on his shirt.

"Not when my dick is up your ass."

Once he took a look around the area, Jeff leaned over the table. "You're lucky you're so fucking good looking, Stanton, because you're fucking high maintenance."

"Moi?" Mickey pressed his fingers against his chest. "That's crap. I'm so easy to please."

"Yeah, when we do it in risqué places." Jeff took another paranoid glance around.

"Hey, this," Mickey tugged at his own uniform shirt, "is just my stinkin' job, not my whole life."

"Then why do you want us to screw wearing it?"

"'Cause it's hot. I've had a cop fetish since I was ten."
"Yeah, huh?" Jeff finished his water.
"Yeah. Always played cops and robbers and wanted the cops to punish me, handcuff me, and beat a confession out of me. Mm."
"Shh. Food's here." Jeff pointed as Conchita brought over their meals.
"Here you go, men."
"Thank you. You're a doll for getting it out so fast." Jeff smiled at her.
"Enjoy."
"I love the food here." Mickey began devouring his enchiladas.
"And they love us. I hate wondering if someone has spit in my food." Jeff took a big bite of his taco.
"No secret sauce here." Mickey dabbed his lip with a napkin. "We should ingratiate ourselves with our local fire department."
"You mean the two hunks?" Jeff smiled.
"I mean the two hunks." Mickey continued to stuff his face in case an emergency call came across the radio and they had to drop their food and run. "You know they cook dinner and lunch at the fire station. We could happen to stop by at meal time."
"Why don't we just go out with them socially?"
"Yeah?" Mickey sipped his water.
Conchita brought a pitcher and refilled both their glasses.
"You're wonderful," Mickey acknowledged her.
"You're making me blush." She winked and walked to the next table.
"If I was straight, I'd do her." Jeff looked over his shoulder.
"Anyway…" Mickey rolled his eyes. "You want to see Hunter and Blake socially?"
"I wouldn't mind. But other than a few chance meetings on the job, do we really know them?"

Mickey was down to his last bites quickly. "We could get to know them better."

Jeff paused to listen to a call broadcast over radio. He resumed eating calmly, looking up at Mickey.

"You're hot for Hunter," Mickey hissed.

"I am not," Jeff replied, shaking his head.

"No? Why not? Big beefy fireman?"

"I never know what you want me to say?" Jeff pushed his empty plate aside and took out his wallet.

"I keep you on your toes, Officer Chandler."

"That's an understatement." Jeff counted out some singles for a tip.

"We got five minutes. Sit." Mickey slouched, moving his legs to lean against Jeff's under the table.

Jeff mirrored his posture, sitting low in the chair. "I'm fucking wiped. I'm not so sure about this three/twelve bullshit."

"Want to go on four/tens?"

"Can we just do that?"

"You don't like the extra days off?" Mickey drank more water.

"I do, but twelve hours is an eternity." Jeff watched two men pass, staring at them warily.

"Talk to the sarge."

"Would we still work together?"

"How the fuck should I know?"

Jeff straightened his back and leaned over the table. "I love working with you, Mickey. You're so much fun."

Mickey met Jeff over the table, nose to nose. "Likewise."

At their seductive pose, Jeff appeared paranoid and moved back. "Let's hit the road."

After they paid the check and were once again in their black and white patrol car, Jeff cleared their lunch break and headed to their district to cruise the streets. Mickey rested his hand on Jeff's broad thigh, rubbing it affectionately.

"Want to head to Venice Beach and check out the eye candy?" Jeff asked.

"Is anything holding?" Mickey turned to the computer screen that was bolted to the dash between them and typed in some codes to get his information. "Since July fourth, it's really calmed down."

"Yeah, that usually means something huge is going to happen."

"Shut up. I'm not in the mood for a big shooting." Mickey tapped at the keys. "Nothing in our district."

"Eye candy it is."

Mickey returned his hand to Jeff's leg. "I feel like I've known you for longer than three months, Jeff."

Jeff peeked over at him as he drove. "Are you going anywhere with this?"

"Well, yeah." Mickey laughed softly.

"You want us to move in together."

Rubbing Jeff's thigh, he replied, "Smart cop."

"Are you ready to be exclusive? Or just sick of living with your sister?" Jeff parked the patrol car with a good view of the beach and paved path. He kept the motor running with the air conditioning going as nearly nude men and women walked, jogged, or skated by.

Mickey noticed Jeff's attention resting on a very buff stud who was giving him the eye through the windshield. "This isn't about Aura. It's about us. I'm ready, but obviously you're not."

"I don't know. I just moved here from Seattle, Mick. I feel like I haven't had a chance to explore."

Mickey took back his hand and rested it on his own lap.

Jeff looked at him. "Mick, don't go all pouty on me."

"I guess we haven't talked about it, you know, how we feel about each other."

Laughing, Jeff said, "No. It's been pure sex and very little else between us so far."

Mickey paused as the dispatcher announced a new stolen vehicle, information only. "I want to talk to you more. But you fuck me senseless, then go to sleep."

"Twelve hours is a long day, babe." Jeff's eyes wandered

out the window again.

"Well, I suppose at least I know where I stand." He crossed his arms over his chest. Angry, very angry.

Jeff tried to adjust his vest in the confines of the tight seat, pushing it up off his hip. "Mickey, please don't make it an issue between us. We love working together, don't we?"

Suddenly he felt like telling Jeff to fuck off, but didn't answer, instead staring out at the ocean waves.

"Mickey?"

"Why do you have to see other men?" Mickey growled a little more defensively than he'd intended.

"Hang on." Jeff held up his hand. He picked up the mike and responded to their call sign. "Eight-Adam-One."

"A report of shots fired in the area of Hancock Park."

"Roger, Code One." Jeff hung up the mike and put his seatbelt back on.

Mickey rubbed his jaw as they left the beach area. "This isn't an end to the topic."

"I didn't think it would be." Jeff checked the time on his watch.

Mickey thought they had something special. He'd already dated around. There was no Mr. Wonderful or Perfect out there. Jeff Chandler, with his tightly packed body, thick brown hair, and sea green eyes, *was* his Mr. Wonderful. It hurt to find out he wasn't Jeff's.

As they approached the park, Jeff opened the window of his cruiser, listening. "Who's the complainant?"

"Who fucking cares?"

"Mickey," Jeff admonished. "This is why I hate talking."

Mickey read the call off the monitor. "Anonymous."

"Just an area check then." Jeff slowed to a crawl, looking into the park.

For the last few hours of their shift, Mickey tried not to be upset, but it didn't work.

∽∾

While Jeff changed, standing in front of his locker, he kept an eye on Mickey. He didn't want to hurt him. He adored him. But was he ready to "settle down"? Moving south from Seattle was like going on a journey to a foreign land. He'd left behind the wet, cold, skinny, pale men of Rain City and discovered the bronze, masculine beauties of La La Land.

Was it wise to hook up with the first dishy male treat he'd made it with?

Jeff had to admit seeing hot gay firemen kissing after a tragic death of a colleague had a profound effect on him. There were very macho gay males around here that made his mouth water. Shouldn't he explore?

Seeing Mickey dressing in his street clothing, a seductively tight pair of white shorts and a navy blue LAPD t-shirt that had been cut into a midriff showing off Mickey's perfect egg-carton abs, Jeff hurried to finish.

"Hey. Don't walk off." Jeff threw his waist pack with his off duty weapon over his shoulder and slammed his locker shut.

Mickey paused, giving him a roll of his bright blue eyes.

Meeting him, Jeff touched the small of Mickey's back, feeling his warm skin, and urged him out of the locker room. They bid goodnight to the few cops going off duty.

Once they were in the parking lot, in the darkness of the short summer night, Jeff stopped by Mickey's pickup truck. Nudging Mickey to lean back against his rig, he used his fingertips to run along the carved muscles of Mickey's exposed stomach. "Come to my place."

"I can't believe you're asking me over after what you said."

"I just don't know what I want to do. It doesn't mean I don't want to *do* you."

"Are you listening to yourself? You sound like a pig."

"Oink." He licked Mickey's neck.

"Better stop. There're a couple of guys walking out to their car."

Jeff stepped back, waiting as the other officers going off duty entered their private cars and left. "If the guys don't know we're fuck buddies by now, they're stupid cops."

"I just don't want the sarge separating us because he thinks we fool around on duty."

For some reason, that struck Jeff as hilarious. He broke up with laughter and bent over as he roared. After he calmed down, he choked out, "You mean giving each other head every chance we get?"

Mickey whacked him in the arm.

Calming down, Jeff took another scan around the area. They were alone for the moment. He dug his hand into Mickey's blond hair. "Sleep with me."

"Are you using me, Jeff?"

"No. I'm crazy about you." Jeff massaged Mickey's neck tenderly. "Mickey…" he purred, brushing his lips against Mick's.

"Fine. Go." Mickey nudged him.

Jeff allowed his hands to glide down Mickey's shoulders and chest slowly before he parted from him. There was no question Mickey was his type. Six feet tall, solid muscle, blond hair, blue eyes, and movie star good looks. Mickey Stanton turned him on to the extreme. *What the hell am I looking for? Mickey is all I need. Isn't he?*

Making his way to his Mustang, Jeff rested his gun pack on the passenger seat and started the ignition. Licking his top lip as he imagined the sex to come, Jeff was already turned-on. Just the scent of Mickey's body was enough.

They met at Jeff's place. With the help of a large cash inheritance when his grandmother died, Jeff had purchased a three-bedroom townhouse, complete with a clubhouse, spa, and pool. Mickey lived with his older sister, Aura, in an apartment in Cerritos.

Parking, waiting for Mickey at the door, Jeff unlocked it and tossed his heavy gun pack on the coffee table as he passed it. "Beer?"

"Please."

Jeff removed two cold ones out of the fridge. It was nearly eleven, but they needed to unwind before they slept.

Seeing Mickey staring down at the two concealed weapons as they lay together on the table, Jeff handed him the bottle. The minute Jeff's hand was free, he rubbed his palm over Mickey's crotch.

At first Mickey purred, pressing his hips tightly into Jeff's hand, but as if he reconsidered, he stepped back. "I don't like being jerked around."

"I'm not doing that. Not intentionally." Jeff sipped his beer, watching Mickey's expressions while being distracted by his body.

They stood in the dim room, drinking. It seemed his reluctance to commit was making a huge impact on Mickey. Jeff wasn't prepared for that kind of reaction. It had only been a short while since they had begun a sexual relationship.

When they were first assigned together, Jeff had no idea Mickey was gay. It had taken many nights of sitting together, chatting in private before that knowledge was released.

Jeff put his empty beer bottle on the table and closed the gap between them. With his right hand, he dug into the blond hair on the back of Mickey's head, and placed his left on Mickey's ass, drawing their crotches together. Mickey took one last swig, finishing his beer, reaching to set it down.

"Remember when we realized we were both gay?" Jeff whispered, running his hand over the tight globe of Mickey's bottom. "Parked in that vacant church lot? Late at night?" He pressed his lips against Mickey's neck. "The minute we figured it out…remember what we did?"

Mickey released a sensual sigh.

Jeff felt both their cocks pulsate as they pressed together. "We wrapped around each other, on duty, and kissed for almost a half hour in the front seat of our patrol car." He licked his way to Mickey's jaw. "And groped each other's dicks through our uniform trousers…remember?"

Mickey's arms hung limp at his sides, covered with roping veins from his working out.

Jeff lowered his right hand to Mickey's shorts. He flipped open the button. "Your tongue fucked my mouth. It drove me insane." Dragging the zipper down, Jeff dipped his fingers into Mickey's tight clothing. "On duty, in uniform, in our patrol car."

Jeff released Mickey's erection from his briefs, sliding over its length. He chewed his way to Mickey's mouth, running his lips over his coarse shadow. "How many blowjobs have you given me on duty, Mick?" Jeff knew this kind of talk would drive Mickey wild. He ran his tongue over Mickey's bottom lip.

"A dozen?" Jeff took Mickey's lip between his teeth gently for a quick tug. "At least?"

Mickey moaned, his head fell back and his cock bobbed.

"You sucked me every chance you got. Every open premise, back stairwells of tenement houses, the bathroom at the precinct…" Jeff increased his stroking, rubbing his fingers over Mickey's oozing slit, feeling his own cock pressing against his shorts. "And now you want to butt fuck me on duty, you dirty cop…dirty, dirty…"

Mickey grabbed Jeff's head and kissed him, opening his mouth and ramming his tongue inside Jeff's mouth. The force of Mickey's attack propelled Jeff back, slamming him into the coffee table, upsetting the empty beer bottles. They stumbled over the leather chair and hassock as Mickey moved them to his bedroom.

Mickey dragged Jeff's shirt over his head and dropped it on the stairs leading to the second floor. Their mouths still sucking and licking at one another, Mickey tore open Jeff's shorts as Jeff yanked Mickey's t-shirt over his head.

Jeff ran his hand over Mickey's torso and his smooth, taut skin. He was so hot for this crazy blond cop he could spurt. They tripped into Jeff's bedroom, kicking off their shoes and socks, dragging each other's shorts down their thighs. Parting from Mickey's mouth to get him naked, Jeff panted hard, his excitement piqued. Grabbing the material of Mickey's Calvin's, Jeff ripped them down his legs. His own clothing coming off as quickly, the minute they were both nude, they wrapped around each other and connected their mouths again.

The grappling was so rough it was painful. Their growing beards scratching each other's face, the grinding of their cocks was manic in their need to penetrate, to come.

Jeff was going insane. He let loose an animalistic growl and shoved Mickey back onto his bed. Horizontal, they continued to suck on each other's tongues and lips, writhing on the mattress. Unable to take much more, he parted from Mickey's mouth and dug into his nightstand. Under him, Mickey gasped for breath, pumping both their cocks together as he waited.

Shaking from the excitement, Jeff slid the condom on and slathered himself with lube. Once he was ready, he shoved Mickey's legs back roughly, exposing his ass. Grinding his teeth at the longing, Jeff slid inside and hissed out a breath of air, his skin lighting on fire.

"Hard…I want it hard, Chandler…fuck me hard."

Bracing himself on his arms, Jeff dug in deep, his jaw clenched, his chest heaving. Mickey clamped around Jeff's neck and drew him down to his mouth, trapping Mickey's cock between them. The minute it had, Mickey pumped like a mad man, sucking on Jeff's tongue and mouth, groaning loudly.

Sweat running down Jeff's face and chest, he slammed his hips into Mickey as each sensation rose to a peak.

God, he loved fucking this man! Nothing compared to it, nothing!

The intensity beginning to overwhelm him, Jeff felt a rush of tingles up his spine and almost screamed from the pleasure. There was no dainty foreplay between them, never had been. It was direct and to the point, just like their life on the job. Get it done! Get it done right, and get it done now!

Mickey parted from their kiss to breathe and gasp as his cum shot out between them with blasting force.

Delighting in the throbbing heat of Mickey's pulsating

dick and the feel of his spunk filling the gap between their drenched bodies, Jeff's cock went wild inside Mickey's hot hole. Instantly, he felt the pleasure churning in his balls. He arched his back and closed his eyes, thrusting as deep as he could inside Mickey. Opening his mouth, Jeff grunted as he came, "I love fucking you, you mother-fucking gorgeous cop!" he roared like a lion's bellow, hearing it echo in the dark room. Even after he came, he gave another violent thrust against Mickey's sweat soaked body, relishing in the slapping of their wet skin. "Motherfucker," he gasped, hanging his head as he got over the strength of his climax.

Pausing to savor the aftershocks and dull throbbing, Jeff opened his eyes. Mickey was staring at him. The love and adoration in them was so obvious Mickey didn't have to say a word to communicate it to him.

Moving more tenderly now that they had come, Mickey drew Jeff down to his mouth and licked at his lips and dewy face.

"I adore you, Jeff."

Swallowing down his dry throat, Jeff nodded. "Same here, Stanton. Believe me." Still inside, he ground his pelvis against Mickey's ass, wishing he could stay in until he became fully erect again and continue screwing him. It was that good. He always wanted to be inside this man. It was an obsession he knew Mickey was reflecting. They were so similar in so many ways, Jeff had no doubt Mickey was as addicted to his cock as he was to Mickey's.

Mickey wrapped around Jeff's back and held him tight. Closing his eyes, Jeff rested his weight on top of him, exhaustion finally catching up. Feeling his limp cock sliding out of Mickey's body, he allowed Mickey to unwind his bent legs. They kissed tenderly until they almost fell asleep as they were.

Motivating himself, with a supreme effort, Jeff raised himself off of Mickey's prone body. Getting to his feet, he stared down at the sight of a well-fucked man on the bed. Very nice indeed. "Can you move?"

Mickey moaned in reply.

Jeff extended his hand to him. As Mickey clasped it, Jeff hauled the big man to his feet. "Wash and sleep. I can't even see straight at the moment I'm so exhausted."

"Fuck…" Mickey moaned in agreement.

Taking turns at the sink and toilet to brush their teeth, scrub up and urinate, Jeff shut the light and dragged himself to bed. As he dropped down on it with a thud, Mickey did the same. A click of the off switch on the lamp on the nightstand before he settled down and his eyes were closed. Behind him, Mickey spooned him, dragging him against his body.

The feel of Mickey's skin, his soft breath on Jeff's back offered incredible comfort to him. It was strange perhaps, since he was a cop, but sleeping with an officer had its perks. Jeff never felt safer than when he was with Mickey, his partner, and his guardian angel.

# Chapter 2

Daylight filled the room. Mickey squinted his eyes against the brightness. Leaning back, he read the digital alarm clock. Five after nine. A day off. Thank fuck.

Yes, twelve-hour days were torture, but the time off in between was bliss.

Rolling his head on the soft pillow, he found Jeff still sound asleep, lying on his stomach. Jeff's arms were relaxed over his head. His tanned shoulders and upper back were exposed from the sheet that road low on his hips. Mickey smiled in contentment. The first minute Mickey set eyes on this lateral transfer from SPD he was in lust. Sergeant Bryant had Jeff work with each member of the squad to give him a chance to get to know them. Mickey was so jealous he had to wait his turn he went crazy. Finally, beautiful, brown-haired, green-eyed Jeff Chandler sat in the passenger's seat next to him for twelve hours. Yes!

Mickey was hard most of the shift. Jeff's dimples appeared when he smiled. He had such classic good looks that he could have been a pin-up boy or a magazine photo. He hardly looked real.

And LA had so many pretty men it was difficult for anyone to stand out. Jeff stood out.

The minute he spotted Jeff in their roll call room, he had nudged one of his fellow squad members, Flo Bower. Flo knew he was gay. One of the few he'd revealed his secret to. "Look at that, Flo. Is he one of ours?"

"I have no idea. Wow."

"I got dibs," Mickey whispered. It made Flo laugh.

And when Sergeant Bryant assigned him and Jeff as an Adam car, Mickey almost spontaneously combusted. *That man? Next to me? All the time? Be still my heart!*

Mickey knew damn well he'd struck gold. Even if he never told Jeff he was gay, they would be friends. *Oh, yes.* He'd have it no other way.

Jeff stirred in his sleep, moving to his side. Now Mickey could ogle Jeff's chest. How he loved to suck those nipples.

They got along so well, right from day one. Mickey asked Jeff out after shift for a beer. Being the new guy, Jeff didn't hesitate. The entire squad met at a sports bar with a video arcade. With a football game blaring from the big screen televisions, he and Jeff sat side by side on motorcycles that simulated racing. Four across, they shoved in their quarters in the slot and went crazy watching their animated images either pass each other or wipe out on the screen.

Jeff was good fun. He never hesitated to try anything even though he was the stranger.

Mickey stared at Jeff's dark brown stubble on his jaw and his hair a mess from his deep slumber. As far as Mickey was concerned, Jeff was one sexy fucker. All male. A strong, big, delicious top. Mickey was tired of being top male in all his encounters. Yes, cops were the pinnacle of the food chain, eating all the others below them, and because of that, civilian guys always wanted Mickey to dominate. Mickey liked it, but having a guy like Jeff take over? Fuck him into submission? Sublime.

*Let's live together, Officer Chandler.* Mickey wanted this man in his bed every morning. Oddly enough, he was always in Jeff's bed. Aura never saw him anymore except to stop by for his mail. All his spare uniforms were in Jeff's closet.

When Jeff's eyes opened, Mickey almost jumped at the unexpected flash of green irises.

"Morning."

Mickey gave him a seductive smile and moved closer.

"Morning."

Jeff turned to have a peek at the clock. "It is a day off, right?" He yawned, rubbing his face.

"Uh huh." Mickey connected their bodies.

"Let me piss and brush my teeth."

"Okay." Mickey followed Jeff to the bathroom.

They alternated using the toilet and the sink. Mickey spat out the toothpaste and watched Jeff in the mirror. Wondering if Jeff had woken up on the wrong side of the bed, Mickey rinsed his mouth and said nothing.

After Jeff urinated, he washed his hands and looked at himself in the mirror.

About to ask if Jeff wanted him to leave, Mickey got his answer when Jeff grabbed his cock. Blinking in surprise, he teased, "Ow?"

"It didn't hurt, ya baby." Jeff gathered all of Mickey's genitals into his palm.

"What are you planning on doing with it now that you've got it?"

Jeff grinned wickedly. "Get back to bed. Now."

Mickey backed up as Jeff's grip on his balls didn't relent. When he felt the bed at his legs, Mickey stated, "Uh, you do realize I can't go anywhere without my dick."

Jeff shoved him backward roughly.

Reaching out behind him, Mickey braced his fall and slowed down his progress to getting horizontal once more. With his feet still on the floor, he relaxed, placing his hands behind his head to wait and watch.

Jeff knelt on the carpet between Mickey's thighs. When he pushed his legs apart, Mickey flinched.

"Tightly wound this morning, Stanton?" Jeff laughed.

"Just trying to get used to an aggressive wolf."

"Grrr…" Jeff grinned devilishly and began devouring his balls.

Mickey felt chills race over his body. Closing his eyes, he was happy to receive. Too many times he'd been the one to give. The one to play alpha male. Did all gay civilians think cops only liked topping?

The teasing was beginning to make him squirm. Jeff had a technique of using his teeth that kept Mickey on the edge between pleasure and pain. He'd never experienced anything like it. Mickey tilted his head backward, looking at the strip of condoms and lube that was out of reach on the nightstand. He wanted Jeff to use it. In a gesture that was purely symbolic, Mickey reached his arm toward it, well short of coming close enough to touch what he desperately needed. He heard Jeff laugh. Turning his attention back to this sex machine, Mickey asked, "What are you laughing at?"

"You." Jeff licked Mickey's cock with a long slow lap. It was standing straight out from his body and bobbed from the tease.

Mickey drew his arm back down to his side slowly.

"Want me in?" Jeff ran his tongue into the oozing slit of Mickey's cock.

Knowing the answer to that absurd question was obvious; Mickey didn't give Jeff the satisfaction. Though he knew damn well he would give him satisfaction in the end. Literally.

"Beg me." Jeff held Mickey's cock perpendicular to Mickey's body and stroked it with his tongue from the base to the tip, using his scratchy jaw to rough it up a little. Some S&M teasing that they both adored but would never admit.

With each flick of that velvety tongue mixed with the sandpaper of Jeff's chin, Mickey's hips jerked up. Watching Jeff's expression of pure, savage lust, Mickey was indeed ready to beg. Even his ass began to throb in longing.

"Mickey…" Jeff hissed, tickling his tongue under the head of Mickey's cock.

Mickey's dick swelled from the touch. His chest rose up and down as his breathing intensified.

When Jeff began tormenting Mickey's anus, rubbing his index finger around the rim and pressing against it, Mickey shivered visibly.

"You want my cock inside you, Mickey?" Jeff sucked the head of his dick, wetting it and then allowing it to slide out of his lips again. Then he blew on it teasingly, drying it off.

*God! I love you, you fantastic fucker!* That was all Mickey wanted to say at the moment. But he needed to play the game. A game he craved so much—the game of sex.

Trying to slow his panting, Mickey laced his fingers behind his head for a better view. Now Jeff's demonic grin was visible behind Mickey's cock.

"Playing hard to get, Mick?" Jeff kneaded his balls, rubbing warm friction against the root to Mickey's ass as he chewed on the head of Mickey's cock lightly.

A blast of sensation echoed through his body. Mickey dropped his head back to the bed and closed his eyes as he endured it. The craving to reach down and pump his dick was overwhelming but he knew Jeff would get too much of a laugh if he did that.

Jeff raised Mickey's legs off the floor and pressed them backward against Mickey's body.

Feeling Jeff's tongue enter his ass, Mickey gave in. "Fuck me! All right?" Jeff's tongue only got more assertive. Mickey gripped the bed, his knees, anything to keep from howling in anticipation of what was to come. Peeking down again, Mickey found his dick blushing reddish purple it was so fucking hard. "Chandler! Goddamn it. I said fuck me." Jeff chewed on the root of Mickey's cock as he returned to the front of Mickey's body. His balls were next to be consumed. Mickey's dick dripped as it stood erect.

When Jeff made his way up Mickey's shaft, Mickey almost came as his cock sunk all the way to into Jeff's throat.

"Agh! Jeff!" Mickey's head spun. He was right on the edge.

When Jeff completely released contact to walk around the bed to the nightstand, Mickey rubbed his face only to prevent jacking off. The craving to come was so intense, Mickey knew the minute Jeff entered him, he was going to spurt.

Tilting to watch, Mickey licked his lips at the sight of Jeff slipping on a condom. Jeff's dick was so hard it too was blushing and solid. As Jeff made his way back around the bed again, Mickey gripped his knees and spread wide. "Come on, baby. Come and get it."

Jeff got to his knees and slid into Mickey's well-worked hole effortlessly. There was no need for prepping, Mickey had taken it up the ass so many times from Jeff he was always ready.

The sensation of being filled made Mickey groan in ecstasy. He loved it, fucking loved it! And no one fucked him like his partner in crime, no one.

Jeff positioned himself to aim for Mickey's magic spot. The second Mickey felt Jeff's cock ride over his prostate, his body jerked up in reflex. "Ah! Yes! You fucker, you know just how to get me crazy!"

All Jeff did was give him a wicked chuckle in reply before he rammed inside again.

Mickey knew it was going to be amazing. As Jeff thrust between his legs, he grabbed Mickey's cock tightly.

That was it. Mickey couldn't hold back another minute. Bucking into Jeff's palm, his jaw felt so tight he thought he'd gnash his teeth from the power. Christ, no one made him come this hard! It began in his balls, which seemed to be connected to the sensation in his ass, which blasted up his torso to his face. It was an entire body, out of body, experience that Jeff seemed to be the only one to create in him. And he knew damn well Jeff knew it.

"Aaaauuughfuckk!" Mickey roared as it sent him into orbit.

As he rocked and convulsed like he was having an attack, Mickey climaxed. Hot cum hit him under his jaw and sprayed his neck. As Jeff milked Mickey's cock, he hammered into him, hissing air between his clenched teeth.

Forcing himself to return from his swoon, Mickey propped his head up to watch. The expression on Jeff's face was awe-inspiring: eyebrows knitted together, his teeth showing under his snarl, and his cheekbones etched deeply as he inhaled. Mickey felt a very strong throbbing preceding what he knew was going to be magma flowing. He held his breath in anticipation of Jeff's orgasm and watched as it hit him in glee.

"Fuck!" Jeff choked as he grunted, slamming his hips against Mickey's body. Howling in pleasure, Jeff threw his head back and arched his spine, as if trying to meld into Mickey's body as one. He certainly believed they were connected deeply. And to Mickey the link was more than physical; it was a spiritual bond he had never felt with another soul. The sex only seemed to reinforce their powerful commitment to each other.

Mickey felt Jeff's cock pulsating like mad inside him. "Oh, yes… That's what I was waiting for."

Another solid thrust of his hips and Jeff pressed as deep as he could inside Mickey, grinding against his body as the aftershocks rocked him.

Smiling in delight at seeing such an intense climax, Mickey already felt his dick respond to the sight. When Jeff's eyes finally opened, Mickey grinned wickedly at him. "Dirty cop."

Jeff laughed wearily.

After a moment to recover, Jeff pulled out, sitting on the carpet on his heels, catching his breath.

Mickey scooted off the mattress to kneel beside him. Tenderly, he caressed Jeff's coarse jaw. The act caused Jeff's eyes to meet his. Mickey loved him. There was no question he loved Jeff. Could he say it? Put his heart out there to a man who wasn't sure he wanted to commit? No way.

Jeff touched Mickey under his chin. When Mickey looked he found his own cum on Jeff's finger.

"Good one, Stanton?" Jeff laughed.

"It's always a good one with you, Chandler."

Jeff licked Mickey's cum off his finger sensually.

Mickey cupped Jeff's face and brought him to his lips. The minute their mouths connected, Mickey knew he was already gone. There was no way he had ever loved anyone the way he loved this man.

⁂

Jeff wrapped around Mickey for that kiss. Post-coital affection. Yes, he loved it. So? Did that make him a woman? Inhaling deeply, he enjoyed Mickey's scent. All over. He could nestle into his armpits and drift off to sleep. Parting from their kiss to gaze into his blue eyes, Jeff brushed Mickey's blond hair back from his forehead and smiled at him. "I need to wash up. I still have a fucking condom on my dick."

Mickey hauled Jeff up to his feet and held his hand as he led him to the bathroom.

Staring at Mickey's tight ass as he walked, Jeff adored the fact that he had just been in it. "Christ, you look good from behind, Stanton."

Mickey tilted over his shoulder. That sexy smile of his melted Jeff. Turned him into mush.

What was he looking for? Who the hell was out there as good as Mickey? He was the complete package. Six feet tall, built like a fucking quarterback with thick, wavy blond hair, sky blue eyes, and a big dick. And that was just the outer wrapper. Inside, Mickey Stanton was a loving, loyal, generous friend, and a damn good cop to boot.

Jeff had dated civilians in Seattle and hated it.

*"What kind of gun do you carry? Why do cops always give out speeding tickets to good people? Have you ever shot anyone? Ever beat a confession out of a 'perp'?"*

Perp? Who the hell said that? No one he knew of. *Perp.* The minute a man said 'perp' to him, Jeff was gone.

When he first became a cop, everyone warned him he'd lose all his civilian friends. That was a lie. He kept all his pre-cop civilian friends. All of them. Of course, now they were all long-distance friends. Telephone calls and e-mails.

None of them knew he was gay. No one suspected a thing. Only his family knew. That was it.

Even in a liberal city like Seattle, where there was a

huge gay population, being an out, gay cop wasn't exactly good for your health. He had hopes LA would be different, but cops were cops: macho men who strutted around talking about fucking women. The married ones cheated every chance they got and, inevitably, cops had a very high divorce rate.

When Mickey stepped into the shower, reaching out for him, Jeff smiled in delight.

Jeff spread his legs and placed his hands on the door and tiled wall. They had a shower routine. One Jeff savored.

Watching Mickey pour liquid soap onto a washcloth, Jeff waited for his scrub down. It began at his neck and worked its way south. He closed his eyes as Mickey washed him. In response, his cock grew hard and they usually jerked off or sucked each other. It didn't matter that they had just fucked like mad. Showering with Mickey always made him hot.

The soft material of the washcloth rubbed between Jeff's legs. *Oh yes...that's it, Mickey.*

It didn't take much. Jeff was fully erect again.

Mickey continued down each of Jeff's legs to his feet. It was erotic and relaxing at the same time. Nudging him, Mickey let him know to turn around. Jeff faced the rear wall in the same position. His back and ass were washed briskly. When that tickling cloth rubbed against his balls and anus from behind, he let out a low moan.

Mickey chuckled.

"Here."

Jeff opened his eyes and took the cloth—Mickey's turn. Reloading with coconut-scented soap, he began at Mickey's neck, going through the same routine with him. It was tender and sweet after all the violence they had to deal with at work. The contrast wasn't lost on Jeff. He craved the compassion, especially if the week on duty was particularly brutal. It was as if their time together kept his viciousness in check. Yes, he was a big tough cop, but that was only who he was at work.

Mickey moaned as Jeff cleansed him. They both looked forward to this ritual.

Once Jeff had scrubbed him front and back, he poured shampoo into his hand and washed Mickey's blond mop of hair. Mickey moaned in pleasure, arching back into Jeff's hands as Jeff massaged his scalp for him.

"Rinse." Jeff washed his hands under the spray.

Mickey closed his eyes and allowed the water to run over his head.

They swapped places. Jeff turned his back to Mickey and closed his eyes. The first touch of Mickey's hands to his hair made his skin erupt with goose flesh. The shampooing always came with a scalp massage to die for. It sent tingles all over his body. "Christ, Mick…"

"Mmm," Mickey hummed in agreement.

When Mickey tapped him to rinse, Jeff felt like he was in a trance from the massage. Making sure all the soap was off him, Jeff shut off the taps and they stood dripping, staring at each other. He opened his arms and Mickey sealed his wet skin against Jeff's front. They kissed. It was as slow and as tender as the quiet, peaceful scrubbing.

This was what days off were all about to Jeff. Unhurried lovemaking. He enveloped Mickey in his embrace, squeezing him tight. Tiny whimpers erupted from Mickey as they rubbed their wet crotches together.

When Jeff parted to look into Mickey's eyes, he felt spellbound by the emotion in him. Who was he kidding? Mickey loved him. Jeff fucking knew he did.

Glancing down, Jeff watched as Mickey pressed their erections together tightly in two hands. The act made Jeff shiver in delight. They were sex fiends. Two testosterone filled sex-aholics. So? Did it matter? It was their business. Yeah cops were nosy, cops loved gossip, couldn't help themselves from poking their noses into other people's business. But not theirs. The sex he and Mickey had was between them. And neither could get enough.

When they weren't actually having sex, they were

talking about it. When they weren't talking about it, they were thinking about it. Maybe that was what macho men who were drawn to the paramilitary and military services were like. Too much fucking testosterone for anyone's good.

But having a man who wanted it as much as you did? A partner who never said no? Bliss.

He clasped his palms around Mickey's. Going wild, almost jumping off the ground he wanted to hump so hard, Jeff felt Mickey squeezing tighter, so he did as well. The sensation of friction was amazing. "Goddamn it, Mick!"

Mickey gave a one-syllable laugh as he continued to fist them frantically. Jeff knew they liked it rough. The harder and more violent, the more intense the orgasm. Yeah, so what?

Grinding his jaw as it became unbelievable and the sensation of being this close to coming but not quite there had arrived, Jeff wished he could hover on that plateau for hours. "Yeah, yeah…" he panted in time with Mickey's fisting.

"Oh, Christ, Chandler…oh, fuck…"

That was Mickey's signal. Jeff forced Mickey's hands to move even faster, a beige blur of knuckles. "Come! Come!" Jeff urged; he was there.

Mickey let go, his deep masculine grunting echoed off the wet tiles. As his spunk erupted over both their hands, Jeff joined him, loving the climax like a drug. Forcing his eyes to open when they inevitably closed during the act, Jeff watched their sperm co-mingle and ooze down the backs of their hands.

As Mickey caught his breath, Jeff released his grip on his hand and dropped heavily against Mickey's body as he recuperated.

Mickey hugged him, rubbing his back gently as they both caught their wind.

Jeff knew it was perfection between them. He just had to get his emotions caught up to his libido.

# Chapter 3

Dressed in a pair of shorts, Jeff filled their mugs with coffee while Mickey fried eggs in a pan on the stove.

Pouring milk into Mickey's cup, he set them near the flatware already on the table. "Do you need to stop home?"

"I should. I need some clean clothing."

The toast popped. Jeff took the bread out of the toaster and buttered them up. "I can do a load of laundry. I need to do one anyway."

"Okay. I still wouldn't mind getting some things." Mickey used a spatula to set two eggs on each plate.

"Thanks." Jeff moved out a chair and waited for Mickey to join him before he ate.

He loved Mickey in that cut off, midriff t-shirt and tight shorts. Though much of his skin showed, there was just enough of him covered to tantalize.

Once Mickey sat across from him, Jeff began eating. "Good. Thanks."

"It's just an egg." Mickey smirked at him.

"Still tastes good. And it's just how I like it." Jeff dabbed his toast into the runny yolk.

As they ate quietly, Jeff wondered how much thought Mickey had given to that conversation they had had. The one about commitment and cohabitating. He hoped Mickey wasn't thinking about it at all. They really were doing well with the arrangement they had. Why ruin a good thing? If things went bad, Mickey had his sister's apartment to run to when he needed to cool off. If they moved in together, in a permanent situation, and things got rocky, what then?

"Do you want to do anything else today?"

"Like what?" Jeff wiped his lips with a napkin.

"Hit the beach?"

"Definitely!" Jeff sipped his coffee. "I can't get enough of the sun and warmth."

Mickey laughed at him. "Rain City blues?"

"Fuck yeah. I hated the weather up there." He pointed to his arm. "See this? This is a tan. T-A-N. You know what they call it up north?"

"No. What?"

"Rust."

Mickey laughed, his eyes sparkling.

"You think I'm joking." Jeff bit his toast. "It's fucking wet up there. Wet and cold."

"That does suck."

"I swear, Mick, I'll never complain about the heat here."

"Then you'll be the only one." Mickey finished his eggs and set his fork and knife on the plate, drinking his coffee.

"I know it gets hot here. I still don't care." Jeff stacked his plate on top of Mickey's. "I'll wash, you cooked."

"Thanks." Mickey's gaze seemed unfocused.

Jeff knew he was deep in thought. He couldn't even bring himself to ask what he was thinking about. "So? Which beach? Malibu? Venice? Long?"

"Malibu. Forget Venice." Mickey narrowed his eyes at him. "You'd be ogling pecs all day."

"Oh? No nice looking men in Malibu?" Jeff teased.

"Less. At least it's not muscle beach."

Jeff had an urge to reassure Mickey, but he wasn't so sure he liked Mickey's possessiveness. Couldn't they just be themselves? Standing, he took the plates to the sink to wash.

"Just stick them in the dishwasher."

"Two plates?" Jeff shook his head. "It'll take me two seconds."

Mickey set both their empty mugs in the sink and leaned against the counter as he washed.

When he felt Mickey's hand caress his bottom, Jeff winked at him adoringly. "Horny again?"

"Just looking at you makes me horny."

"Yes, I'm at my sexiest with my hands in the kitchen sink."

Mickey moved to stand behind him, rubbing his hard-on into Jeff's backside.

As Jeff swished a sponge around the plate, Mickey's fingers dug into his gym shorts. Pausing, he closed his eyes as Mickey massaged him front and back. Mickey got him so hot it made him crazy. Leaning his hands on the sink, Jeff enjoyed Mickey's fingers wrapping around his shaft and Mickey's cock rubbing his ass crack.

He shut off the running water and closed his eyes again, allowing Mickey to give and permitting himself to receive. Lowering Jeff's shorts down his hips, Mickey pushed his dick pushed between Jeff's legs and freed Jeff's cock from his shorts. Jeff peered down as Mickey's hand worked him. He trapped Mickey's cock, locking it inside his thighs.

Gripped to the kitchen sink, Jeff ground his jaw as the pleasure rose. Behind him, Mickey was ramming his dick up under Jeff's balls, his hand becoming a blur as it jacked Jeff off in a frenzy.

Jeff groaned, his knees going weak as Mickey lit the fire in him yet again. He came, his cum spurting like a fountain, splashing over the ledge and into the sink. When it oozed over Mickey's fingers, Mickey jammed hard against Jeff's body. Mickey's cock shivered and a river of hot liquid dripped down Jeff's inner thighs.

Catching his breath, Jeff gulped air as Mickey rested his head on Jeff's back. When his cock was released, he blinked and looked down at it. Mickey backed up, separating from him.

As he recuperated, Jeff leaned his forearms on the sink, staring at the wet silverware in the bottom of the stainless steel basin. He felt Mickey mopping up cum from his thighs with a napkin. He spread his legs as far as he could with his shorts at his knees. "Thanks."

"My pleasure."

Once he was tended, Mickey hoisted Jeff's shorts back up his hips. Jeff tucked his cock into his briefs and turned on the water to continue where he'd left off. Once he finished, he wiped his hands on a towel and checked he wasn't covered in sperm.

Tossing the towel over a cabinet door, Jeff ran his hand through his hair. "Right. The beach."

"The beach." Mickey smiled.

"You still have your bathing suit here?" Jeff asked.

"I think so." Mickey headed to the staircase.

"If it's here, it'll be in the bottom drawer of the dresser." Jeff followed him.

"K."

Pausing at the threshold of his bedroom while Mickey gathered his things, Jeff had a strange thought. Were they already living together? When the hell had that happened?

∽∾

Mickey packed a rucksack with towels and sunscreen. His Speedo under his shorts, he left his wallet in the bedroom and propped his sunglasses on top of his head. "Do we want to take any bottled water?"

"Huh? Oh. Sure." Jeff headed down the stairs.

Mickey followed, feeling an odd vibe suddenly. "Jeff? You still want to go to the beach?"

"Yes." Jeff handed him two bottles of water.

Dropping the pack on a chair, Mickey stuffed the water inside, zipping it back up. "Officer Chandler, what the hell just happened?"

"Huh?" Jeff spun on his heels. "Happened?"

Mickey shook his head. "Never mind." He slung the pack on his shoulder and muttered, "Who's driving?"

"I will."

Mickey was hoping he would. Walking to the front door, he made sure his mobile phone was on and put it into the tiny front pouch of the backpack. Mickey looked back at him. "What are you doing?"

"What?"

"You're taking your gun? To the beach?"

Jeff looked down at the waist pack with his off duty weapon in it. "I...in Seattle I always carried it with my badge."

"What are we going to do with it when we go swimming?" Mickey couldn't believe how distracted Jeff had become. Three climaxes later, he would have thought Jeff would be all over him with kisses and hugs. *You call this gratitude? More like lost in the Twilight Zone.*

"Shit. Don't we have to take them?"

"Put the damn gun somewhere and let's just go." Mickey checked his watch. When Jeff stood there and did nothing, he dropped the backpack and stormed over to him. Something happened. Mickey had no idea what, but a switch had been flipped in Jeff and he could read his expression of apprehension a mile away. He wasn't stupid and he knew this fucking cop way too well. "Okay. What's going on?"

Jeff met his eyes but said nothing.

Crossing his arms over his chest, Mickey felt like screaming. "Jeff!"

"I'll put the gun away."

"Take mine too." Mickey picked his gun pack up from the coffee table where he had left it the night before and handed it to him.

Nodding, Jeff jogged up the stairs.

In the silence that followed, Mickey asked himself, "What the fuck?" Wracking his brains, Mickey tried to figure out what went wrong between the kitchen climax and the move to go to the beach. He was completely at a loss. Rubbing his face he retraced their exact movements and replayed the words in his head. What was it? He was lost. There was no way he could understand where this moment had gone bad.

But that was becoming typical Jeff. One minute hot, next cold. It was wearing on him and all he wanted was simplicity.

When his mobile phone rang, Mickey turned to the backpack and knelt down to open the zipper part. He recognized his sister's phone number. "Hello, Aura."

"Hey, Mouse."

"Hey." Mickey stood stiffly, very angry at Jeff, leaning his back against the front door.

"I assume you're at Jeff's."

"Yes. We were going to hit the beach." Mickey's eyes darted to the staircase Jeff had ascended.

"Must be nice having weekdays off. You don't have the crowds."

"It's summer, Aura. Believe me. It'll be packed."

"So, are you living there now?"

"Good fucking question." Mickey stood off the door and thought about it. Was that what was bugging Jeff? Was that the reason for his weird mood? It made so much fucking sense. Son of a bitch! His bathing suit... Was the fact that he had his bathing suit here what turned Jeff into an ass?

Mickey kept his eyes on the stairs and assumed Jeff was emptying the bullets from the guns and locking them up.

"Uh oh. Trouble in paradise?"

Hearing noises from the upper floor, Mickey whispered, "I can't really talk now, Aura. But he's pissing me off."

"When are you coming home again?"

"Tonight. I don't think I should sleep here every night. He's beginning to resent it or something."

"Fuck him."

"I have. It hasn't helped." He heard her laugh. "I have to go, sweetie."

"See you tonight for dinner? I can cook."

"You don't have to cook for me after a full day at work."

"I like to. I don't like cooking for one."

"Let me get back to you." Mickey met Jeff's eyes as he rounded the bend at the bottom of the staircase.

"Okay, Mouse. But at least give me some notice so I can stop at the grocery store."

"I'll try. Bye." Mickey closed his phone and glared at Jeff.

"Who was that?"

"What the fuck do you care?"

Jeff approached him menacingly. "Don't mouth off. It's just a simple question."

"I don't even want to go to the fucking beach with you at the moment, Chandler." Mickey stuffed the phone back into the pack.

"What the fuck did I do?" Jeff puffed up his chest.

Mickey had seen him do that on duty. Trying to look bigger and meaner than he really was. It worked with the stupid suspects, but it didn't work with him.

Standing to face him, Mickey argued, "Your fucking attitude, Jeff. It sucks sometimes."

"I didn't say a fucking thing!"

"You think I'm stupid?" Mickey crossed his arms over his chest.

"You know what? Just go the fuck home."

"Gladly!" Mickey stormed past him to the stairs to get his keys and wallet. "Where'd you put my fucking gun, asshole?"

"Wait and I'll get it for you, *asshole*," Jeff mimicked.

Mickey's chest was heaving. He was so angry he could kill Jeff. *What the fuck? What the fuck? You want me for sex, but that's it? Fuck this!*

He ascended the stairs. Mickey was livid. There was nothing worse than feeling used. Nothing. And he wasn't the type to allow himself to be walked over, hardly. He was too fucking proud to put up with that kind of treatment. *No fucking way, Chandler!*

Stuffing his keys and wallet into his shorts' pockets, Mickey waited as Jeff opened a strong box in his closet with a key. He tossed the pieces of Mickey's Glock onto the bed, including the magazines and the one round from the chamber.

Mickey assembled it quickly, fury rising. Once it was

complete, he jammed the magazine into the butt and chambered a round with a threatening *ka-chunk* sound. He held it in his hand, his index finger off the trigger, glaring at Jeff. The weapon feeling heavy, yet very familiar in his grip, he knew it made him look fierce, and was reluctant to hide it in his gun pack at the moment. The resentment in him was too great, and the urge to use it to intimidate Jeff was almost too strong to resist.

Jeff glanced down at the black gun first, before making contact with Mickey's eyes. "What the fuck did I do to you?"

"I'll say it again, Chandler, I'm not an idiot. I get it, okay?"

"Get what?"

"*I'm good for a fuck!*" Mickey roared, his hand tightening on the gun. "*A fuck*, Chandler!"

"Put that goddamn gun away. Now!"

It was Jeff's police ordering voice. Mickey knew it well. Mickey ran his fingers over the textured grip. Domestic violence with a handgun. The image did flash across his brain. How many shootings in LA were domestic? A lot. Good. Maybe the sight of a loaded pistol was just the fucking wakeup call Jeff needed.

As Mickey thought about it, he realized how idiotic that idea was.

"What are you going to do, Stanton? Shoot me?" Jeff splayed out his hands.

Feeling guilty for his thoughts, Mickey threw the gun on the bed rendering it harmless and placing them both back on level ground.

When he did, Jeff walked over to him. "I thought we were going to have a decent day at the beach. I get ready, lock up the guns, and after some phone call you're furious with me."

"Is that how you see it?" Mickey grinned but he wasn't happy. It was more a grimace than a smile. How stupid did Jeff think he was? More like Jeff was feeling the sting of rejection this time. *Take that, ya bastard. How's it feel?*

"Yeah. Where did I mess up? I was locking up the guns and we were on our way out."

"You're a fucking idiot."

"Now I'm an idiot?" Jeff threw up his hands. "Just go."

When Mickey reached for his gun, Jeff flinched and backed up. Not wanting to terrify Jeff, he locked back the slide, removing the chambered round to calm Jeff down. "How could you ever think I would harm you?" Just the thought that Jeff might think he could actually point the thing at him brought a lump of emotion to Mickey's throat.

"You been to any DVs lately?"

Knowing that meant Domestic Violence, it didn't surprise Mickey in the least they had the same thoughts. He slid the gun and loose bullet into his its waist pack and fastened it around his hips. Without looking back, he descended the stairs. Opening the rucksack up, he dumped out what was Jeff's including the water bottles and took his own items out. "Can I collect the rest of my shit some other time? I can't stand the sight of you at the moment."

"Whatever."

Without making eye contact, Mickey left. The heat outside was brutal. LA in August. Maybe the Seattleite thought it was pleasant, but Mickey had lived here all his life. LA summers sucked as far as he was concerned. Half the state was always on fire. He climbed into his pickup truck and started the engine. When he forced himself to look back at the front door, it was closed. The pain of leaving Jeff behind when they had planned on spending their free time together bit hard. It was always the remorse after the battles that bothered Mickey the most. He hated when they were angry at each other. It drove him crazy and made him hostile and preoccupied.

He parked at his apartment building in Cerritos. Three fucking days off without Jeff? How bad did that suck?

Slamming his truck door, he armed it and stormed to the lobby door from the parking garage. He was so angry he was grinding his teeth. After unlocking the door, he opened it so hard it clattered against the wall with a bang. Throwing doors back as he progressed, Mickey bypassed the elevator for fear of breaking it because he'd punch the buttons too hard, and walked up the staircase which was on the outside of the building. Two flights up, he impaled the lock with another key, shoving it back and slamming it loudly behind him.

Standing still, breathing fire, Mickey took a minute to react and unfastened his gun pack. He tossed it on the table with his wallet and keys. He needed to vent somehow. He needed a punching bag. Instead, he changed out of his bathing suit and into his running outfit and pocketed his key.

In the burning heat of that August day, Mickey ran his tension off with the sweat that poured from his body.

And all the while he did, he thought of Jeff Chandler and what it would take to urge the man he loved that their relationship was right and he needed to see it. But you can't force someone to love you when they don't.

"You're just a good screw, Stanton," he muttered bitterly, "take it for what it's worth and forget it."

But he couldn't. He loved Jeff too much to either give up on him or forget him. He knew he'd be in agony for a very long time.

He was possessive, jealous, quick to anger, all those wonderful qualities women hate in men, and men don't like in other men either. But that was who Mickey was. Yet, he knew if Jeff wanted a devoted friend, loyal lover, or partner for life, he could be that as well. That was the trade off. "Am I worth it, Chandler? Huh?"

All the inner chastising and arguing was defeating the purpose of the run. Mickey wasn't releasing any stress at all, he was beating himself up with physical punishment, but getting nowhere in his mind.

He wanted more from Jeff than Jeff was willing to give him. That was the fact. And if Mickey did not face that fact, he would lose Jeff forever with his pushing.

Wiping at his eyes as they teared, and sweat burned

them, Mickey battled the oppressive heat and put miles behind him trying to cope.

*※*

*Fuck this. I'm still going.*

Jeff went to the beach. Parked in a pay lot, he slid his flip-flops on and carried his pack over his shoulder. Pushing his sunglasses higher on his nose as they slid down from his sweat, he raised his head to the gorgeous white sand and aqua blue ocean. Walking on the hot, dry sand, he scoped out a good location. Seeing some handsome young men playing volleyball, he decided that was the perfect spot for some boy watching. Spreading out his towel, kicking off his sandals, and pulling his t-shirt over his head, Jeff coated himself with sunscreen as he ogled the handsome men hammering a white ball back and forth over the net.

He shimmied out of his gym shorts and rubbed lotion up to his bathing suit. Capping the bottle when he was done and wiping his hands on his towel, he noticed two young women leering. He ignored them and lay back on the towel to rest.

Mickey. Mickey, Mickey, Mickey…

Jeff struggled to figure out what he had done to tip him off. How on earth did Mickey read him so easily? The minute Jeff grew nervous about him already moved in, Mickey noticed. And Jeff had no idea he had let on. He wasn't even going to say anything about it. Not a thing. So what if Mickey had a few belongings at his place. That didn't mean they were officially cohabitating.

Closing his eyes, Jeff had a sudden flash of Mickey under him on the bed, teasing the hell out of Mickey before fucking him senseless.

*Shit.*

Jeff rolled to his stomach to hide his erection. Propping his chin up in his hands, he watched the men playing volleyball. They were good looking. Tan. Perfectly fit. What a difference from Seattle. It was night and day.

Why shouldn't he play a little? Was it fair to jump into

a committed relationship? Just like that?

*I'm in fucking LA! I could fuck my way across the damn city.*

The ball rolled toward him.

Jeff leaned up and touched it, getting a grip on it. When he sat up to toss it back, one of the fantastic men was standing in front of him.

"Hey."

Jeff's skin tingled. "Hey. You need this?" He laughed.

"Can't play without my ball."

*I knew they were gay. Goddamn!*

"Here." Jeff tossed it to him. "I wouldn't want to hold onto your ball any longer than I should."

A gorgeous Hollywood smile followed. The man's ass wiggled as he strutted back to his boyfriends, looking over his shoulder like a seductress.

Jeff relaxed on his towel, facing them, his arms wrapped around his knees. Now they were all looking back at him. Kindreds. Instant knowledge. The gay handshake. It was exquisite.

Loving the performance, four perfect tens showing off for his pleasure, Jeff was distracted by the two women who had eyed him earlier.

"Can we keep you company?"

"Uh. No. I'm okay."

"You sure? We don't mind."

Before he could say another word, the white ball rolled near him. Jeff stood up to go for it. Once he had it in his hand, he met up with the man. "Thanks."

"You looked like you could use rescuing."

Jeff noticed the women backing off to their own towels.

"I'm Jeff." Jeff extended his hand.

The handsome man took it. "I'm Sean. Come over and I'll introduce you."

"Boys, this is Jeff. Jeff, this is Carlos, Alejandro, and Todd."

"Hey." Jeff didn't know which one he wanted to fuck

first. They were all outstanding.

"Hey, Jeff." Carlos closed in on him, his eyes flicking down to Jeff's bathing suit.

Jeff knew he was hard. Big deal.

"We were going back to Todd's place. Want to come?"

"Hell yeah." Jeff grinned.

"Get your stuff."

Jeff walked back to his towel, packing his backpack. The two girls were scowling at him. He ignored them.

The men had wrapped up the net and began walking down the beach. Jeff caught up to Sean. "Where's Todd's place?"

"Just a mile down there."

"Oh, cool." Jeff was glad he didn't have to drive.

"We come down to this area and play all the time."

"That's good to know." Jeff's feet dug into the hot sand. In front of him were Carlos and Alejandro, teasing each other and chuckling softly as they walked. Jeff was ready to combust. *Now this is the gay scene I was looking for.*

As they approached, Jeff realized the home was already overflowing with people. Loud music blasted out from the open sliding door and windows and empty cups and beer bottles littered the deck.

His smile faded. What he imagined was going to be a nice quiet sex session suddenly appeared to be a monster party.

Sean gestured for him to climb the stairs to the deck. Beach towels were draped over the rail in rainbow colors. Women were in bikinis, smoking. Instantly, Jeff caught the scent of weed.

He stopped in his tracks.

Sean bumped into him at the abruptness. "Keep going."

Jeff's ass was rubbed seductively. He was urged step by step into Sodom and Gomorrah. "Crap."

Once inside the living room, crammed with everything from preteens to thirty-somethings, Jeff instantly knew he had two offenses. Underage drinking and pot smoking.

A glass of unknown liquid was handed to him. He declined.

Looking around in despair, Jeff knew this was a bad idea.

When a mirror loaded with cocaine made its way to him, he backed up from it quickly. "Fuck."

Todd snorted a line with a rolled up twenty, handing it to Jeff. "No. Thanks."

"Don't do blow? What do you do? We have everything. Want some ecstasy?"

"No. Don't tell me that." Jeff moaned and rubbed his face.

"Why? You're not like a cop or something, are you?" Todd laughed.

Jeff met his eye, not laughing.

The smile dropped from Todd's face. "No. Please tell me you're not a cop."

Someone overheard and choked out the words, "A cop?"

The place went dead silent, except for the music.

Jeff spun on his heels and exited the house from where he had come in.

Todd panicked, "Jeff, man, are we in trouble?"

"I'll give you the time it takes for me to get to my car to get rid of the shit."

"Fuck!" Todd raced back inside, screaming for everyone to go.

Backpack over his shoulder, and his head hung low, Jeff scuffed his feet in the hot sand to his car. He had no intention of reporting them. He just wanted to get the hell away from the house.

Opening his car door, throwing his backpack on the seat, he brushed the sand from his feet before stepping into his shorts and putting his t-shirt back on. Sitting behind the wheel, he turned over the engine to get the air conditioning running. Once it was blowing cold air, he shut the door and sat still for a moment. "I'm such a fucking idiot."

After his shower, Mickey had his feet up on the coffee table and a DVD in the player. It was a movie he'd seen before, but he just wanted something other than television on to numb his brain. Hearing the doorbell, then a knock on the door, Mickey stopped the movie and walked through the living room. He opened the door.

Jeff was standing there.

"Can I come in?"

Mickey stepped aside. As Jeff passed, Mickey caught the scent of sunscreen. "You ended up at the beach after all?"

"Yeah. Not for long."

Mickey closed the door. "What do you want?"

After tossing his keys on the coffee table, Jeff faced him.

The pain was so obvious in Jeff's expression it made Mickey's breath catch in his throat. Without another word between them, Jeff sprung at him, slamming Mickey back against the closed door.

Jeff sucked at his mouth while he dug under Mickey's midriff t-shirt. Mickey ducked under it as Jeff yanked it over his head. Instantly, he went back to Jeff's mouth, feeling Jeff's tongue swirling around his own. He gripped the edge of Jeff's shorts and dragged them down his thighs. Jeff dug his hand into Mickey's, wrapping around his cock.

Who was he kidding? They couldn't keep away from each other? Did he think Jeff could prevent the attraction they had? Yeah, maybe it was just sex at the moment, but Christ! What sex it was! It was like nothing Mickey had ever experienced in his lifetime and he was addicted. Jeff Chandler was his heroin.

He moaned at the rush and splayed out against the wood framed door, his arms over his head, his eyes closed. *Take it! Take it. Stay mad at him? Hate him? Am I nuts? All I want is for him to touch me, fuck me...I hate you, Chandler!*

Jeff turned into an animal at the submissive gesture. He growled, making the hair stand on Mickey's neck. Jeff tore off Mickey's shorts and sank to his knees wearing only his bathing suit. A second later his cock was inside Jeff's mouth.

With both his hands, Mickey dug his fingers through Jeff's dark hair, urging him tighter, fucking his mouth. *That's it, baby, make it up to me. Suck me, you asshole, suck me hard.*

Mickey knew what Jeff wanted. His ass. But first Jeff had to earn it. He had no doubt Jeff would, with interest.

Whimpering like he was in heaven and hell at the same time, Jeff sucked hard.

It was so rough, so deep and fast, Mickey was about to drop from the swoon. Getting a grip on Jeff's hair, he aggressively fucked his mouth, making sure he got his money's worth from this act of make-up sex, which is exactly what it fucking was.

"Take it! Suck it, Chandler, you fucking dirty cop! Suck it!"

Jeff went mad, deep-throating Mickey until he was nearly chewing on Mickey's balls along with his dick. Jeff's grip on his hips was painful it was so tight. As Jeff began using suction along with his teeth to add the edge of pain, he piston-fucked Mickey's cock until his head was spinning in pleasure.

"Holy fuck, Chandler!" Mickey's balls went tight and his body jerked with his orgasmic spasm. Knowing he was about to shoot a load, Mickey opened his lips and drew in a deep breath before he came. Pressing Jeff's head against him for total penetration, feeling his cock pulsate inside Jeff's mouth, he cried out from the intensity. Nothing compared to sex with this hot cop, *nothing!*

Before he recovered, Mickey was thrown to the carpet on his back. His legs were pressed into a wide straddle and back against his chest. "Get the lube." Mickey gasped for breath. "Get the fucking lube!" He knew the pent-up state Jeff had gotten himself into; he was ready to fuck him bareback.

As if Jeff couldn't hear or see at the moment through his blinding passion, he paused, jerking on his own cock, staring at Mickey's ass.

Barely able to function himself, Mickey cursed under his breath and got to his feet, racing to his bedroom. Lubrication and a condom in his hand, he spun around to find Jeff looking like a crazed beast.

Mickey froze, his heart pounding so loud it was like a drum in his ears. The man at the doorway looked like a completely out of control sexual beast. The hunger on Jeff's face and his body's posture were that of a wildcat on the hunt for flesh.

Jeff stalked him, naked, his cock protruding like a pole from his body. Moving close, Jeff thrust his pelvis out in a very overt gesture. "You better get a condom and lube on me, Stanton, or you'll be on the ground raw any second."

The power emanating from Jeff blew Mickey away. Was there ever a hotter fucker on the planet than this LAPD sex god?

Mickey tore open the rubber and slid it on Jeff's cock, shaking as he coated the latex with slick gel.

Before he had capped the tube, Jeff shoved Mickey onto the bed violently.

Licking his dry lips as his heart raced, Mickey backed up, staring at this maniac through his own bent knees. He knew he'd love what was coming, he just couldn't help but play the goddamn game.

Jeff grabbed Mickey's legs and jerked him closer. Mickey leaned on his elbows, waiting, watching. As he went through the act of mounting Mickey, the prize for all Jeff's posturing and pomp, Jeff crushed Mickey's legs tightly to his body.

Mickey actually flinched when Jeff's rounded head forced its way inside his rim. Inhaling deeply to relax after being completely knotted up from his own orgasm, Mickey knew if he reacted to Jeff's aggression it would only turn Jeff on more. So he did. He hissed and released a breath of air through his teeth. Peeking at Jeff, he found Jeff's smirk of delight.

Pushing at Jeff's arms as if to stay him off, Mickey

continued to light the fire in his lover. He knew his man. He knew him well. Sex was power. A very strong drug of power. And Jeff loved to dominate.

Another thrust sent Jeff's cock deeper. Mickey bit back his groan of bliss and tried to make his face a mask of apprehension. He knew Jeff would see right through the façade, but he loved it. Loved it!

"You can dish it out but can't take it, Stanton," Jeff sneered.

"Fuck you."

Mickey felt Jeff thrust in deeper until he was completely burrowed inside his ass.

Pleasure ripped through Mickey like a lash of a whip. In playful retaliation, Mickey jammed his hips upwards, connecting his ass to Jeff's pelvis, making Jeff whimper and stiffen up.

Jeff's reaction sent Mickey's dick upright, throbbing and eager for his second orgasm.

"Balls deep, Stanton, balls deep," Jeff growled as he ground down on Mickey to the hilt, the veins in his neck showing as his entire body tensed and his arms muscles swelled. Mickey felt the pause like it was a lit fuse. He was about to shout, "Fuck me, you asshole!" but soon he didn't have to.

Once Jeff had braced himself, he gripped Mickey's hips and began ramming inside him ruthlessly.

Getting ready to hit pay dirt, Mickey arched his back, moving his body to get Jeff to rub on his prostate. As if Jeff knew, he shifted his position. Bingo. "Oh, motherfucker… no one fucks me like you do, you nasty cop."

Jeff whimpered in reply as if he couldn't form words, his face was a mask of orgasmic pleasure.

As that delicious sensation raised him to what he had thought were unreachable heights, Mickey grabbed his own cock and fisted it in time with Jeff's pumping hips. Forcing his eyes open, he watched the intensity washing over Jeff's fine features. Suddenly, Jeff's teeth appeared between his lips and his eyes clenched tight. "Fuck! Fuck!" Jeff appeared to be going into an altered state.

"Yes!" Mickey roared. "Yes!" Watching the climax hit Jeff and feeling his body convulsing with it, he blew cum all over his own chest.

"*Fuck!*" Jeff bayed like a wolf, ramming his body again and again into Mickey's.

"Baby! Yes!" Mickey loved it. Fucking loved it!

"Oh, God! Oh my fucking God!" Jeff groaned in agony, dripping with sweat. Leaning his hands on the bed, he hung his head and gasped for air. His arms were shaking as he held himself up and his legs were quivering from the aftershocks.

"Good one, motherfucker?" Mickey snarled as he grabbed his face and drew Jeff to his lips. Jeff staggered on his arms as he lost his balance, but Mickey had him. Curling up to meet Jeff's mouth, Mickey felt him still pulsating inside him as he kissed him, tasting the sweat off his top lip. *I love you, you fucking asshole! Wake up and see what we have!*

Jeff pulled out and dropped on top of Mickey's body. Squeezing him tight, Mickey wrapped his arms and legs around Jeff's tall frame, nuzzling into his neck and sniffing at his perspiration. Slowly Jeff began to come to life. Leaning up on one arm, he looked down at Mickey in what appeared both adoration and exhaustion.

Mickey ran his hand along Jeff's face and into his damp hair. The sex had left them both drenched in sweat.

"I'm sorry."

"It's okay, Jeff."

Shaking his head as if he were struggling, Jeff opened his mouth but only air came out.

"Jeff. I get it." Mickey knew the relationship part of this partnership was a struggle for Jeff. He had to learn to be patient.

Lying his cheek down on Mickey's chest, Jeff wrapped around him.

Mickey caressed Jeff's hair and neck gently. They needed to clean up, but neither felt like moving at the moment. Calming down, Mickey savored Jeff's sweat and heat on him. He wanted nothing more than to hold him in his arms. It was all he ever wanted to do on their time off. Lie naked together, Jeff's weight on top of his, his perspiration commingling, their hearts beating in tandem. He didn't care if it was sappy or romantic. He loved this man. The more physical contact they had, the deeper that attachment grew. Jeff was his soul mate, Mickey knew that.

Finally after ten minutes, Jeff sighed, "I'm falling asleep." He managed to lift his chin, kissing Mickey's chest. "I have to get rid of the rubber."

Nodding, Mickey helped Jeff to slide off his body, finding the floor with his feet. Once Jeff had staggered off to the bathroom, Mickey sat up, rubbing his face tiredly.

He met Jeff in the bathroom and waited for him to urinate and wash his face and body. Jeff handed Mickey the washcloth. Thanking him, Mickey used it to clean up and watched as Jeff left the room. That nervous pang of apprehension returned, but he tried to deal with it.

When Mickey emerged, Jeff was sitting on the bed, slouched over, his posture looking defeated or just tired.

Mickey sat next to him, leaning on his shoulder. "Just tell me what you want."

"I don't know." Jeff scrubbed his eyes and coarse jaw with one hand.

"I know you're new to LA and it looks like some theme park for gay sex and thrills but, believe me, it ain't."

An ironic smile found Jeff's face.

"It's no different here than the great Northwest, Jeff. Men are men."

"Yes. I know you're right."

"I'm sure if you were a regular at a gay club in Seattle you could fuck a different man every night."

"That's true."

"Is that what you did up there?"

"No. I never went inside a gay bar. I was afraid someone would recognize me as a cop and I'd be screwed, and not in a good way."

Mickey smiled at Jeff's wink. "Then, what are you looking for? An open relationship?"

"Maybe."

Nodding, feeling a stab in the chest from the comment, Mickey thought about it. "I'm not."

"I know."

"I won't ask you about moving in again, Jeff. I'll leave that decision in your court. You know my thoughts."

"I do." Jeff held Mickey's hand.

Mickey promised himself he would not feel rejected or hurt or used. Promised himself. But he did.

He wouldn't ask himself why the sex and relationship they had wasn't enough. He wouldn't cry at night when Jeff wasn't in his arms.

*Keep telling yourself that, Stanton.*

"I hate asking you to wait in limbo."

Mickey hated it too, but wasn't sure he had any choice. Trying to have faith in their connection, he met Jeff's green eyes. "Why? Do you think you're not worth the wait to me?" Mickey noticed the wheels churning in Jeff's head. "You are. I'll answer it for you."

"Why? What's so great about me?"

Mickey tried not to break up with laughter. "You're either modest or dying for me to compliment you on your many virtues."

Instead of smiling, Jeff turned his eyes away. "I'm not that wonderful, Mickey."

"Says you." He kissed Jeff's hand.

Jeff's eyes once again gazed at him. "Why do you want a stinking cop for a boyfriend?"

"Because I'm a stinking cop." Mickey cupped Jeff's hand in both of his. "Only a cop can relate to another cop, Jeff. And only a gay cop can relate to another gay cop." Seeing Jeff's ironic smile, Mickey knew he understood.

"Don't you get sick of the questions about what kind of gun you carry? For fuck's sake, Jeff, I feel like I'm some kind of freak when I date a non-sworn guy. And they get fucking paranoid. Like every joint they smoked in high school I'm going to find out about and turn them in. Fuck that. I want a cop." *I want you.*

They heard the front door.

"Aura." Mickey's eyes went wide.

"Shit. My clothing is on the living room floor."

"Mouse?" she yelled.

"Yeah. Hang on!" Mickey rose up and tossed Jeff a pair of his shorts. "Put these on." He pulled a fresh pair of his own on quickly.

Mickey poked his head out of his room. Aura was holding up a pair of his briefs. "Uh, lose something?"

Jeff peeked at her from over Mickey's shoulder.

"Oh. Hi, Jeff. Now I get it." She laughed and dropped the briefs quickly. "Yipes!"

Mickey hurried to clean up the mess they had made.

"I told you to call me so I could pick up groceries, Mick." Aura set her purse down on the coffee table.

"I'll order a pizza." Mickey balled up all their clothing and tossed it into his bedroom.

"So? How are you guys doing?"

"Good." Jeff smiled sweetly at her.

"The famous LAPD crime solving duo?" She laughed on her way to her bedroom. "Batman and Robin? Saving Gotham City?"

"That's us, sis," Mickey replied as she closed her door. "Pizza okay with you, Jeff?"

"Perfect. I adore your sister."

Mickey cocked his head to the side. "In a brotherly way, or?"

"In a brotherly way." Jeff kissed his cheek.

"Good." Mickey found the phone book. "Pepperoni?"

"Anything. I'm easy."

"Yes. I've heard that about you."

Jeff smiled sweetly at him.

∽∼

While Mickey was on the phone, Aura reappeared, out of her work attire and in a pair of shorts and tank top. Jeff could see the similarities between brother and sister. Aura had the same dirty blonde hair and blue eyes, a slender figure and an oval face. She was two years older than Mickey, a whopping twenty-eight.

She plopped down beside him and gave him a smile filled with the naughtiness he loved. "Good sex?"

He laughed and replied, "Is that a statement or a question?"

"You're glowing. It's a statement. I can't remember the last man I stripped at the front door."

Mickey announced, "Pizza on the way."

"I would have cooked."

"I got it, sis."

Mickey sat across from them.

"Am I taking your place?" Aura gestured to the spot on the sofa.

"I can survive over here for five minutes." Mickey grinned at her.

"I thought you two were connected at the hip."

"Somewhere around there." Mickey covered his smirk.

"Is there wine left? Or did you two polish it off?"

"Not us." Jeff shook his head.

"Mouse?"

"Still in the fridge. Go get it."

"Good." She rose up and left the room.

"I can't believe she calls you mouse." Jeff giggled.

Mickey shrugged. "She's called me that since I was born. She loves Mickey Mouse."

"Get over here." Jeff patted the cushion next to him.

Mickey crossed the room. When he dropped down beside Jeff, he put his arm around his shoulders and licked his cheek.

"Behave. Don't get naughty in front of my sister."

"Why the hell isn't she married? She's so pretty."

"Please tell me you're not attracted to her."

"I'm not." Jeff grabbed Mickey's balls.

"Hello!" She laughed as she entered the room.

"Sorry." Jeff took his hand back.

"So, I *was* sitting in your seat, Mouse." She sat in his, sipping her wine.

"I know this shouldn't be awkward," Mickey sighed, "But…"

"Awkward?" Aura chided, "Since when do I care if you grope each other?" She took another drink from her glass. "You're just usually at Jeff's place. I never see you two together. Oh, sorry. Do either of you want some wine?"

"I'm okay." Jeff held up his hand.

"I'm fine too." Mickey relaxed on the cushions. "So? When are you seeing Mom and Dad?"

"I don't know. When are you seeing them? Do they know about Jeff yet?"

Mickey peeked at him. "No."

"Am I a secret?" Jeff asked.

"No. You're not a secret; you're just not common knowledge yet."

"Oh." Jeff dug his hand into Mickey's hair from behind, watching Aura's reaction. She seemed to like it.

"Are you guys sleeping here tonight?"

Mickey exchanged looks with Jeff. "We haven't discussed it."

Jeff shrugged. "We can, but all our stuff is at my place."

"Yes. It is." Mickey raised his eyebrow, indicating he was amused, but there was a slight serious overtone to that amused smirk.

"So, I guess we'll be staying over at my place."

"Okay." Aura kept the wine glass covering her mouth.

"Why," Jeff asked, "you want to hear me humping your little brother?"

"Jeff!" Mickey smacked him in the chest as Aura broke up with laughter.

"Mouse, you are one lucky SOB." Aura's light eyes gleamed.

"This is too weird. After the pizza, we're gone." Mickey rubbed his arms like he was cold.

"Don't go on my account. Maybe we could watch a movie together."

"What movie?" Mickey rested his hand on Jeff's naked thigh.

"One of your gay romances?" Aura gave them another wicked smile.

"Do two men having sex together turn you on?" Jeff was enthralled.

"If it does?" She took another sip of wine.

"Aura," Mickey moaned, "stop embarrassing me."

"I'm curious, Mick." Jeff elbowed him. "Let her answer."

Giving a long pause before she did, Aura sighed, "*Yes.*"

Mickey choked in shock as Jeff cracked up. "I had no idea two men together turned women on."

"You kidding me? I've got girlfriends who would pay me good money if I let them watch you two."

"Aura..." Mickey rubbed his face in agony.

"Yeah? Pay to see us?" Jeff asked.

"Hell yeah." Aura finished her wine, setting the glass on the coffee table between them. "Men want to see two women together."

"I have no interest in seeing two women together," Mick replied.

"Not you. Straight guys." Aura rolled her eyes.

"No shit?" Jeff felt a slight tingle at the thought of straight women watching him and Mick screw.

"No shit, Jeff." Aura curled one of her legs under her. "I love watching Mick's gay movies. I do all the time when he's not here."

"Shut up." Mickey coughed in a laugh.

"I do." She shrugged. "I go to gay websites, read gay erotic romance…"

Jeff couldn't believe what he was hearing. He just kept smiling at her in amazement.

"You think telling my lover about your deviances is a good idea, sis?" Mickey teased.

"My deviances? Are you being silly on purpose?"

Leaning over his lap toward her to speak on a more personal level, Jeff asked, "What will you do if your boyfriend thinks it's gross?"

"First of all, what boyfriend?" She snorted, adding, "I'd have to date a man that thought it was okay. After all, my brother is gay."

Jeff dropped back to slouch on the cushions, thinking about it. Finally he said to Mickey, "Your sister is a gay man in a woman's body."

Aura roared with laughter while Mickey's eyes widened in surprise.

"Nailed!" Aura gasped between laughter. "Christ, Jeff, you're one perceptive cop."

"I don't believe this conversation." Mickey shook his head.

"Tell Mom she has two gay children, Mouse. She'll enjoy hearing that one."

Jeff grinned at Aura first, then kissed Mickey's cheek.

"Mm," Aura hummed.

"Behave," Mickey chided them both.

⁂

Twenty minutes later, there was a knock at the door.

"I got it." Mickey rose up and found his wallet. When he opened the door, a young man was standing outside with two cardboard pizza boxes. "Hey." Mickey propped it open with his back.

"Twenty-five dollars and thirty-five cents, man."

Mickey handed the young guy thirty dollars. He exchanged the bills for the boxes, giving them to Jeff who took a close look at the youth before he walked away.

Typical surfer boy: earring, pierced eyebrow, blond with blue eyes. Mickey watched as he counted out the change.

"Here, dude."

Mickey handed the young man back three dollars. "That's for you."

"Thanks, man." The young surfer gave Mickey's crotch a good once over.

Watching him walk down the outer stairs, back to his car with the plastic blue and red sign on it, Mickey figured the guy had to be gay. The inspection of his crotch had been pretty overt. "Bet you get lucky on occasion, my friend."

"You say something?" Jeff asked as he set the boxes on the table.

"Huh? No. I'm starved."

"Come and eat," Aura offered, opening the lid of the cardboard box.

When Mickey sat down and joined them, Jeff asked, "You fantasizing screwing that pizza kid?"

"No, but I think he was imagining doing me. Gave my dick a good once over."

"You gay guys have it so easy." Aura gnawed on the pizza.

"Sorry, sis." Mickey put a slice on his plate. "Does smell good."

"What? The pizza or the kid?" Jeff laughed.

"The pizza, asshole." Mickey stuck his tongue out at him.

"You will use that later," Jeff warned.

"Jesus!" Aura choked. "I'm glad you spend your time at Jeff's. You guys are bad."

"Aura, you have no idea." Mickey grinned at her as he bit the cheesy slice.

He caught Jeff's wink and winked back.

# Chapter 4

Mickey was once again in Jeff's bed in his townhouse in Anaheim. Their toothbrushes shared a ceramic holder, their hairbrushes a drawer in the vanity, and their briefs intertwined in Jeff's bureau. *But I don't live here.*

Lying on his back, staring at the ceiling light fixture, Mickey pretended he understood the skewed logic solely to prevent him and Jeff from arguing and going their separate ways, which would be tough assigned to the same patrol car.

A tangle.

That's what it was really. An emotional knot without an easy solution. *Time, time, yes give him time.* Mickey wasn't known for his patience. Not by a long shot.

Fast and satisfying. It was how he liked his sex and his life. That child in him, the *I want it, I want it now*, 'id', was forever there.

"I'm a Freudian nightmare."

"Hm?" Jeff opened his drowsy eyes.

Mickey ignored him. He'd soon be back asleep. Jeff always fell asleep first.

What gnawed at Mickey the most was his own ego. He knew he was a catch. Since he was out, outside of work, and available, many men had licked their chops at him. It was Mickey who had ended all his past relationships. Too clingy, too weak, too cop-obsessed. The reasons for splitting from other men pre-Jeff were too numerous to expand on. He wanted a cop. Period. And finding a gorgeous, available, gay, LAPD officer, wasn't as easy as it sounded. It was nearly impossible.

And the idea of going to some gay cop group? That instantly outted you. Out. You were branded. Though he didn't exactly hide in the shadows, he was very selective about who he told. Flo Bower was very cool, and very discreet. She was also bi. So, he kept her secret, she kept his.

Who else on the department knew? Jeff Chandler.

It was nobody's fucking business who he fucked.

He didn't need the harassment either. Cops were cops were cops were cops….

A deep, loud sigh bellowed from his chest.

"Mickey…" came a moan of anguish, "sleep."

"I can't."

"Take a pill."

"What pill?" Mickey rolled over to stare at Jeff's face in the dimness as it crunched into the bedding.

"A sleeping pill."

"I never take pills."

"Take a fucking pill…" Jeff groaned, digging his head under the pillow.

"Fine. Where are they?" He threw back the sheets.

"Bathroom. Medicine cabinet."

Mickey scuffed across the carpet and turned on the light. Squinting at the glare he pulled open the cabinet's mirrored door and tried to find the right vial. When he did, he read the directions. He shook out two and capped the bottle, replacing it. Popping them into his mouth, he stuck his head under the sink faucet and swallowed them. "Hate taking fucking pills." He rubbed the water from his chin. Shutting off the light, he returned to the bed and dropped down on it heavily.

"Why can't you sleep?" Jeff rolled to his side.

"I don't know."

"Something on your mind?" Jeff rubbed Mickey's chest.

"You don't even want to go there." Mickey checked the clock; it was nearing one.

"You got that right." Jeff shifted on the bed, getting comfortable.

Mickey stared at the light fixture again. The outside moonlight lit part of the wall and ceiling in elongated rectangles. Hearing rustling, he felt Jeff's hand sneak across his hips to his pubic hair. "Jeff Chandler's awake. That means he's horny."

Jeff chuckled softly. "Your fault. You woke the beast."

"Is that what you call it? I never knew you had named your dick."

"Shut up." Jeff laughed again.

Trying to relax, Mickey closed his eyes. The tips of Jeff's fingers combed through his short and curlies. It was comforting.

Very gently, Jeff massaged Mickey's pelvis and brushed against his soft cock. Soothing was morphing to stimulating.

Mickey whimpered quietly, spreading his legs, meeting Jeff's hot body in the process. Jeff continued a circling motion, riding up Mickey's lower abdomen, pressing his fingers through the skin to Mickey's wall of muscle underneath. A surge of blood caused Mickey's cock to move. Tilting his head into the pillow, Mickey tried not to get hot, to simply enjoy the loving gesture. Jeff's caressing dug back into his pubic hair, rubbing it in such a way as to make Mickey just crazy enough not to want him to stop.

When Jeff's index finger and thumb judged the width of his dick, Mickey knew he was a goner. Had a boner. Damn. Oh well.

Jeff's hand retreated and he rolled to his side, connecting their body's closer. "You need to come?"

"It might help." *When don't I need to come?*

"How many times have you climaxed today?"

"Are we keeping count?"

"No." Jeff reached his hand down Mickey's body for a good grip.

"You don't have to. I know you were asleep. I'm sorry I woke you."

"We're off tomorrow. We can sleep in. Big deal."

"In that case." Mickey threw off the sheets and interlaced his fingers on his chest. *Service me, lover.* "Go for it."

Jeff leaned on his elbow, smoothing up Mickey's shaft slowly. "You have a fantastic prick, Mick."

"Yeah? You like it?"

"Gets me hot touching it."

Jeff's hard-on rubbed against Mickey's hip. "I'm up

for it if you are."

"You sure? How many times can you get fucked a day?"

"We did it early this afternoon. I feel fine." Mickey wanted Jeff in.

"I'll go easy."

"Sure you will, Chandler." Mickey laughed.

"Forget it. Too much preparation. How about this." Jeff wriggled out of the sheets and straddled Mickey's face.

"Fuck yeah!" Mickey's body raced with pleasure. "Sixty-nine...an oldie but goodie."

"Shut up and suck," Jeff said with his mouth full.

Suddenly stimulated well beyond sleep or sleeping tablets, Mickey spread Jeff's ass cheeks and burrowed his face into it. He ran long wet laps of his tongue from Jeff's balls to his rim. Jeff's hips were already moving into an imaginary lover. And Mickey's cock was enveloped to the root. Pushing Jeff back slightly, Mickey was able to get a hold of his cock. Tilting it toward his mouth, he aimed it in and sucked hard. Jeff moaned, sending vibrations through Mickey's length. He had forgotten how challenging this was. At times the pleasure from Jeff's lips was so outstanding, Mickey paused, forgetting to give back, until Jeff's hips urged him on, reminding him.

Mickey slid the heels of his feet backward so his knees bent and he could feel Jeff's hair tickling inside his thighs. "Ah," he moaned, Jeff's cock still in his mouth but sagging out of it as Mickey's own impending orgasm began to distract him completely.

"Suck!" was garbled from Jeff's full mouth.

Waking from his stupor, Mickey gripped the base of Jeff's dick with both hands and went for it. This time Jeff stopped. "Suck!" Mickey laughed as he tried to shout with a huge dick in his mouth.

"Fuck it!" Jeff pulled back, gasping, holding Mickey's cock and Mickey assumed he was waiting for his climax before he continued. "Suck it, Stanton!" Jeff ordered.

Mickey went wild. No distractions now. Jerking his

head up and down, closing his eyes, Mickey squeezed the base of Jeff's dick and drew it in and out to the tip. A surge of pre-cum hit, then Jeff's hips jerked forward and Mickey felt the entire length vibrate under his lips.

"Fuck! Augh!"

Mickey tugged on Jeff's balls as they hung low in front of his face. Massaging them, cupping them in his hand as he sucked, Mickey loved the way they rolled inside their sack of loose skin. He used some of his saliva and rimmed Jeff's ass gently. A long low moan of pleasure was his reward. Soon Jeff's hips aggressively pumped into Mickey's mouth. Mickey had to use both hands on the base of Jeff's dick not to be choked by the size of Jeff's cock and power of his thrusting.

"Yes, yes…" Jeff coaxed softly. "That's it, baby…just like that."

Mickey gripped the base of Jeff's cock tighter, jerking it with the timing of Jeff's pumping hips. A pre-cum spurt hit Mickey's tongue and then Jeff's cock began pulsating as Jeff's balls went tight. "I'm there! I'm there!" Jeff announced as he rammed his cock deeper into Mickey's throat.

Holding back Jeff's hips so he didn't asphyxiate from having his entire mouth filled and his nose crushed against a taut body, Mickey backed Jeff up enough to breathe through his nose. Finally he was able to slip Jeff's cock from his mouth and catch his breath. "Jesus, Chandler! You almost suffocated me."

"Sorry. Damn, it felt good though."

As Jeff recovered, Mickey used his hands to keep milking Jeff's cock gently, lapping off the fresh drops as he did.

After a brief pause, where Mickey assumed Jeff was locating his brain cells after a mind-blowing climax, his prick was devoured.

"Bout time." Dropping his head back on the pillow, Mickey kept the tip of Jeff's cock in contact with his lips and waited as Jeff drew down on him as if he could suck all of his cum out in one hard slurp. When Jeff shoved his hand between Mickey's legs and rubbed hot friction on his root and ass, Mickey moaned in pleasure. "Oh yes. X marks the spot." He relaxed his back muscles and his legs went into a limp straddle. "Suck it, Chandler. Suck it like you mean it, ya bastard."

Hearing Jeff's full mouth snarl made Mickey smile. A finger instantly shoved its way up his ass in retaliation for the comment.

It sent a zinging pleasure through his cock. And shut him up.

A blowjob was always intense from Jeff. Mickey knew Jeff fucking loved to suck him. They weren't happy unless someone was penetrating somewhere, and Jeff in particular loved Mickey's cock in his mouth at every occasion that presented itself, as well as on the job.

Mickey felt his cock hit the back of Jeff's throat as his ass was impaled by his index finger. The base of his dick was squeezed in tandem with everything else that Jeff was doing. Mickey was in awe of his skills in the oral department. If nothing else, he could fall for Jeff just for his talented mouth. Luckily there was a hell of a lot more to Officer Chandler than his dexterous tongue.

When Jeff moaned from the pleasure of giving head, Mickey knew he was done for. He arched his back and gripped Jeff's hips tight, gasping in delirium at the amount of pleasure his body gave him in the midst of a very adept man. He shot out his load and quivered from head to toe at the satisfaction.

After lapping at the tip for the last few drops, Jeff flopped back on the pillow beside him. "Sleep," he groaned.

Still rocking his hips side to side from the orgasm, Mickey made hushed, lovesick noises as he recovered. His chest tightening from emotion, Mickey rolled over, embraced Jeff and spooned him as tightly as he could. "I love you, you fantastic motherfucker," he cried and meant every goddamn word.

Giving a weary laugh, Jeff, sighed, "Go to sleep, Stanton."

Burrowing his face in Jeff's hot skin, Mickey drifted off into a deep sleep, sexually sated beyond his wildest dreams.

# CHAPTER 5

Once again light was the morning's weapon of choice that woke Jeff. Stretching, yawning, rubbing his face, needing a shave desperately after two days without, he tilted over to his bedmate.

*Wait a minute. Wait just a fucking minute. Mickey Stanton told me he loved me last night.*

A big smile covered Jeff's face. "I knew it." Leaning up on his elbow to stare at him, Jeff's smile slowly softened as he thought about it. *Wait a minute…Mickey Stanton told me he loved me last night? Shit.*

Did he love Mickey?

He covered his face in both hands and flopped to his back to think.

Another man, another cop, had told Jeff that before. He'd fallen for it and got burned so badly his heart was covered in scar tissue. Love? *That was a four-letter word… uh oh.*

*What am I supposed to do?* Jeff massaged his eyes through the lids. "Christ, Mickey."

"You talking to me or yourself?"

Stunned he was awake and heard him, Jeff spun his head to see him. *Damn!* "Myself."

"You said, 'Christ, Mickey' to yourself?"

Seeing Mickey's "I'm going to get mad" expression, Jeff positioned himself to face him, lying on his side. He knew how sensitive Mickey was and dreaded another argument and falling out. Trying to cover his stupidity, he tread lightly.

Slowly Jeff cupped Mickey's equally unshaven jaw, and felt the prickly bristles stick his palm. "You sleep well? With the pill and the extra orgasm?"

"Why did you say, 'Christ, Mickey'?"

*Oh no. Let it go! I can't keep arguing with you, please!* Jeff coiled around him trying to think fast to cover up his blunder. "Christ, Mickey, I think you're gorgeous. Christ, Mickey, you have a fantastic body. Christ, Mickey—"

"Shut up. Get away from me." Mickey pressed the flat of his hand against Jeff's chest and pushed.

*I knew it. Here we go again.* Jeff locked his fingers together behind Mickey's back, preventing him from moving anywhere far. "All right…look at me."

Under an angry eyebrow, Mickey's blue iris connected with his.

"You told me you loved me last night." Jeff said it like it was a good excuse. "I just wasn't expecting it."

"I never pegged you for a dumb cop."

"I'm a smart cop, just a dumb boyfriend."

"Boyfriend?"

"I knew you'd glom onto that. Semantics, Mickey! Acknowledge and move on."

"Augh! You frustrate the shit out of me, Chandler!" Mickey wriggled to escape.

"You're not fucking going anywhere, Mick. So stop fighting me." Jeff had no idea why Mickey was so sensitive to everything he did. It was beginning to drive him crazy and he didn't like walking on eggshells. Couldn't Mickey see what they had was incredible? Did he always have to ruin it with words?

"Your way! Always your fucking way!"

Jeff wrestled Mickey back until he trapped Mickey underneath him, their crotches boiling hot on each other, separated at the chest where Jeff pinned Mickey's shoulders to the bed. "Why do you get so fucking crazy? Can't I have a conversation with you without you acting like ya got PMS?"

Mickey went ballistic at the comment. He roared and

wrenched to get free but Jeff wasn't allowing him to go anywhere. "Keep still before I hurt you." Shaking his head in disbelief, Jeff moaned, "I feel like I'm dealing with a woman sometimes, Stanton! Calm the fuck down."

His eyes wild with his fury, Mickey's top lip curled back, revealing his perfect white teeth. His chest was expanding like bellows as his temper raged. "Get fucking off me."

"No." Jeff laughed. "You told me something last night, and I want to talk about it."

"I take it back. I fucking hate you, asshole."

"Sure ya do, Mick. And your hard dick is telling me that right now." Jeff wriggled against it.

"A fuck! Okay? That's all we are to each other. A goddamn mother-fucking fuck. Now get off me!"

Jeff couldn't hold Mickey by the shoulders and control him any longer. Mickey had two inches on him in height and twenty pounds of muscle on him in weight. To keep Mickey under his domination, which for some reason was paramount at the moment, Jeff grabbed his throat.

The look on Mickey's face explained just what a bad idea that was. Mickey ripped Jeff's hand from his neck and heaved Jeff off the bed.

Flailing as he fell, Jeff landed on his ass and gaped at Mickey in astonishment. He knew Mick was strong, but that power came out of nowhere.

Mickey stood over him, his hands on his hips, glaring at him. "What the hell do you think you're doin', Officer Chandler? Dealing with a fucking dope dealer in East LA?"

Jeff scrambled to his feet. "Sorry, Mick. I didn't mean to chokehold you." Jeff held up his hands to try and appease him but he knew this anger was coming from much more than a physical power struggle. It was emotional and Jeff just didn't know how to deal with it.

In a flash, Mickey had Jeff by the throat and pinned him against the closet door with a slam. "You want to fight me, asshole?"

Loving aggression, especially from this gorgeous blond

hunk, Jeff was salivating. Suddenly Mickey was this huge, powerful cop, taking shit from no one. Jeff's dick was so hard he was in agony. "Oh, jeez, Mickey…" Jeff breathed in desire. "You mother-fucking god…"

The look on Mickey's face was pure astonishment.

The high Jeff got from Mickey manhandling him was like a rush of pure adrenalin. He gripped Mickey's rough jaw in his hands and kissed him. Instantly, Mickey released his hold on Jeff's throat and grabbed him around the waist. Jeff hopped up and locked his ankles around Mickey's hips, so impressed with Mickey's strength he was whimpering like a baby as he kissed him. "Fuck me. Fuck me, you dirty cop. Why do I always top you? Huh? Will you take my goddamn ass once in a while, Stanton?"

Mickey carried him over to the bed and fell on it, crushing Jeff under him with his bulk. Jeff unlocked his legs from Mickey's hips and grabbed his own knees, spreading his thighs wide in invitation. "Fuck me! Goddamn you, asshole! Can you screw me, or are you a fucking girl?"

"Who are you calling a girl?"

"You, bitch!" Jeff teased.

"You want it, asshole?"

"I want it in the asshole? Are you stupid?" Jeff loved goading him and knew it would drive Mickey wild as well.

"Stupid? I'll show you who's the stupid, bitch!" Mickey scooped up the condoms and tore at one with his teeth. They were both trembling from the violence and heat. Jeff glanced at his own dick. The head was blushing purple from the craving and blood engorged in it. Mickey pressed Jeff's legs achingly wide and pushed inside him like he meant to impale him.

Unprepared for the sensation, Jeff shouted out. It had been a long time since someone topped him. A very long time. As the shock and pain slowly changed to friction and pleasure, he grabbed his own dick and fisted it frantically. Above him Mickey was grunting and hammering his pelvis against him. Mickey tilted his hips and suddenly Jeff was ignited as the grinding hit pay dirt. *"Ah!"* He shrieked at the pleasure and ejaculated hard. His cum splashed his face as it shot past him to the bed.

Mickey choked on his moans and his expression became a mask of Eros while his cock throbbed rapidly as it erupted. Gaping at him in awe, gasping for air, Jeff was in shock at the intensity of the orgasm and the sight of Mickey's unmatched pleasure.

Mickey hung his head, sucking in the oxygen and droning out loud, long, deep, agonizing groans.

Drops of Mickey's sweat hit Jeff's skin. Jeff was spinning. "Oh, my fucking God, Mick…"

Mickey slid out, sitting on his heels on the floor beside the bed. He laid his head on the mattress, trying to catch his breath.

Jeff couldn't move at the moment. His hand rested on his chest to feel the elevated rate of his heartbeat.

Never in his life had he had sex like this. This was a whole new level. In his wildest dreams he never imagined his own body, with the help of the hottest fucking LA cop on the planet, could achieve such heights. The orgasms were so intense he felt as if he was having an out of body experience. There was no way for him to describe it or put it into words.

"Stanton…" Jeff panted.

Mickey raised his head off the bed with an effort.

"I need you, you fucking hot, dirty cop."

As he slowly climbed across Jeff's prone body, Mickey laughed wickedly. When they were nose to nose, Mickey sighed. "I know you do, Chandler. I know you do."

⁓≈

The day was already scorching, nearing the mid-nineties. Mickey held a backpack with their towels, sunscreen, and water, while Jeff carried a bamboo mat and a Frisbee. They walked along the silky, white sand to an open spot.

"Perfect." Jeff met Mickey's eyes and gestured to the two gorgeous lifeguards manning a tower.

"Excellent." Mickey helped Jeff set out the mat and kicked off his flip-flops.

Once they had stripped off their t-shirts and shorts, Mickey took out the sunscreen bottle and began coating Jeff's back. Both of them faced the two lifeguards as they did.

Jeff whispered over his shoulder, "Jesus, are they the stuff of gay fantasies or what? Get a look at the younger one, Mick. He's beautiful."

"I know. Christ, I'm already hard as a rock." Mickey rubbed the thick cream into Jeff's skin, massaging his shoulders as he stared at the pretty boys in red bathing suits.

Jeff picked up the container of sunscreen and spun around to face Mickey. With a demonic smirk on his face, Jeff spurted the white cream on his own chest.

Knowing exactly what he was up to, Mickey started laughing. "Fuck, Chandler. You're incorrigible."

Jeff aimed the bottle at Mickey making it blob like cum onto his tanned body.

Staring at Jeff adoringly, Mickey relaxed on his back with his knees bent and allowed Jeff to rub the spattered cream into his chest. As he watched Jeff, Mickey could see the raised mound under his own tight bathing suit and Jeff's as well.

Closing his eyes, Mickey lost himself in Jeff's touch as Jeff worked his way down Mickey's body. Listening to the ocean's roar, the gulls calling, children shrieking with laughter, and planes flying overhead in the crystal blue sky, he was in heaven.

When the contact stopped, Mickey opened his eyes. Jeff was rubbing the previously splashed cream on himself while he stared at the lifeguards. Mickey took a look. Neither lifeguard was staring back as both men were surveying the crowd.

That slight pang of irritation hit him again. Yes, he and Jeff had something strong, but it always would rely on Jeff's fidelity, or lack of it.

Once Jeff had finished coating himself, he wiped his

hands on a towel and shifted his sunglasses to the top of his head. Lying on his stomach, he rested his head on his arms, facing Mickey.

He rolled over and pecked Jeff's cheek quickly.

Jeff's eyes sparkled from his smile.

Seeing the comfort Jeff had at the touch, Mickey turned to lie on his side and caressed Jeff's back. The amount he adored Jeff was something he was struggling to cope with. He kept praying it was mutual.

"Three twelves coming up."

Mickey knew Jeff was referring to tomorrow when their long twelve-hour shift would begin. "Yes."

"You want to change to four tens? Ask the sarge?"

"Do you?" Mickey ran his fingertips down Jeff's spine to his black bathing suit.

"I don't know. It's sometimes like opening Pandora's Box when you ask for a change of shift."

"I love the time off in between." Mickey peeked up and noticed the pretty lifeguard was looking at them. When Mickey gave him a seductive smile, the attractive man turned away shyly.

"Forget it. Let's not mess it up, then." Jeff sighed heavily. "You know, that feels great."

"Good." He continued to stroke Jeff's bronze back. "There's no harm in enquiring, Jeff. I can just throw it out there."

"I'm afraid if you say something to Sgt. Bryant, then he'll know we're interested in a change and we'll get one whether we like it or not."

"It does sometimes happen that way. I've learned one thing about the police force. You have very little say, in the end, what you do."

"It was the same in Seattle. You just get what you get. You can ask for a shift or a squad, but in the end, they do what they want."

Mickey ran his fingers width-wise across Jeff's back, up and down, from his shoulders to his waist.

"You're putting me to sleep."

Mickey smiled. "I can't get enough of touching you."

"You're such a romantic, Stanton."

"You tell anyone that and I'll have to kill you." Mickey stretched out to look at the blue sky, scooting over to connect to Jeff's arm. He rested his hand on Jeff's bottom and closed his eyes.

"I feel like a lazy fuck. We should at least go for a run or something."

"Later." Mickey squeezed Jeff's ass cheek.

After dozing off, Mickey heard a loud blast from a whistle. Opening his eyes, he tilted his head up to see the lifeguards running down the sand.

Jeff sat up, turning to look over his shoulder. "What's going on?"

"I don't know." Mickey leaned on his elbows to get a better look. "Fuck. It's a fight."

"Shit." Jeff flipped over and knelt up. "We have to help the guards, Mick."

"I didn't bring my ID or badge."

"Big shit. Come on." Jeff hopped to his feet and took off running.

Mickey sprinted by his side. It appeared three men were in dispute of some kind and fists and feet were flying like in a kung fu movie.

The two lifeguards were trying to get in between the combatants. Mickey grabbed the most aggressive of the three and growled, "Cut this shit out. We're off duty LAPD."

"He fucking started it!" the man Mickey was holding spat as he pointed.

Mickey could smell the alcohol on his breath.

Jeff had one of the other men in an arm-bar hold, keeping him subdued. The third man was obviously injured and was being tended by the two lifeguards.

"Fuck you! You were making a pass at my wife, asshole!"

Jeff shook the man who shouted that line. "Calm

down."

"I didn't know she was your wife, dickhead!"

"Will you shut up?" Mickey jarred the man. "Calm down or we'll call a marked unit and haul your ass to jail."

Jeff asked the lifeguards, "Is that guy all right?"

The larger of the two held his rescue buoy over his head, signaling the next tower. "No. I'm calling him a medic unit."

"Which one of you hit him?" Jeff asked. When no one answered, Jeff said to Mickey, "If they're calling a unit, we have to get the cops here for a report."

Mickey had a slight panic attack. The idea that someone from their department would see him and Jeff in their skimpy bathing suits, together on the beach, would probably out them. He was certain.

"Shit, Jeff." Mickey loosened his grip on the man he held as they all calmed down.

"We don't need the cops, man." Jeff's guy appeared petrified.

"We are the cops, man," Jeff sneered at him. "When the medics show up, can you get them to call 911?" Jeff asked one of the lifeguards.

"I can do better than that." The younger, pretty one held up the rescue can in a different position.

Mickey looked out into the distance at the next tower. A signal came back that the lifeguard's sign had been received.

"They'll call the cops." The pretty lifeguard met Mickey's eyes. "I mean, more cops." He grinned flirtatiously.

*Fuck, he's gay?* Mickey was about to swoon at the knowledge.

As the story of the battle unfolded, Mickey kept looking back at the street level, hoping like hell the cops who showed up were cool. Suddenly he felt very stupid to have gotten into this situation in the first place. They were off duty. They shouldn't be working.

"Mick."

Mickey met Jeff's eyes.

"Look."

Mickey spun around and found Blake and Hunter on their way over. "I don't believe it."

"Our lucky day?" Jeff grinned.

When the two firemen drew close, Mickey read the surprise in their eyes. "Do you two fight crime in your Speedos?" Hunter shouted as he approached.

"Mr. Rasmussen, what a pleasure to see you." Jeff gave him a wicked grin.

"What have we got, Tanner?" Blake knelt down by the injured man.

"He was clocked pretty good in the head. It might just be a bruise but I wanted you guys to check him out."

"Hello, boys," the pretty lifeguard smiled in delight.

"Josh," Hunter greeted him, "Are you behaving yourself?"

"Never!"

Mickey listened in awe. *Josh, Tanner, Hunter, Blake? Are we all gay? I'm going to cream.*

He gaped at Jeff and Jeff gave him his own curious look. A pair of older cops finally showed up. Mickey didn't know them. They looked completely irritated to be out of their air-conditioned patrol car and walking through the sand in their black shoes. Mickey imagined they were called off their doughnut break to handle another garbage call. He knew the type well.

When they were close enough to take over the scene, Mickey released his hold on the guy he had kept from escaping.

After a mumble of greeting, the old, out of shape cop asked, "Who did what?" with the interest of someone who was already back at the doughnut counter.

Tanner relayed what he knew. "This guy flirted with that guy's wife. Then these two started punching each other."

Mickey noticed one of the cops giving him a strange look. Trying not to draw attention to himself, he stood next to Jeff. "Don't tell them we're cops."

Jeff whispered back, "Don't they already know from the dispatched call?"

Mickey hoped not.

Hunter packed his medical kit and said, "This guy's okay. I'm leaving it up to him if he wants to go to the hospital."

"No. I don't." The man stood up, still holding an ice pack to his eye.

The big cop with the protruding gut said, "All right, just give me your names." He flipped out his pad.

Jeff tapped Mickey's arm. "Let's get out of here."

Mickey nodded. He couldn't agree more.

"Mick!"

Mickey turned to look. Blake was catching up to him. He and Jeff paused as he stepped closer.

"Hunter and I have been meaning to talk to you. We would really like to get together with you two socially."

"Yeah?" Jeff's eyes lit up.

"Yeah. When can you go for a beer?"

"We're starting our three twelves tomorrow. We just had three days off." Mickey noticed Hunter and the two lifeguards laughing and smiling together.

Blake took out a pen and paper. "Here's my cell phone number." He scribbled it down. "On your next days off, call us."

"I was telling Mick we should go eat dinner with you guys at the station." Jeff took the paper Blake handed him.

"You should. You know you guys are welcome anytime. We try to eat at around five, but if we get a call, it'll be later."

Mickey paused as the other three men walked over to them, leaving the little battle for the uniformed cops to handle. Before the lifeguards came too close to hear, Mickey whispered in Blake's ear, "Are Tanner and Josh gay?"

"Josh is, I think Tanner is straight." Blake peered back at the men as they approached.

Tanner held out his hand. "Thank you, gentlemen."

Mickey took it, shaking it. "Our pleasure. I'm Mickey Stanton, and this is my partner, Jeff Chandler." Mickey figured saying they were partners could mean two different things. If Tanner was straight, he could decide which version he was the most comfortable with.

Josh snuggled against Jeff flirtatiously. "You two gorgeous hunks are LAPD cops? And I watched you rub sunscreen on each other?" Josh fanned himself dramatically. "That'll hold me for a week."

"Mr. Elliot, behave," Tanner chided.

When Jeff held Josh's face in his hands, Mickey flinched in jealously.

"You are gorgeous, Josh," Jeff gushed. "You're in the wrong business. You should be in gay porn."

"I hear there already is an actor with my name." Josh batted his long lashes at Jeff, giving Mickey the urge to shove them apart.

"There is." Mickey didn't smile when he said it. "But he's blond."

Josh sauntered over to Mickey. "What's wrong with blond?" Josh gestured to Mickey's hair.

"Joshua," Tanner admonished in a deep voice.

Hunter choked in amazement, "Put a leash on him, Tanner."

Josh spun around, connecting his gaze to Tanner. "He's already got a leash on me."

Mickey's eyes widened. Tanner and Josh?

Jeff moaned, "Please, can we all get together…please?"

Blake said, "Hunt, I gave them my cell phone number."

"Good." Hunter nodded.

"You want mine?" Josh purred.

"I'll give them mine, trouble." Tanner crossed his arms.

Jeff took the same piece of paper that Blake had given him and asked, "Anyone got a pen?"

Hunter handed Jeff his. "Shoot, Tanner." Tanner relayed his cell phone number to Jeff as he copied it down.

"Great. Hopefully with all our crazy schedules we can manage one night together." He handed Hunter back his pen.

"Growl!" Josh licked his lips.

Tanner wrapped his arm around Josh's neck from behind. "Will you control yourself?"

"Are you joking?" Josh laughed. "Firemen? LAPD cops? Gorgeous fucking heroes? All gay men? And you ask me to calm down? Tanner, I'm so revved up at the moment I'm about to pop."

Mickey peeked back at the two old-timers. It seemed they had gotten what they needed and they were scuffing their way off the sand. When he gazed back at their group, he smiled happily. "I hope we can all manage to get together. I'd really enjoy that."

"We will." Blake patted his back. "We have to get going."

"Us too." Tanner nudged Josh. "Say goodbye and get back to work, sexy."

"Bye, boys." Josh waved, licking his chops.

"See ya." Hunter waved as he and Blake walked off the beach.

Mickey and Jeff watched them leave. When Mickey felt Jeff touch his hand, he woke up from his daydream. They walked back to their bamboo mat and sat down on it.

Jeff wrapped his arms around his knees and stared out at the water. "That was really surreal."

"No kidding." Mickey stretched out his legs. He caught Jeff's eyes darting to the tower where Josh and Tanner were back on duty. "You'd fuck him, wouldn't you?"

Jeff spun around to face him. "Who?"

"Josh."

"Wouldn't you?"

Mickey dropped to his back heavily. It was no use. He couldn't win this game.

≈≈

Jeff drove them back to the townhouse. Mickey had gone quiet again. It was beginning to feel like a vicious cycle.

Yes, he would fuck Josh Elliot. In a heartbeat. The guy was so fucking pretty Jeff knew he'd jack off imagining topping him. What was he supposed to do about it? He couldn't help his feelings. He was only human. And male.

*I'm not a woman, Mick! I want to fuck around.*

Once Jeff parked and stood at his front door, unlocking it, he passed into the living room, feeling the coolness of the interior.

Mickey walked straight up the stairs to the bedroom. Rubbing his face in annoyance, Jeff needed a shower to wash off the sand and lotion, but needed a beer first. He removed one from the fridge and used a bottle opener to pry off the cap. Leaning back on the sink, he took a long drink of the cold ale.

He heard Mickey coming down the stairs. About to offer him a beer, he noticed him holding his backpack and two of his uniforms they had picked up from the cleaners, still on hangers and in plastic.

"What are you doing?"

"I think I should sleep at home tonight."

"Mick!" Jeff moaned in exasperation.

"Jeff, look, you can't be what I want you to be." He walked toward the door.

Jeff set his beer down and took off running, stopping him. One hand on Mickey's hip, the other trying to take the uniforms from him, Jeff said, "Why do you always have to go off on me? I have never even cheated on you."

"Not for lack of trying."

"What are we supposed to do tomorrow?" Jeff shook Mickey by the waist. "We'll be working twelve hours together."

"I'll talk to Bryant."

"No! Mick!" Jeff tore the uniforms out of Mickey's fingers and tossed them over the arm of the couch. He slid the backpack off Mickey's shoulder, dropping it to the floor. When Mickey's arms were limp at his sides, Jeff slid his fingers under his shirt and used his thumbs to massage his sides gently. "Mickey," Jeff purred, kissing his chin. "Why so extreme? Can't we just chill?"

"You want to screw other men, Jeff."

"I want to screw you." Jeff raised Mickey's shirt up his torso and sucked on his nipple.

"I'm sick of this pathetic game."

"Don't play it." Jeff ran his tongue over the hard nub.

"I feel used. Don't you get it?"

Jeff stuffed his hand down the front of Mickey's shorts, inside his bathing suit. "Don't feel used."

Mickey grabbed Jeff's wrist to stop him.

With his palm cupping over Mickey's genitals, Jeff asked, "Are you really trying to pull my hand out?"

"Yes."

Jeff stared deeply into Mickey's eyes. "You…you don't want to make love?"

"I want to go home."

Jeff removed his hand angrily and pushed back from Mickey. "See ya."

With a deep sigh, Mickey picked up his pack and uniforms, and headed to the door.

Wanting so much to shout out to stop him, Jeff watched him leave in agony. Once he was standing in the silence, he heard Mickey's pickup truck door close and the engine start. Walking to the window, Jeff peeked through the blinds as it backed out of his driveway. Mickey's actions hurt. Deeply.

Walking to the kitchen, Jeff picked up his beer and took a swig from it, thinking. What the hell did Mickey expect? An engagement ring?

# Chapter 6

Mickey arrived at work early so he wouldn't have to stand near Jeff in the locker room and change. Hanging around in the roll call room, he caught up on the bulletins he'd missed on his days off.

"Hey, Mickey."

He glanced over his shoulder. "Hiya, Flo."

"How was your time off?"

Mickey shrugged.

"Do anything?" Flo sat down at one of the tables.

"Went to Malibu Beach, slept a lot." He took the paperwork with him and joined her at the table.

"Anything good happen on our days off?" She leaned on his shoulder to read with him.

"Same old shit." He passed her the information as he finished reading them.

When someone stepped into the room, Mickey glanced up. Jeff was there. Christ, he looked amazing in his blues. His eyes lingered on the bulge in Jeff's pants under his gun belt.

"Hey." Jeff approached.

"Hey."

"Hi, Jeff." Flo smiled. "Did you have a nice weekend?"

"Half and half," Jeff replied, sitting on the table in front of Mickey.

When Jeff ran his fingers through Mickey's hair, Mickey looked at Flo for her reaction.

She was grinning. "I knew you two would be at it."

Mickey nudged Jeff's hand away. "Not at work."

Jeff leaned down to kiss Mickey's forehead.

"Hey!" Mickey shoved him back. "Not. Here."

Slow to respond, Jeff slid off the table casually and leaned against the wall next to him.

Out of the corner of his eye Mickey could see Jeff rubbing himself over his zipper flap. The surge it sent to his dick was intense. *You fucker. You motherfucker.* No one knew how to cock tease him better than Jeff did.

Men filed into the room, talking, joking, catching up. Mickey didn't look at Jeff's face once. He did notice as it became crowded Jeff stopped touching himself.

Roll call commenced and the sergeants assigned them to their usual cars and updated them on training and anything noteworthy. Ten minutes later they were walking to their patrol car.

It was Mickey's turn to drive and Jeff's turn to write reports. They alternated. While Jeff tucked his kit bag into the trunk, taking only a small briefcase into the front seat with him, Mickey gave the car an inspection as well as checking the shotgun, which hung from a rack inside it. They both ended up getting into the car at the same time. While Mickey fastened his seatbelt, Jeff logged them into service on the computer.

When the engine was started, the dispatcher's voice came over the radio.

"You going to give me the silent treatment all day?"

"Maybe." Mickey rested one hand on the steering wheel, powering the windows down until the air conditioning blew cold.

A deep sigh escaped Jeff. The minute they were available, dispatch called them for service. Jeff picked up the mike and responded. When Jeff said, "copy," after the call, Mickey reminded him, "We say 'roger' down here."

"Whatever." Jeff leaned his arm on the passenger's side door and gazed out of the window.

Mickey put the car in drive and left the precinct parking

lot, trying not to be so preoccupied it put him in danger.

After a few boring calls that amounted to nothing more than talking to people, a report of an occupied stolen car came over the air.

Jeff grabbed the microphone. "Eight-Adam-One, we're in the area."

"Eight-Adam-One, in the area."

"What was it again?" Mickey scanned the surroundings.

"Black 2005 Ford Focus, license plate 'U-Tube'."

"That should be easy to spot."

They cruised up and down the main streets before hunting the side streets.

"Turn right."

Mickey whipped the wheel and veered onto a secondary street. "What did you see?"

"Black four-door. Keep going."

Speeding up, Mickey came to the end of the block.

"There it is. Right turn"

They weren't close enough to see it clearly. Mickey flew down the side street at fifty. The black car veered off again.

"Fuck. They're running. That has to be it." Jeff grabbed the handle over the door for balance as Mickey accelerated to catch up.

The minute they had it on a straightaway, they knew it.

"Bingo." Jeff grabbed the microphone as Mickey hit the lights and sirens. "Eight-Adam-One, we've got the vehicle northbound on Butler at Missouri."

"He's flying." Mickey tore after him.

"Eight-Adam-One, in pursuit," Jeff advised dispatch.

Instantly, the air lit up with backing units racing toward them.

"Location, Eight-Adam-One?"

Jeff grabbed the dash to steady himself as they took a corner on two wheels. After a breath, Jeff said, "Eastbound—Santa Monica Boulevard."

Mickey's adrenalin was pumping. He knew the amount of traffic would be brutal where they were headed. Where wasn't it in LA?

Jeff threw the mike out of his hand. "Now! Before they bail!" He jumped out of the moving car.

Mickey jammed the transmission into park, flew out after him and drew his gun as the stolen car stopped for a traffic jam.

With Jeff on the passenger's side and him on the driver's, Mickey aimed the gun at the driver. "Let me see your hands!" Mickey roared.

Two hands appeared out of the broken window.

Mickey depressed his shoulder mike. "Eight-Adam-One, two at gunpoint."

"Code Three, all units responding, Code Three."

Staying in position, Mickey waited as two more patrol cars screamed into the intersection and the men jumped out with their guns drawn. Once six cops were aiming their weapons at the two in the car, Mickey heard Jeff shout, "Passenger! Get out of the car! Hands over your head!"

Mickey's heart was pounding and he was dripping with sweat. His sole attention was on the driver's hands which were still visible outside the window.

"Passenger! Down on the ground! Now!"

Jeff's orders were loud and clear and, without looking, Mickey knew damn well they were obeyed.

Another few moments passed and Mickey heard Jeff's shout. "Clear, Mick!"

Mickey knew that Jeff's suspect was in custody. "Driver!" Mickey ordered, "Step out of the vehicle." He adjusted his hands on the gun.

The man did nothing. Fuck! Mickey repeated it, louder. "Driver! Get out of the vehicle!"

Another quick look around and Mickey saw twelve cops pointing their guns at the car. He took a step closer to see into the driver's window.

"Get out of the car!" Mickey roared.

"My seatbelt is on, man!"

"Use your left hand and go slow. Unbuckle it." Mickey aimed his gun at the man's head, watching his hand move.

Very slowly the man undid the buckle.

"Open the door!" Mickey stepped closer.

The man swung open the door. Something was not right. Mickey sensed it. The man was too slow in obeying his commands. "Get out of the car! Now!" He couldn't shout any louder. Still the man didn't move. Mickey could see both his hands clearly. They were empty.

Another cop closed in, his gun now aimed at the suspect. Mickey holstered his weapon. When he had his hands free, he grabbed the suspect by the shoulder and tore him out of the car, planting his face on the tarmac. "Don't move your hands," Mickey snapped, pressing his knee into the man's neck, he handcuffed him. He did a pat down for weapons and felt the butt of a gun in the man's front waistband. "Gun! He's got a gun," he alerted the cops around him. "Don't fucking move!" Mickey ordered the suspect. Jerking the guy to his side, Mickey gripped the handgun and tore it out of the man's pants. He stuffed it into his own belt and continued to check for more weapons. When he was satisfied the driver was clean, he grabbed the man's arms, stood him up against the stolen car, and did one more check for weapons.

"He's clear." Mickey handed him off to another cop who put the suspect into the back seat of their patrol car. Once they had cleared the rest of the stolen ride for occupants, including the trunk, Mickey took a minute to wipe the perspiration from his face.

He removed the suspect's gun from his belt and opened the revolver's barrel dumping the six, thirty-eight caliber rounds into his palm. After he'd bagged both the ammo and the gun, locking it in the trunk of his car, he walked over to where the suspect was sitting in another patrol car and opened the back door. "What were you thinking?" Mickey asked him. "You do what a cop says, or you're a dead man, you got it?"

The suspect gave Mickey a strange look.

"Are you on dope?" Mickey prodded. "Didn't you hear me when I was telling you to get out of the car?"

"I was thinking about shooting myself, okay?" the suspect snarled.

"Shooting yourself? Over a stolen ride?" Mickey knew the guy was no older than his mid-twenties.

"I'm sick of jail."

"Then stop stealing cars." Mickey slammed the door shut and noticed Jeff watching him. When they met gazes, Jeff approached. "You okay? What was the deal with that suspect?"

"Contemplating suicide." Mickey wiped at the sweat as it poured from his face. "Lucky me, huh?"

"Fucker almost had suicide by cop. He had ten guns pointed at him." Jeff softened his tone. "You were awesome, Mick. Absolutely amazing."

"Who's got the first suspect you took out of the car?"

"He's in Flo's at the moment."

"Someone call an impound?"

"Yes."

Mickey nodded and walked to Flo's car. She was standing outside the back door, guarding the suspect. "We'll take him."

"You sure? I can transport."

"No. We got it." Mickey opened the back door. "Get out." He grabbed the man's arm and walked him to their own patrol car. Mickey leaned him over the hot trunk and patted him down before he put him inside.

"Mick."

"What?"

Flo held up a baggie. "He tried to ditch this in my backseat."

"Nice one. Put it in the car." Mickey nodded to his driver's seat. "Got anything else?" he asked the suspect, putting on a pair of gloves and nudging his legs wider.

"Needle in my front pocket."

Exhaling deeply, Mickey muttered, "I appreciate you telling me that. I mean it."

"No problem, man."

Mickey turned the man's pocket inside out gingerly and was able to remove the hypodermic needle without getting jabbed.

Jeff appeared with a narcotics baggie. Mickey dropped the needle in a 'sharps' container in the trunk of their car. "There's dope on my front seat. Flo found it after he dumped it."

"Got it."

"Have a seat." Mickey opened his back door and held the man's head as he maneuvered him in. Once he had shut the door, Mickey complained, "Fuck, it's hot."

Seeing everything was taken care of, even traffic officers assisting with the busy main street as a tow truck claimed the stolen car, Mickey dropped behind the steering wheel and cranked up the A/C, trying to get cold air to blow down his vest at the neck.

Jeff climbed in next to him. He picked up the mike and asked Mickey, "Ready to transport?"

"Yeah." Mickey put the car in drive.

"Eight-Adam-One, ten-fifteen to the station."

"Roger, Eight-Adam-One, ten-fifteen."

Jeff put the mike back on the hook and rubbed Mickey's thigh. "You are awesome."

"Just doin' my job, Chandler."

"But you do it so damn well."

"You're the one who spotted it in the first place."

"Dumb luck. I'm not the one who had a suicidal suspect with a gun to deal with. I had no idea what was going on and why he wasn't obeying your orders."

"At first I thought it was because he had his seatbelt on. He was afraid to move to open it. But when he still wasn't listening to me, I knew something was wrong."

"Awesome." Jeff's hand rubbed and squeezed Mickey's

thigh hungrily.

Mickey knew Jeff was excited. He smiled. *Well, as long as everyone managed to live through another scary call, I suppose it's okay to like Jeff touching me.*

"Awesome," Jeff repeated, grinning ear to ear.

※

After hours of writing extensive reports for two suspects, a stolen vehicle and narcotics, Jeff suggested they take a food break. "I'm starved."

"For anything in particular?" Mickey started the car in the precinct parking lot.

"Yeah," Jeff purred, sliding across the bench seat and wrapping his hand along the inside of Mickey's thigh.

Mickey looked around the area. Jeff did as well. He could see it was clear so he grabbed Mickey's jaw. When he kissed Mickey, he cupped his palm over Mickey's crotch and squeezed. "You hot, motherfucker." Jeff ran his lips across Mickey's freshly shaven skin.

"I'll make you suck it," Mickey warned, his eyes still surveying the surroundings.

Jeff went for his zipper.

"Not here. We're in the precinct lot, Jeff."

"Go park at the church."

"In broad daylight?"

"In the back. It's surrounded by trees."

Mickey put the car in gear. Sitting back in his seat, Jeff kept up the stroking of Mickey's hard cock, rubbing his own simultaneously.

They pulled into a small Presbyterian Church lot. Mickey drove around it and backed into the furthest corner of the chain-linked area. He put the car in park and looked at Jeff.

Without another word, Jeff wrapped his arms around him, kissing him. Inhaling Mickey's aftershave, Jeff opened his mouth wider, allowing Mickey's tongue easy access. Their little dance inside his mouth always thrilled him. He loved the way Mickey kissed. It was rough and masculine, yet showed that tender side Jeff craved from him. Going mad already, he stuffed his hand between Mickey's legs and dug under his dark blue slacks. As he rubbed Mickey's balls, Jeff urged Mickey into a deeper kiss by cupping behind his head. Soon their moaning drowned out the sound of the dispatcher broadcasting information.

Parting from the kiss, Jeff savored Mickey's lips as they mouthed his cheek and neck. He opened Mickey's gun belt and peeled it back. Next was his leather belt, button, and zipper. Hunting under Mickey's briefs, feeling his sweat and heat, Jeff was squirming in the seat and knew his own satisfaction would have to wait.

The minute the head of Mickey's dick appeared, Jeff dove down on it.

Mickey tensed his legs and his feet dug under the pedals.

Between Mickey's Kevlar vest and the steering wheel there was barely an inch of extra space for Jeff's head. Holding Mickey's dick upright, Jeff thrust up and down on it quickly, squeezing the base of Mickey's cock as he did. "Mmm…" Jeff moaned, shifting his legs as his own cock was bent awkwardly and he was dying to come.

"Jeff… Ah, Jeff…"

Mickey breathed out in pleasure, as Jeff tasted his cum in his mouth. Sucking like mad, Jeff made sure he drank every drop, slowing his pace down and mouthing it gently.

"Sit up."

Jeff popped up instantly.

Another patrol car was making its way over.

"Fuck!" Jeff faced forward in the seat as Mickey fastened his zipper and gun belt. Jeff tugged down the visor and checked his face in the mirror, wiping his mouth, running his hand through his hair.

The car pulled up to Mickey's side and the window lowered.

"Hey."

"Hey, Chris…" Mickey spoke casually.

"Good job earlier."

"Thanks."

Jeff tried not to look Chris in the eye. He had no idea if he'd seen him sit up or not.

"You guys still milking the call?"

"Yeah, a little. Just taking a break." Mickey rested his hand on the wheel, the picture of nonchalance.

"You may as well clear. Nothing's holding."

"Oh." Mickey looked over at Jeff. Jeff could tell Mickey was a nervous wreck, though outwardly he was acting perfectly normal. "You wanna clear?"

"Sure." Jeff pressed the correct code into the computer screen and hit the send button.

"Where are you guys thinking of eating lunch?"

Mickey shrugged. "I don't know. Any suggestions?"

"I was just going to get a burger over at the Astro Burger."

"Don't they spit in your food at those places?" Jeff asked, leaning down to see Chris through the driver's side window.

"No, they're all right. I go to the one on Santa Monica Boulevard. They know me."

Mickey turned to whisper, "We could go to the firehouse. It's nearing five."

"Great idea."

Leaning his arm on the driver's door, Mickey said, "We'll pass on the burger. Catch ya later."

"See ya."

Mickey rolled up his window and drove off first since he was facing the right way.

Once they were out of the lot, Jeff exhaled a deep breath. "I was fucking sure he saw me sit up."

"Me too, but obviously he didn't."

Jeff slouched in the seat. "You think one of these days someone will catch us?"

"Not if we're careful."

Jeff found Mickey's hand and held it on his lap. Hopefully the blowjob made up for some of the bad feeling Mickey had last night. Jeff didn't know any other way to make it up to him.

Mickey parked the patrol car in the back of the fire station next to several personal cars. As they walked up to the door, Mickey adjusted his gun belt.

"You all right?" Jeff gave him a wicked smile.

"Yeah. I'm good."

They rang the bell and waited.

A woman approached, opening the door. "Hey, guys!"

"Hi." Mickey stepped inside the hall. "We were wondering if Blake and Hunter were here."

"They are. You're just in time for dinner."

"Excellent!" Jeff keyed his mike and asked for a meal break. He was given one by dispatch.

"I'm Hailey."

"I'm Mickey and my partner's Jeff."

When Jeff came around a painted cement wall, he smelled the aroma of food and found three men seated at a long table in a lounge. "You firemen are so spoiled."

"Hey!" Hunter and Blake stood to greet them.

"'Bout time you guys made it over here." Blake shook each of their hands. "Have a seat. I was just serving dinner."

"Hey, buddy!" Hunter led Jeff to a chair next to them. "This is Dwight. Dwight, Jeff and Mickey."

They all shook hands in greeting.

"I've seen you guys out there," Dwight said.

"Yes, we're all over the place lately." Mickey sat down and looked back at Blake. "So, Chef, what's for dinner?"

"Baked ziti," Hunter moaned. "Taste." He held out a full fork.

Jeff looked at Dwight and Hailey first, having no idea who knew who was out or in. "I'll wait for mine. Thanks. It smells amazing."

"Blake is the best cook." Hunter ate the food off his fork.

"Here you go, gentlemen." Blake set a full plate in front

of each of them.

"Wow, Blake, I'm impressed." Jeff quickly stuffed the food into his mouth. "Mm!"

"Juice? Or water?" Blake searched the cupboards for two glasses.

"Juice, please," both Jeff and Mickey replied.

As Blake poured for them, Hunter asked, "So? How's your day going?"

Jeff pointed his fork at Mickey. "He did something awesome."

"It was no big deal, Jeff."

"Sure, Mick." Jeff thanked Blake for the juice when he set it down.

"What's no big deal?" Blake asked as he continued eating.

Jeff chewed and swallowed first. "Mickey pulled some guy out of a stolen ride. He was armed and contemplating suicide. He had a gun on him."

"Jesus!" Dwight shook his head.

"He wasn't responding to my commands," Mickey said. "I figured something was up."

"I wouldn't want your job." Hailey met Jeff's eyes.

"And I wouldn't want yours," Jeff responded. "I notice the flag is still at half mast."

"Yes. But today will be the last day." Blake appeared upset by the topic.

"We still need to go out for a drink and have a detailed discussion about that, Blake," Jeff said as a warning. After a practical joke had gone bad, one of their fellow firefighters killed himself in a blaze. Blake had executed the prank. Jeff knew how guilty Blake felt over Tom Young's death. But that was before they knew gay-bashing Tom Young was planning on kidnapping Hunter, torturing him, and killing him.

"Blake." Jeff made sure Blake met his eyes. When he had them, Jeff, said, "We do need to talk about that."

"I know. I know." Blake nodded.

Jeff watched Hunter and Mickey exchange worried

glances.

The sound of tones and a dispatcher's voice came over the air.

"You need to get that?" Mickey asked.

"Nope. Not for us." Blake continued eating.

"When are your next days off?" Hunter finished his plate and stood for seconds.

Mickey sat back to think. "Uh…we just started our three twelves, so in three days."

Blake said, "Perfect. That's our first day off as well."

"Good." Jeff nodded.

"Anyone want more?" Hunter asked.

"Hell yeah." Jeff stood with his plate.

"Come to my place?" Blake offered. "We can barbeque on the patio."

"Perfect," Mickey replied.

Jeff looked back at the table as Hunter spooned more food onto his plate. "How's Blake handling it?"

Hunter shrugged. "Good and bad."

"I want him to hear the details about what the detectives found in Tom's apartment. He needs to know."

"Do I need to know?" Hunter appeared pale. "What the hell was that Nazi planning on doing to me?"

As if Jeff just realized what he said, he touched Hunter's arm. "I'm sorry. Maybe I should just shut my mouth."

"How bad was it?" Hunter set the spoon back into the casserole dish.

"Bad. Never mind." Jeff returned to the table.

"What do you say, Hunt?" Blake asked, "Tuesday afternoon at our place?"

"You two live together?" Jeff asked in surprise.

"Yes," Blake answered.

Mickey's eyes became angry instantly. Jeff stayed silent and ate.

Taking a pen out of his pocket, Blake wrote down his home address and phone number. "Just call if you can't make it."

Mickey took the paper and folded it into his pocket. "We'll bring booze. Anything else? Dessert?"

"Sure. Booze and dessert." Blake smiled.

More tones blasted over the PA. Dwight and Hailey rose up. "We got it. You guys eat." They ran to the engine bay.

"Thanks!" Hunter shouted after them.

After they had left, Jeff asked, "Did they mind we made plans without them? I felt a little guilty."

Blake shook his head. "Don't. Dwight is married and busy at home, and I doubt Hailey would be interested now that she knows Hunter is gay."

Mickey laughed. "Broke the poor girl's heart, Hunt?"

"I doubt it." Hunter smiled sheepishly.

"This is great," Jeff praised as he finished his second helping. "I think we'll be here all the time now."

"Good. You know we love it." Hunter winked at him.

"We should invite Tanner and Josh."

As Blake said those names, Jeff caught Mickey's glare. "What?" Jeff threw up his hands in frustration.

Blake paused and met with each of their eyes. "A problem?"

"Yeah." Mickey snorted. "Officer Chandler wants to fuck Josh Elliot."

That comment made Hunter roar with laugher.

Jeff wasn't so sure it was a joke.

"Who doesn't?" Hunter exclaimed when he calmed his hilarity. "The guy's so fucking pretty."

"Think we can?" Jeff whispered.

Mickey shoved out his chair and brought his plate to the sink.

"Just leave it, Mickey. We'll do the cleaning up," Blake said.

Hunter leaned against Jeff's shoulder. "You don't mean you literally want to fuck Josh, do you?"

The skin of Jeff's face went red hot. Didn't he?

"Aren't you and Mickey…" Hunter made a gesture with his hands that appeared to mean 'together'.

Jeff was back in the doghouse. Mickey glared at him from where he leaned against the sink.

"Uh…" Jeff didn't know what to say to redeem himself.

"Yes," Mickey shouted. "He means literally, Hunter. He wants to fuck around. Jeff thinks the men here in LA are something special and he has the desire to sample as many as he can."

"I didn't say that." Jeff felt like he was being crucified unjustly. He didn't want fuck everyone. Maybe one or two.

Blake blew a breath between his teeth. "Good luck with Josh Elliot. I got the feeling after that call on the beach that he and Tanner are a couple. But I haven't verified that."

Hunter added, "Believe me, you don't want Tanner Cameron as an enemy. He's fucking big."

Mickey muttered, "I'm clearing the break," as he clicked his shoulder mike to tell the dispatcher.

Instantly, they were sent to a waiting call.

Feeling like the worst heel, Jeff carried his plate to the sink. Mickey avoided him.

"Thanks, boys. It was good food." Mickey rubbed Blake's back affectionately.

"We'll expect you at my place Tuesday, unless…" Blake took a quick look at Jeff, "things change."

"We'll be there," Jeff assured him. "Come on, babe." He reached out to Mickey who passed him by, pure venom and cold shoulder.

"See ya." Jeff waved, pouting as he walked behind Mickey to the car. "Stanton!"

Not turning around, Mickey threw up his hand as if he'd had enough.

Once they were side by side in the patrol car, Jeff moaned, "I won't fuck Josh, okay? Jesus!"

"Fuck who you want. I'm done with this relationship." Mickey threw the car in reverse.

"Don't say that." Jeff touched his leg.

Mickey shoved his hand off. "I'm talking to the sarge this evening and getting us separated."

"No. Mickey. No." Jeff's heart was breaking.

"Shut up. Stop talking to me." Mickey glanced at the computer screen to read the call.

Once Mickey had them driving in the right direction, Jeff leaned closer so he could read it as well. Residential burglar alarm.

Jeff rubbed his face in agony. He was so upset he couldn't think.

⁓⁓

Parking a few houses away from the actual home they were going to check, Mickey turned on his portable radio as he approached the posh house. There was a beautiful manicured garden and a black Mercedes parked out front. Jeff followed Mickey to the front door. They knocked. Mickey turned the handle finding it locked. Without a word, Mickey began checking the windows and making his way around the house.

Jeff tried not to brood. There was an easy way to fix this. Tell Mickey he wanted to be exclusive. Jeff just had to decide that he did. He would not lie to Mickey to keep him.

When they rounded the back of the house, Mickey tried the slider. "It's unlocked."

"Okay." Jeff took out his gun.

Mickey keyed his mike. "Eight-Adam-One. Open premises on our alarm."

"Eight-Adam-One, open premises. Would you like the air held?"

"Negative." Taking his gun out of the holster, Mickey pushed back the glass door and entered the kitchen.

Jeff followed behind him quickly. The home was perfectly tidy and open-plan.

They cleared the bottom floor. He heard Mickey shout, "Clear," as he went room to room.

Jeff climbed the stairs first, the gun pointed down. Pausing at the top landing, he entered a bedroom and had a look for hiding burglars. "Clear," he said.

He heard Mickey walking down the hall. Right after

he entered another room, he shouted, "Clear."

Soon they had inspected the entire house. No suspects or foul play existed. Jeff holstered his gun. Clicking the mike, he told dispatch, "Eight-Adam-One, under control."

"Eight-Adam-One, under control at the Code Three-Oh."

Jeff noticed a photo. Walking to the dresser, he picked up an eight-by-ten unframed picture that had been propped against the mirror. "Wow."

Mickey snapped his holster strap over his gun. "What?"

"Check this out." Waiting, Jeff held it for Mickey to see.

As if he just realized it was something good, Mickey took it out of Jeff's hands.

Seeing Mickey drool, Jeff asked, "What do you think of those two?"

"Definitely 'wow'." Mickey's mouth hung open.

"You think they live here?" Jeff leaned against Mickey to stare at the picture with him. It was of two men, one licking the other's cheek. The one doing the licking was gorgeous. Long dark hair flowing down his shoulders and back, the blond he was lapping at smiled broadly, loving the affection.

Mickey whistled. "I could jack off to that."

"No kidding." Jeff rubbed his hard dick.

"Where was it?"

Jeff took it and propped it up against the mirror again. Before he left the room he looked for more clues. Mickey was already walking down the stairs. Jeff hurried after him.

When he arrived at the bottom level, he found Mickey staring at the coffee table. A large picture book was displayed on it. The title read, *American Male-Men.*

"Go on." Jeff nudged him.

After taking a look around, Mickey picked up the heavy book and flapped open the cover. Both he and Jeff moaned at the naked men. "Nice…" Mickey sighed.

"Gay guys live here? I'm not writing them a ticket."

"Look." Mickey pointed to a photo in the book. "That's

the same guy from upstairs."

"Let me see that." Jeff drew the page closer. The man with the long hair sat on a white stallion. "He looks like a woman."

"Maybe his face does, but look at his body. Holy shit. All fucking man."

"Any of his cock?" Jeff waited as Mickey fanned the pages.

"There he is again."

The same long-haired man was in a bed with the sheet drawn to his pubic hair. "Mick, I'm going to die. Who is he?"

"Fuck if I know."

Jeff spotted something on the wall. "Mick. Look."

Setting the book back in its place, Mickey met Jeff where he stood. "An LAPD academy photo. The guy's a cop?"

Mickey inspected the faces of the group. "That guy is not in this class photo."

"Maybe his partner's a cop." Jeff nosed around.

"Here we go." Mickey held up a small framed photo.

Hurrying over, Jeff pressed against Mickey's arm. In the photo was the pretty long-haired man, with slightly shorter hair, and a stunning macho man holding him. "That's the cop."

"You know him?" Jeff walked back to the class photo. "It's an older graduating class. Look at the date."

"You think he's still on the department?" Mickey moved to the kitchen. Mail lay on the counter. "Steve Miller and Mark Richfield."

Jeff found him where he stood. "Which is which?"

"You do ask some dumb questions. How the hell should I know?"

"Let me see." Jeff took the pile of envelopes. "Duh. Mark is the model. Look, this one's return address is an acting agency."

"So, Miller is the cop." Mickey tapped his chin. "Steve Miller? Nope. Doesn't ring a bell."

"Wow. A gay cop dating that?" Jeff pointed over his

shoulder. "Lucky bastard."

Mickey shoved him. "Why don't you leave your number so you can fuck him?"

"Come on, Mick. When did you get so sensitive?" Jeff set the stack of mail down.

"So sensitive? Jesus, Jeff. You treat me like shit. What the hell do you want from me?"

"Treat you like shit?" Jeff crossed his arms defensively. "What the fuck? I do not. You're the one ruining it. I thought we had a good thing."

"You keep telling me you want to screw everyone else. Good thing?"

"Maybe I'm just saying that." Jeff unwound his angry posture. "I'm just all talk, Mick."

"Bullshit. If Josh Elliot dropped his pants in front of you, you'd stick it in."

"So would you!"

"No. I love you. I wouldn't fuck anyone else."

"Mickey…" Jeff pouted out his bottom lip. "Don't be mad at me."

Mickey twisted away from him.

Coaxing Mickey to face him, Jeff wrapped around Mickey's heavy bulletproof vest and leaned his own on him, pressing Mickey back against the sink. "Baby, don't break up with me." He made for Mickey's lips, running his hand down the front of Mickey's zipper flap. At the taste of Mickey's mouth, Jeff moaned softly, pulling Mickey's zipper down and reaching his fingers inside.

As if he couldn't resist, Mickey dug his hands into Jeff's hair, deepening their kiss.

Jeff opened Mickey's gun belt. It sagged heavily down his hips. On his knees in front of him, Jeff released Mickey's cock from his briefs. Knowing this was Mickey's second, and no BJ for him yet today, Jeff didn't know what more he could do to make it up to him. As he sucked Mickey deeply, Mickey combed his fingers through his hair, encouraging him.

"Bloody hell."

Jeff gasped and spun around slipping clumsily on the tile, only to flop onto his bottom on the kitchen floor.

Two men were staring at them from the doorway, both dripping in sweat and wearing only gym shorts. Jeff immediately recognized them from their photos.

"Oh, shit." Jeff scrambled to his feet as Mickey tucked his dick away and fastened his pants and gun belt.

The long-haired man gaped at them in awe. Jeff assumed he was the model, Mark Richfield. That left the LAPD cop, Steve Miller. "We're dead." Jeff gulped.

"What are you guys doing in here?" Steve asked.

Mickey cleared his throat. "Uh, your alarm went off. The back door wasn't secured. Please tell me you're not an LAPD lieutenant."

Steve chuckled. "Not LAPD anything anymore."

"Are we dead?" Jeff asked meekly.

"Well!" Mark's eyes were bright green. "It's not every day one comes back from a run to find two gorgeous cops performing a lewd sexual act in their kitchen."

"You're British?" Jeff exclaimed.

"Down boy." Mickey grabbed his arm.

"You're not dead." Steve removed two water bottles out of the fridge, handing one to Mark. "I didn't even know the alarm was set. I take it you checked the place out."

"Yes. Nothing is out of the ordinary." Mickey sounded like he was trying to be professional, which under the circumstances, Jeff thought was ludicrous.

"Sorry guys." Jeff smiled shyly. "We do get carried away a little."

"I didn't mind." Mark winked. "Lovely. Like a living fantasy. I'm sorry you stopped."

"All right, Mark." Steve rolled his eyes.

"We'll get out of your way now." Mickey nudged Jeff.

"Thanks for stopping by." Mark followed them to the door.

"Again, we're really sorry." Jeff paused.

Mark read his nametag. "Not to worry, Officer Chandler."

"Jeff." Jeff extended his hand.

"Mark. And your friend is?"

"Mickey Stanton."

"Mickey. Very nice to meet you." Mark squeezed Jeff's hand.

After Jeff checked to see where Mickey was, he whispered to Mark, "By the way, Christ, you're fucking gorgeous."

Mark blushed, lowering his long dark lashes. "Thank you. Perhaps you and your friend can stop by for a drink sometime. Off duty."

"Yeah?" Jeff's heart pounded.

"Of course. Steven, do you have a piece of paper to write our number on?"

Licking his lips, Jeff watched the drops of sweat run down Mark's angular cheekbones. *Christ, you're amazing.*

"Here you go, Jeff. Call anytime."

"Really?"

"Really." Steve laughed. "We can share LAPD war stories."

"Cool. Thanks. And thanks for not turning us in. Seriously."

"No problem, copper," Mark purred.

"Bye." Jeff folded the paper and put it into his wallet. When he made it to the front of the house, he found Mickey had already gotten the car and pulled it up to the residence. Once he climbed in, he was about to laugh about the incident when Mickey snarled, "Get a phone number for pretty Mark Richfield, Jeff?"

Jeff's kind smile dropped. This possessiveness was not good. Maybe he and Mickey should split up.

He stayed quiet the rest of shift, doing the work without the chitchat.

# Chapter 7

After twelve grueling hours, Mickey was exhausted. Avoiding Jeff's gaze as they changed out of their uniforms, Mickey left first, his off duty gun pack over his shoulder, his keys in his hand. He sat behind the wheel of his Ford pickup and started it. As he drove down the street, he noticed Jeff walking to his car. It hurt so badly to see him alone he bit his lip to suppress the pain.

Unable to prevent it, as he passed, Mickey met Jeff's eyes. The look of devastation killed him. "Oh, God." Mickey battled with his emotions the whole drive home. "What am I doing? What am I doing?" he moaned.

Parking in the apartment lot, Mickey scuffed his tennis shoes up the outer staircase to his apartment door. When he opened it up, he heard noises inside. Closing it behind him, dropping the gun pack down on the coffee table, he stood at the door to Aura's bedroom. She was sitting up against the headboard watching a DVD. One of his.

"Hey, Mouse. Is Jeff here?"

Kicking off his shoes, Mickey dropped down next to her. "No." He laid his head on her lap and watched the movie.

She ran her hand through his hair. "What did you do now, you dork?" she accused.

"I'm pushing him away from me and it's killing me."

"Why are you doing that?" She paused the DVD.

Rolling to his back to be able to see her, Mickey sighed. "He won't commit to me. He keeps flirting with other guys. It gets me so jealous I could kill him."

"Oh, Mouse…" She combed her fingers through his hair. "You do realize you've only been dating a few months. Maybe you're rushing things."

"Am I? No. Why the hell doesn't he love me yet?"

"He loves you."

"He never said it. Not once."

"He doesn't have to say it. I can tell."

Mickey wondered if he was being premature in ending things. A hot tear ran down his cheek before he could hide it.

"Don't be upset, Mouse."

"Where am I going to find another like him, Aura?" He wiped at it roughly.

"Don't look for his replacement. He's right there."

"He keeps making comments that hurt me."

"Like what?"

"He wants to fuck a lifeguard, a model, Christ, any pretty boy he sees he wants to have."

"So? I'd like to screw like that too, but it doesn't mean I will."

Thinking it over, Mickey stared at her. "You think he just fantasizes about it? But he won't?"

She shrugged. "I don't know him well enough to guess. In some ways, we're all sexual opportunists. I think even the most loyal spouse, given the right set of circumstances, would cheat."

"And that's supposed to make me feel good?"

"It's reality."

Mickey sat up. "I'm going to bed."

"Good night, Mouse."

"Night."

⁂

Jeff sat at his computer. A beer on a coaster on his desk, he typed Mark Richfield's name into Google. Reading the snippets of notes on his architecture designs, his modeling career, his signing on with Artists and Models for Hire, he found a link for YouTube. Clicking it, a short film downloaded. He choked in awe at the content and watched Mark writhing in bed with Carl Bronson and Keith O'Leary of *Forever Young*, that racy cable television drama everyone was talking about.

As it played out, and Mark was kissing one handsome movie star, then the other, Jeff stuck his hand into his briefs. He stroked his cock gently, replaying it once more. "How the hell did you guys meet?" The thought of a run of the mill, though exceptionally good looking, LAPD cop happening upon that Greek god was something Jeff wanted to figure out. There was a story there, he was certain.

Shutting off the computer, he sat for a moment, drinking his beer. A stretch and a yawn later, he set the bottle into recycling and ascended the stairs to his bedroom. After he washed up, he climbed into bed. Mickey. He was heartsick without his Mickey.

Reaching for the phone, Jeff picked it up, hesitated and set it back down again. He moved the sheet to his knees, spread his legs and massaged his cock. Coming would help him sleep. After pulling on his length for a few minutes, Jeff gave up. He rolled to his side and tucked the pillow under his head. Running his hand on the empty sheet next to him, he missed his lover. A lot.

"Mick…come on. Give me some time. Three fucking months? I just moved here." Jeff splayed out and knew he wouldn't sleep. Sitting up, he checked the clock.

※

Mickey yanked his shorts on as he headed toward the knocking noise. He rubbed his head, angry at being awoken from a sound sleep. When he opened the door, Jeff lunged at him, throwing Mickey back against the wall with a bang. Jeff connected to his mouth, stuffing his hand down Mickey's shorts.

Suspecting it had to be him in the first place, when Jeff attacked him, Mickey was still stunned. Jeff wrapped his arm around Mickey's neck, trapping him. As Jeff licked and sucked at his mouth, Mickey groaned in agony.

"Baby," Jeff hissed, "I need you."

Mickey embraced him, devouring Jeff's mouth and tongue as it went wild with his own. He tore Jeff's t-shirt over his head, stripping his gym shorts down his thighs. Spinning them around so he was dominating Jeff, pinning him to the wall, Mickey rubbed Jeff's cock and balls, kneading them in his palm as he sucked at Jeff's tongue. He parted from Jeff's lips, turned him to face the wall and hammered his cock between Jeff's legs, under his balls, not penetrating. "You want it, Chandler?" Mickey panted.

"Oh, Christ...oh, Christ!" Jeff growled, grinding his ass against Mickey's cock.

Mickey loved it. "Keep coming back for more, Chandler?" Mickey crushed him against the plasterboard. From behind Mickey chewed on Jeff's neck as Jeff groaned in agony.

"Fuck me! Fuck me, Stanton!"

Mickey wrapped his arms around Jeff's waist and picked him up off the floor. As they passed the front door, Jeff kicked it closed with a slam. While he dragged Jeff to his bedroom, Mickey squeezed Jeff's cock and balls in his hand, much harder than he ever had previously. He threw Jeff face down on his bed and tore off his own shorts. Pinning Jeff under him on the bed, Mickey ground his cock against his bottom roughly. "How bad you want it? Huh? Tell me how bad you want it, Chandler."

Jeff arched his back under him and roared loudly in frustration.

Mickey shook open his nightstand and fished out the lube and condoms. Once he'd managed to get one on with his shaking hands, he dragged Jeff's ass up off the bed. "Beg me."

"Fuck me! Please." Jeff panted in loud bursting breaths.

"I'll fuck you." Mickey shoved Jeff's face into the bed and jammed his cock into Jeff's ass. Jeff winced and cried out.

"Hard enough, Chandler?"

Jeff covered his head with his hands as he shivered, stifling his screams in the sheets.

Mickey encircled his arm around Jeff's waist and thrust in as he gripped Jeff's cock. Making sure he could rub against Jeff's prostate, Mickey fisted Jeff's prick wildly.

Jeff snarled like a feral wolf, reaching out his hands to strangle the bed.

Mickey inhaled him. Jeff was an aphrodisiac. While he was thinking, *I love you! You god!* he was growling, "Fuck you, you bastard, fuck you!"

Jeff howled in ecstasy as he came, shooting cum into Mickey's hand and on the sheet under him. Mickey convulsed as he climaxed it was so strong. Jerking his hips involuntarily deeper, he penetrated Jeff balls deep and gripped him like iron as his dick shivered inside Jeff's body.

Embracing him in a vise hold, Mickey dragged Jeff to his lap, still deep inside him. Jeff sitting on Mickey's thighs, gasping for air, Mickey's dick pulsated in him for a last few pleasurable throbs. Mickey rubbed his cheek over Jeff's back, kissing and licking his sweat-soaked skin. With both hands, Mickey massaged Jeff's spent cock, feeling the last drops of semen run sticky trails across his knuckles. He loved Jeff so much it was agony.

"Mickey… Mickey…"

Lethargic from the exertion and the twelve-hour shift, Mickey released his hold. Jeff staggered off his lap, disconnecting them and falling to his hands and knees on the floor.

The sex had become a drug. The two of them were addicts. At some sick level Mickey wished he could keep it just physical. The physical was unbelievable. Never, *never* had he experienced sex like this. It was heroin. Morphine. Something treacherously addictive.

Mickey staggered off the bed to the bathroom. Barely conscious, he discarded the spent condom and attempted to clean up. When he returned, Jeff was still sitting on the floor.

Standing over him, Mickey hauled him to his feet. They dropped onto the bed and passed out.

# Chapter 8

The alarm sounded. Mickey moaned in agony. He slammed the snooze button heavily.

"Augh…"

Mickey cracked open his eyelid.

Jeff was there trying to wake up. "Twelve motherfucking hours…" he moaned.

"Shut up." Mickey lay on top of him, nuzzling Jeff's face.

The alarm screamed again after ten minutes.

Frustrated, Mickey hit it so hard it fell off the nightstand.

"Let me up. Gotta pee."

Struggling to move, Mickey rolled to his back, freeing Jeff from his grasp.

He watched Jeff stagger out of the room, naked.

A second later, Jeff shouted out and ran back in. He leaned against the door. "Aura."

Mickey laughed until he thought about it. "Oh, God no."

"Oh, God yes," Jeff whined and found something to cover himself with.

Once Jeff left the room again, Mickey located a pair of clean briefs and tried to be brave. He found his sister sipping from a cup and fresh pot of coffee brewing. "Hey."

"Hey…"

Her smile unnerved him. "Shit. Aura…"

"Don't even think of apologizing."

"I…we…"

"Forgot I was here. I know."

"He…" Mickey pointed over his shoulder, couldn't think of a thing to say, so he retreated.

"I'll make toast for you."

Mickey waved without turning around.

∽∾

After he had shaved and dressed, Jeff sat on Mickey's bed, waiting for him to finish his morning routine. He wasn't about to face Aura single-handed. He might run into a barrage of gunfire on duty, but confronting Aura after the sex he and Mickey had? Pure chicken shit.

Mickey appeared, clean-shaven and washed up. "You want coffee?"

"Yes."

"She's okay with it, Jeff."

"Too okay with it." He laughed nervously, following him to the galley kitchen.

"Hi, again." Aura smiled.

"Hi. Sorry about earlier." Jeff thanked Mickey for the coffee.

"Believe me. It was my pleasure."

Jeff felt his cheeks go crimson.

They chewed the toast quietly. Jeff couldn't take the suspense. "How much did you see and hear, Aura?" He cringed as he waited.

"Me?" She pressed her fingers to her chest, expressing innocence. "See? Hear?"

"Cut it out, sis." Mickey refilled all their cups.

"Well, I 'saw' all of you a minute ago, Jeff. And man, is my brother fucking lucky."

Jeff rubbed his eyes in humiliation.

"And last night?"

Raising his head to spy her smug expression as she chewed her toast, Jeff cringed.

"Are you guys always that violent?"

"Ouch." Mickey shrunk back as Jeff hid.

"I mean, wow."

"Aura…come on."

"Don't blame me. He asked, Mouse. I swear, guys, if I had a video of you two wild animals doing it…"

"Aura," Mickey begged.

"Enough said." She set her cup in the sink. "Gotta go." She pecked both their cheeks.

After she left, Jeff sighed, "I swear, Mick, I forgot she was here."

"I did too. I'm used to doing it in your townhouse."

"How embarrassing." Jeff covered his eyes.

"I wouldn't worry." Mickey sat down next to him. "Why did you come? Just for the sex?"

Turning in his chair, Jeff faced him, holding Mickey's hand. "You know I'm crazy about you."

Mickey shrugged.

"I am. Completely. Mick, you have to admit the sex is…is…"

"Beyond belief?"

Jeff laughed softly. "I don't know about you, but I have never in my life experienced anything like it."

Mickey drew Jeff to his lips. "Neither have I."

After the kiss, Jeff set back to see Mickey's eyes. "Babe. I keep coming back for it. I know it's more than that. I do. But you keep putting all these demands and conditions on everything. I'm scared to death I can't live up to your expectations." Jeff smiled gently. "Except in bed."

Mickey's face darkened again.

Jeff hated when he upset him. "I know I talk…about Josh, or that pretty model, Mark. But in reality, Mickey, they have their own men, their own lives. I've learned you can't assume being gay that you could have the same monogamous relationship as straight couples." He took a deep breath. "I know damn well that if you had the urge to just have a fuck, you could. I never imagined gay men being the type to commit, to say some vow of marriage and never stray. I've learned that lesson the hard way." Jeff grabbed

Mickey's arm to prevent him from turning and running away. "Please understand…Mick…"

"What do you want from me?"

Jeff stood up, hugging him. "We're best friends. Partners on the job, lovers…what do I want from you?"

"If I hear you've had sex with another man, I'll crack up. I won't be able to take it."

Jeff was about to ask how Mickey would find out if he did, but thought better of it. "Can't we just take this a day at a time? Do you have to make some command decision to separate us both at home and on the job? Is that what you really want to do?"

Mickey hid his face in Jeff's chest. "No."

Rocking him, Jeff replied, "Then, let it go a little. Okay?"

The grip around his torso tightened. Jeff kissed Mickey's blond hair and held him. "You're my best friend, Mick. My best friend."

"Your fuck buddy."

"That too." Jeff smiled.

Mickey raised his head. He wasn't smiling.

"Don't you want to be my fuck buddy?" Jeff pecked his lips.

Not answering, Mickey closed his eyes, and rested his chin on Jeff's shoulder.

Holding him tight, Jeff wished he could be what Mickey wanted. Was something supposed to just click and it became the right decision? He just didn't know.

〜

It was Jeff's turn to drive. As Mickey attended the computer, Jeff tapped his fingers on the steering wheel and watched the changing of the guard. Exhausted, slumped over cops going home, and exhausted, slumped over cops coming on shift. A perpetual state of weariness prevailed. Maybe twelve-hour days weren't such a good idea. If they were subpoenaed to court in the early morning, it was murder.

"Ready?"

"Ready." Jeff smiled as Mickey sent their information via computer, logging them into service.

Instantly they were summoned by the dispatcher. Mickey picked up the mike to acknowledge her.

Jeff tried to concentrate on the call while feeling drained from the heat, the long days, and the emotional strain that Mickey was placing on their relationship.

"Roger," Mickey responded, setting the microphone back on the clip. "You know where it is?"

"I think I can find it." Jeff put the car in gear and drove out of the police parking lot.

"You did really well getting to know the area. If I lateraled into SPD, I'd struggle to find my way around."

"I studied the map a lot in the evenings. I hate being lost. Besides, I have you to direct me."

"We need to shoot some practice rounds. Qualifications are looming."

"Shit." Jeff didn't need one more stressor in his life at the moment.

"You a decent marksmen?"

"I'm okay." Jeff paused at a traffic light, looking around at the cars that were in his field of vision. He enjoyed finding occupied stolen vehicles.

"Bet you're more than okay."

Trying to feel confident in their relationship, Jeff smiled sweetly at him.

He pulled up in front of a large apartment complex. After Mickey let the dispatcher know they had arrived, Jeff climbed out and turned on his portable radio.

"Number thirty-two."

"Right." Jeff buzzed the number code on a panel near the lobby door. A crackly unintelligible voice came through it. "Seattle Police." Instantly realizing his error, Jeff shouted, "I mean, Los Angeles Police…" rubbing his face and sighing as Mickey laughed at him.

"Man, she's going to think you came a long way just

for her 911 call."

"Shut up."

A metallic snapping sound alerted them the door was unlocked. Mickey opened it and allowed Jeff to walk through first. They stood waiting for the elevator.

Jeff knew in the past what their "elevator behavior" consisted of. A violent lunge, sucking tongues and groping cocks. It didn't feel as if that was going to happen at the moment.

The elevator opened, an old woman holding a small dog, gasped at them. She hurried past them to the outside door.

Jeff stepped into the box, facing outward as Mickey hit number three. "Jesus, lady, we don't bite."

"Don't we?" Mickey asked as the doors slid closed.

"Well, we do chew and tear a little." Jeff leaned against the back wall as the elevator ascended. "What? No hot kiss and fondle?"

Mickey pecked his cheek.

"Ooh, be still my heart," Jeff teased.

"Tough. It's all you're getting at the moment."

"Brat," Jeff muttered as the doors opened to their floor.

"Moron," Mickey replied.

"Buttface."

"Dickwad."

Jeff laughed as he knocked on the correct door. When it opened, a woman stared at him. "Did you say Seattle Police?"

"Sorry. Brain dead." Jeff asked, "What can we do for you?"

She backed up and allowed them into her apartment. "Last night I broke up with my boyfriend. And this morning I get this nasty message." She walked to an answering machine that rested on a side table in the living room. "I knew it was him from the caller ID so I didn't pick up."

Mickey took out his pad and pen before she played it.

"Ready?" she asked.

They nodded.

She hit the button. A man's angry voice was heard. "Listen, whore, you want to play around? Play around. But if I find out who you're fucking, you're dead. No one fucks with me, girl. No one. I told you I wanted a commitment from you. But you're too busy looking at everyone else to give a shit what I think. So, let this be a warning. If I catch you out with another man, I'll kill both of you."

Jeff felt his face go crimson. That may as well have been Mickey leaving a message for him. He was afraid to look at Mickey's face the guilt was so strong.

She stopped the tape.

Mickey asked, "What's his name and address?"

After she gave it, she said, "I think he's just mad. I don't think he would hurt me."

"Has he ever hit you before? Made threats like this?"

As Mickey interviewed her, Jeff began to feel like it was a conversation about him and Mick's relationship and it made him very upset.

"No. Never. He asked me to marry him. He even bought a damn ring. I just thought it was too soon. I recently moved to LA and I don't think it's right to dive into a relationship without exploring my options."

Jeff rubbed his face in misery. *Christ, we don't need this.*

"If he's home at his address, we'll pick him up."

"What?" She coughed. "Arrest him? I don't want him arrested."

"He threatened to kill you." Mickey pointed his pen at the machine.

"No." She shook her head. "He's just angry because he wants me to be exclusive. He's really in love with me. He wouldn't hurt me."

"What do you want us to do?"

Jeff was dying. He wanted to walk out of the room so badly he had to restrain his impulse.

"Just talk to him. Make him see reason."

"Can I have that tape? For evidence?"

"The tape?" she gasped. "No. I don't want him in trouble. Honest, Officer. He's just the kind of guy that needs security. I know eventually we'll manage to work it out. If I give you that tape and you arrest him? Well, it's over between us, isn't it? And I'm not ready to let him go."

"Oh, God…" Jeff muttered.

When the room went silent, Jeff peeked up. They were both staring at him. "Never mind." He waved at them.

"Then," Mickey asked impatiently, "what exactly did you call us for?"

"I don't know. Talk to him. Tell him not to rush me."

"Can't you do that?" Mickey added.

"He won't listen. He gets all mad at me and won't stay quiet enough to hear me out."

"Fine." Mickey put his pad back into his pocket.

"Thanks. I know it sounds silly. I suppose I shouldn't have dragged the police into this. I didn't realize you would arrest him or something." She walked them to the door.

"Threats to kill are a felony." Mickey paused before he walked to the hall. "If we find him, we have no choice but to pick him up."

"No! I won't press charges. Didn't you hear what I just said? He's just upset."

"If he's not?" Mickey countered. "If he's seriously considering killing you and we do nothing. What then?"

"I know him. He isn't serious. I'm sorry I called you now."

"You did place us in an awkward position."

Jeff watched Mickey's profile. The fucker was so goddamn handsome standing there in his dark blue short-sleeved shirt and navy blue slacks hugging tightly around his massive thighs. Clean-shaven, delicious blue eyes. Jeff's cock throbbed hungrily.

"I didn't mean to. Can we just forget it? If you're going over there, I'll call him and tell him to leave."

Mickey let out a deep exhale in frustration. "I have to

write it up. I'll let the follow up domestic unit decide what to do. You'll probably get a call."

"Whatever," she snorted.

They left her apartment and stood at the elevator silently.

When it opened, Mickey stepped in first, spinning around to face the door. The minute they were closed in, Jeff shoved him back against the wall and kissed him.

Mickey tensed up, not responding.

Jeff leaned back to see his expression. "I knew it."

"Seems your kind are prevalent in this city."

"What if you didn't want a committed relationship and I did?"

Mickey nudged him over and pressed the button for the lobby. "Stop justifying it. I'm sick of talking about it."

"Jesus, Mick. I used to live for riding in a elevator with you."

Once they were on ground level, Jeff walked back to the car, climbing in.

"We have to go try to pick him up."

"I know." Jeff shut off his portable radio and started the engine.

Mickey lifted the patrol car's mike off the dash. He let dispatch know they were relocating to the suspect's address. She acknowledged them.

Driving to this poor schmuck's house, Jeff hoped the woman had called him and warned him. It was a bad idea for the guy to leave that message if he wasn't going to harm that woman. The idiot just made himself a suspect. As Jeff drove, Mickey checked the man's name and date of birth in the computer. "Any priors?"

"Nothing. He's clean."

"Poor SOB."

"No kidding." Mickey kicked his foot against the floor mat. "I'd rather arrest her for being an asshole and leading the man on."

Jeff scrubbed his hand through his hair as he drove.

*This is so not good.*

No one was home at the address. Jeff figured as much.

Parking in a quiet vacant lot, he daydreamed as Mickey typed up the report on the keyboard connected to a frame that held the computer.

Listening to various other cops answering other calls, Jeff felt that if he closed his eyes he could be lulled to sleep. Peeking over at Mickey, Jeff waited until he was finished with the report before he talked. "I was thinking about what the detectives found over at that Tom Young's place."

"Mm?" Mickey didn't look over at him.

"I think it's important for Blake to know the details, but maybe not good for Hunter. The plan Tom made for that kidnap and torture session was pretty gruesome."

"Are we still going there?"

Jeff stared at Mickey's profile. "Why aren't we?"

Mickey shrugged.

In the tight space of the car, Jeff tried to shift his body to face him. "Why do I think things are good, and then I get the cold shoulder from you again?"

Instantly Mickey met his eyes. "You think things are good?"

"Fine!" Jeff shouted, throwing up his hands. "You know what? I'm yours. Okay? We're engaged. Buy me a ring."

"Fuck. You." Mickey glared at him.

"Stanton! What the hell do you want from me? I can't fucking win. Move in. Okay? Move in."

"You have any idea how much I hate you right now?"

Jeff released a loud growl in frustration. "Now you hate me. Fine. Hate me."

"You self-absorbed bastard. Everything's always on your terms."

Jeff showed his teeth as he snarled, grabbing Mickey's uniform shirt collar. "Watch it, Stanton."

Mickey shoved Jeff back, making him hit the driver's door.

In rage Jeff dove at him, ramming him hard into the

passenger's side. It was so tight in the front compartment, with the computer, radio, shotgun, and their girth and height, there was no place to fight. But it didn't stop them from trying.

With the heel of his hand, Mickey pressed Jeff's jaw back as Jeff used all his weight to force Mickey against the opposite side of the car as he was. As he tilted his chin to tear away from Mickey's grasp, Jeff grabbed Mickey's head in both hands and jerked him forward, meeting his lips and whimpering in agony as he sucked on Mickey's mouth.

Mickey forced Jeff back into the driver's seat, stuffing his tongue into Jeff's mouth.

Panting, going crazy, Jeff clamped his fingers into Mickey's hair and pressed their mouths together painfully hard.

Emergency tones came over radio.

They gasped and sat back, gulping the air.

"Code Nine-Nine...repeat, Code Nine-Nine...Edward unit involved in One-Forty-Eight..."

"Fuck!" Jeff slammed the car in gear, hitting the sirens and lights. "Mickey, get me there! What's the quickest route?"

"Turn right here!"

Squealing the tires as they flew on the wrong side of the road around stopped traffic, Jeff was frantic. His adrenalin, testosterone, and fight/flight response was pumping him into pure madness. He just had to get there. The traffic unit wasn't responding to radio's call.

"There!" Mickey pointed to a police motorcycle.

Jeff slammed on the brakes and jammed the car into park. Both he and Mickey flew out of their patrol car and found the officer rolling on the ground with a suspect trying to unholster the cop's weapon.

Jeff roared in fury and grabbed the suspect by the shoulders, dragging him off the officer. Mickey dove on the rogue male, pinning him to the dirty pavement. Pushing the suspect's face into the hot tarmac, Jeff pressed his knee on the man's neck. Mickey wrenched the suspect's arms behind his back and ratcheted cuffs on him. The man under them screamed from pain.

"You son of a bitch!" Jeff dug his knee into the suspect's back.

Mickey slapped Jeff in the arm. "Get him up."

Other units came screeching to a halt, the smell of brake pads and gas fumes permeated the hot air.

Jeff gripped the suspect by his hair and arm and forced him upright as the man shrieked. Jeff threw him over the hood of a boiling patrol car and patted him down for weapons.

"You all right?" Mickey asked the traffic cop.

"Christ, he had me. I thought I was dead. He was pulling my gun out of my holster."

Hearing it, Jeff slammed the man's body into the car again. "You did what, you SOB?"

"Easy man!" the suspect whined.

"Jeff." Mickey grabbed his arm.

Seeing Mickey's calm expression through his tunnel vision, Jeff inhaled a few times to decompress. A second traffic officer and a supervisor showed up amid the patrol units.

Backing up as they approached, Jeff tried to catch his breath. He couldn't even remember how they got there. Someone swapped over the handcuffs and handed Mickey back his pair as the suspect was placed into another car. Dizzy from the adrenalin dump, Jeff moved to the supervisor's patrol vehicle fender where the traffic cop was recuperating. Jeff fell back against it next to him. "You okay?"

The traffic cop was beaming at him and Mickey. "You two were like bats outta hell! Holy fuck. I've never seen anything like it. Thanks, guys."

Jeff took his outstretched hand. "I'm just glad you're all right."

"Chandler?" the traffic cop read his nametag. "Are you new?"

"Transfer from Seattle."

"Fuck. Their loss is our gain."

Jeff patted the traffic cop's shoulder in gratitude and relief.

A sergeant appeared. Jeff bit his lip and wondered if he was going to get nailed for excessive force. He had been so upset to see the traffic cop on the ground battling for his gun he knew he'd lost his head a little. And well, he was pent up from Mickey's lips.

"I need a statement from both of you. We're booking him for attempted murder."

Jeff nodded, checking Mickey's eyes. When Mickey touched Jeff's arm, Jeff stood off the car and followed him back to their own patrol car. Waiting, Jeff watched as Mickey found two statement forms. They leaned side-by-side on the trunk of the car and scribbled down what they had done when they arrived.

Once Jeff was finished, he looked around. Media, medic units, gawking spectators, it was suddenly a fiasco. Making sure Mickey had completed his form, he brought both their statements to the sergeant. "Here, Sarge."

"Thanks. Well done. Good work." He whacked Jeff's shoulder assertively. "Go clear. Thanks for the assist."

About to say goodbye to the traffic cop, Jeff noticed him being checked over by medics. Meeting Mickey at the car again, Jeff climbed in and dropped down on the seat. He was drenched in sweat and spent.

Mickey splayed out on the passenger's side, sipping water from a bottle. He handed it to Jeff.

"Thanks." Jeff swallowed it down thirstily.

"You okay?"

Nodding, Jeff gave him back the water. Mickey took hold of Jeff's arm and raised it up. Jeff felt him brushing pebbles from his skin. "Am I cut?"

"Yeah."

"I think I felt it. I can't remember." Jeff looked out of the windshield at the lunacy still in full swing.

"Let's go."

Backing out, Jeff headed them in the direction of their own sector, trying to recover from the event and the heat. They didn't discuss anything. Not the incident, nor the violent kissing prior to it.

※

Sitting in the car and eating lunch, Mickey wiped at his lips with a napkin and tried to think about what had happened. He knew Jeff. Jeff had gotten himself into an altered state even before the emergency call came over radio.

While he licked the guacamole sauce off his fingers, Mickey hated to admit he loved it when he and Jeff were violent with each other.

After all, they were carnivores; top men. There wasn't much at times separating cops from criminals in one respect. Power. Cops craved it as much as crooks.

Mickey had no doubt he needed to control Jeff, and vice-versa. Though who liked to top the other more during sex was up for debate. Mickey always preferred the bottom, but the last two times he'd topped Jeff, well...

He peered over at him.

Jeff was shoving the last bite of his taco into his mouth. Mickey felt his cock throb. *You big, sexy, macho, killing machine. I love you so much I ache.*

"Let's go to the range."

"Hm?" Jeff licked his fingers. "Shoot? Now?"

"Yeah."

"Sarge will never let us." Jeff crumbled up the wrappers and stuffed them into the bag it came in.

"I can ask." Mickey gave him his trash to add to the bag.

Jeff sucked his soda through a straw. "It's too busy. Forget it, Mick."

"Want to go before shift tomorrow?" Mickey ran his hand down Jeff's inseam.

Jeff stopped slurping his soda and looked at him.

"I wanna see you shoot," Mickey purred.

"Mick's back!" Jeff shouted. "Where've you been, you horn dog? I've been dealing with your frigid evil twin."

"Frigid?"

"Give me one of those things to clean up with. My hands are greasy."

Mickey gave Jeff a foil packet of disinfectant wipe that they always had handy, using one himself.

"Are we okay?" Jeff asked as he cleaned his fingers.

"I don't know. Don't ask."

"Don't ask, don't tell?" Jeff laughed.

"Yeah. Whatever."

"Uh oh, the evil twin is back." Jeff pulled the car up to a trash can, leaned out and tossed the garbage in it. "Three points."

"I'm clearing our break."

"Okay." Jeff drove out of the parking lot and onto the main road.

Mickey picked up the mike and cleared their lunch break with the dispatcher. When she acknowledged it, Mickey hung the radio back up on its hook. "Where you headed?"

"Just cruising."

Slouching in the seat, Mickey looked down at his dark slacks and rubbed at a small, dusty spot on them from their earlier tousle on the street. When he looked up, he found Jeff was trailing behind two joggers. "What are you doing?"

"Recognize them?"

Mickey leaned closer to the window. One male had a ball cap on and a long brown ponytail bouncing out the back of it, the other was shirtless and solidly packed. "Were you looking for them?"

"It's about the same time as the alarm came out yesterday. They had just come back from a run." Jeff shrugged.

"How can they run in this heat?"

"I have no clue. Mick…I'm going to say something to you. Don't get upset."

Mickey threw up his hands in a gesture of futility.

"I don't want to fuck him, but…Jesus, Mick. Look at the guy's ass."

Mickey did. It was outstanding. Both men were.

Finally the long-haired model noticed they were being trailed.

The minute he made eye contact, Mickey rolled down the window. "Are you guys insane?"

Steve spun around. Mark was already jogging toward them.

"Oh, air conditioning!" Mark almost dove into the car head first.

Mickey pressed back into the seat and started laughing.

"Hello, boys." Mark grinned flirtatiously. "To what do we owe the pleasure?"

Mickey leaned closer to Mark and inhaled. "Damn, you smell good."

Jeff placed the car in park and leaned for a sniff. "Mm! Holy Christ…"

Steve dragged Mark out of the window and back on his feet. "Hey, guys."

"Hello, Steve." Mickey smiled. "How can you run in his heat?"

"He's killing me." Mark tried to climb back into the window again. "He's a brute. Arrest him, Officer."

Jeff chuckled. "Mickey, he is so frickin' cute."

Ignoring the comment, yet agreeing with it completely, Mickey said to Steve, "Why do I get the feeling you have your hands full, Miller?"

"You have no idea." Steve rolled his eyes, keeping Mark at bay.

"Let me feel the cool air," Mark complained. "You're the one who loves this heat, not me."

"Come on in, hot stuff!" Jeff waved.

Mark poked his head back inside. "Oh! I could squirm all day on you two. I love cops."

"Behave, Richfield!" Steve moaned.

"You already have a cop." Mickey smiled.

"Ah!" Mark reacted when Steve swatted his bottom. "Now I have wood."

Jeff moaned in agony. "Mark, stop."

Mark begged Steve, "Hit me again, copper."

Steve obliged.

When Mark flinched and whimpered, Mickey was fully erect and stunned.

Jeff punched Mickey's arm at his reaction. Mickey turned to see his expression. Jeff was very amused. "Go on. You know you want to," Jeff urged.

Mark peeked at Mickey. "He wants to what? Ah!" Mark got another swat from Steve since his bottom was easily accessible as he leaned into the patrol car. "Oh, that makes me tingle!"

Mickey shifted in his seat. He wanted to, but he knew it would prove Jeff right.

"Mickey…" Jeff coaxed in a deep voice, "Go on."

When Mark spun around to look at Mickey curiously, Mickey grabbed his face and planted a kiss on his lips.

Mark's eyes sprang open. He got another swat at the same time and hummed in delight.

When Mickey parted from his lips, he grinned at Mark wickedly.

Mark panted in excitement. "I think I came!"

Steve muscled into the window beside him. "What'd I miss?"

"This naughty cop kissed me!"

"Sorry, Steve. He was right fucking there."

"I swear, I came in me pants. Steven. I did."

Jeff groaned and rubbed his crotch in agony.

"He gets into the worst trouble," Steve said, "Just ask Billy Sharpe."

"The sergeant from SWAT?" Jeff asked.

"Yup. Come on, Mr. Richfield. Let's get this run done."

"Bye, boys." Mark threw a kiss at Jeff and pecked Mickey on the lips.

After they jogged away, Mickey took a minute to recover.

"Uh hum?"

Turning to see Jeff's look of satisfaction, Mickey warned, "Not one word."

"Yeah, right."

"I mean it!"

Jeff laughed as he drove down the street.

Mickey touched his lips softly as he thought about what just happened. Yes, it was nice, but he still wasn't interested in screwing anyone but his top man.

⁂

Mickey was finishing up writing a ticket for a traffic accident they had just come from. Jeff drifted off, leaning his elbow on the driver's door handle and resting his chin in his palm. Dispatch came over the air with a call. Jeff perked up to listen.

"Possible Four-Seventeen, description of suspect…"

"I knew it was too quiet." Jeff sat up and fastened his seatbelt.

Mickey picked up the mike to offer up for the call, waiting until the dispatcher had finished her information. "Eight-Adam-One, Code Three."

"Eight-Adam-One, Code Three."

Jeff heard several other units responding to the same call, a man with a gun. As he ran lights and sirens around the tail end of rush hour traffic, which seemed to becoming longer every day, the update reported shots fired.

"Crap." Jeff paused. "Left or right, Mick?"

"Right. First left, then we're in the area."

"Thanks." Jeff knew the streets when he had time to think but struggled with the layout when he had to get there fast. He'd learn it. He'd only been in LA a few months.

Mickey told dispatch they had arrived.

Slowing down, Jeff searched for the person from the description the dispatcher had broadcast. Someone flagged them down. Jeff pulled over as Mickey lowered the window.

"You here for that guy with the gun?" the man panted, the cell phone to his ear.

"Yes." Mickey had clicked into cop mode big time.

Jeff waited for the update impatiently.

"He's down there. Big guy. Wearing a baggy coat in this heat. Wool cap."

"You saw a gun?"

"Yes."

"What color's the coat?"

"Black."

Mickey picked up the microphone and broadcast the information for the other units responding.

"There! There he is!" the man panicked and ran.

"Shit." Jeff jumped out of the driver's side, drew his weapon, and crouched behind the open door. Mickey did the exact same thing on the passenger's side the radio mike to his lips letting everyone know.

Jeff shouted, "Hands up! Get your hands up!" as the man approached.

He was ignored.

"Now!" Mickey roared, his gun aimed over the doorframe.

The guy kept moving toward them, seemingly oblivious to their commands.

"You see a gun?" Jeff asked.

"No." Mickey rose up, both hands on the weapon pointing at the man. "Get your hands up! Now!"

The man looked stunned and held up his hands.

Jeff raced around the car to stand with Mickey. "On the ground!"

"What'd I do, man?"

"On the ground!" Jeff snarled.

Slowly, with his hands over his head, the young man got to his knees.

Jeff heard other sirens shutting down and the heavy sound of hot car engines behind him.

"I didn't do nothin', man!"

"Face down!" Mickey ordered.

The young man lay out spread eagle.

Jeff holstered and sprinted to him, dragging the man's

hands behind his back to cuff.

"What did I do?" he whined.

"Someone said you had a gun."

"A gun?"

Mickey stood over Jeff as he felt around the young man for a weapon. "Nothing."

"I told you I don't have a gun!"

Jeff sat the man up. "We got a report of a man with a gun and shots fired. And a witness pointed you out."

"It ain't me."

"Did you see someone with a gun?" Mickey asked, holstering his Glock.

"No!"

Jeff helped him to stand and unhooked the cuffs. The man rubbed his wrists when he did. Sighing, Jeff whispered to Mickey, "Get a supervisor."

Nodding in agreement, Mickey asked for their sergeant over the air.

"Not him?" one of the cops yelled.

"No, keep looking." Mickey waved the massive army behind him onward.

"Sorry, man." Jeff allowed the young guy to lean against his car. "Can I have your name and birth date?"

"Yeah." He gave it to Jeff.

Mickey reached his hand out to Jeff. "I'll run it."

Tearing the page off his pad, Jeff handed it to Mickey. He sat down on the passenger's seat to check to see if the young man had any outstanding warrants for his arrest.

Sgt. Bryant's patrol vehicle pulled up. Jeff looked back at him as he climbed out of his car and put his cap on.

"Sarge." Jeff nodded to him.

"What happened?"

"We were flagged down when we drove up. A man on a cell phone, who we assumed was the witness, pointed this guy out and said he was the one with the gun."

"And?"

"He was mistaken. No weapon. We had him on the

ground and cuffed him, Sarge."

Mickey stepped out of the car. "He's clear."

The sergeant nodded and had a chat with the young man.

Jeff sighed deeply and leaned on Mickey's arm. "I hate it when this happens."

"Good to get the sarge here. Cover our asses if the kid complains."

"What were we supposed to do, Mick?"

"What we did. We had no choice."

"I feel like kicking that complainant's ass."

Mickey rubbed Jeff's back in comfort.

When the sarge stepped back, Jeff approached the young man. "I'm really sorry." He held out his hand.

"It's okay. I wouldn't want to do your jobs, man." The young guy shook Jeff's hand.

"No hard feelings?" Mickey extended his hand next.

"No. It's all right."

"See ya." Jeff waved as the man walked off. "Fuck. Sarge." Jeff clenched his fists as he faced his supervisor.

"Don't beat yourselves up. If he was the suspect with the gun, you followed procedure. He was a decent kid. Just in the wrong place at the wrong time. You did the right thing calling me."

"Thanks." Mickey smiled at him.

They paused as someone spoke over radio. "They got someone?" Sgt. Bryant asked.

"Yes." Jeff bolted to the patrol car.

Mickey dove into the passenger's seat as the sergeant raced to his own car.

Over the airwaves a panicked officer's voice shouted, "Shots fired! Shots fired!"

"Fuck!" Jeff shouted. "Where is he?"

"Slow down. We're coming up on it."

Three patrol cars were aimed at the same area. None of them occupied. Jeff parked behind them, drew his weapon and he and Mickey took cover behind the black and whites.

Sgt. Bryant crouched with them. "Where are they? Did radio give an update?"

"No." Mickey waited.

Sgt. Bryant asked the dispatch for more information.

Jeff heard popping. "Shit!" He rose up and started running in the direction of the gunfire. Mickey caught up to him. Side by side they raced to the commotion. Behind them the sergeant's puffing breaths were audible.

Jeff spotted another uniformed cop. He whacked Mickey to get his attention and they crouched down instantly. "We're behind you!" Mickey shouted to the kneeling cop. He waved them over.

The sergeant crept with them. "Where is the suspect?"

"No clue."

Gunfire sounded again. Instinctively, they hit the deck. It was close by. Jeff knew it was very close, and though they had concealment behind shrubbery, they had no cover if a bullet came their way.

"Who's shooting?" The sergeant shouted to the dispatcher, "Radio? Any update?"

More popping sounded. Jeff was convinced it had to be an exchange. There were too many shots for it to be one shooter.

"Ten-Nine-Nine! Officer down!" came a frantic transmission from the radio.

Jeff's blood went cold. "Sarge! We have to go in there!"

"No! Stay put until I figure out where they are!"

Mickey grabbed Jeff's shoulder, squeezing it.

Imagining one of his own, bleeding and unable to help him, Jeff went nuts.

The same voice was heard, panic-stricken. "Medic! Send a medic!"

Jeff rose up, Mickey yanked him down.

"Please! Sarge!" Jeff begged.

"You want to walk into an ambush?" Sgt. Bryant announced. "One man down is enough! Sit tight!"

A watch commander's voice was heard over the air. He

asked someone to advise where the suspect was and a safe approach to the downed officer.

"Suspect fleeing southbound!" was shouted over the air.

Jeff was up and running as the street location was broadcast. He suddenly came face to face with a large male in a black coat.

Jeff dropped to his knees and aimed the gun. "Get down! Show me your hands!"

The man spun and ran. Jeff bolted after him. Mickey had caught up, racing at his side.

When Jeff aimed his gun to shoot the guy in the back, Mickey slapped his arm down. "Don't do it!"

"He shot a cop!"

"Jeff! Don't!"

They cornered the suspect in an alley that had no outlet.

Mickey grabbed Jeff and hauled him behind a dumpster. "Face the wall! Get your hands up!" Mickey roared.

The man slowly faced the bricks behind him.

"Easy," Mickey warned Jeff.

They set their guns on target, both hands on their weapons, held up to their eyes, sites on the suspect's back, and walked toward him.

"Don't fucking move," Jeff ordered, "or you're dead."

The man spread his legs, hands flat on the wall above him.

Mickey holstered and looked at Jeff. Jeff nodded, aiming at the guy's head now.

Mickey dove at the suspect, grabbed his wrist, and slammed the man into the wall. Slapping a cuff on one hand, he wrenched the other down and fastened the second one. Jeff walked right up next to the man and pointed the gun at his temple. "How do you like it?" Jeff sneered. "Want a hole here to let your brains air out, cop killer?"

Mickey found the weapon in the man's waistband. After tucking it into his belt, he kept patting him down to be sure the suspect didn't have more than one.

"Holster your gun, Jeff." Mickey looked at him. "Holster!" he shouted.

Sneering at the man, Jeff jammed his gun into his holster.

"Tell radio one in custody, under control." Mickey began walking the suspect out of the alley.

Jeff keyed his mike and relayed the information, "Eight-Adam-One. One in custody, under control," glaring at the suspect, wishing he could kill him.

They met Sgt. Bryant back in the area they had left him. Someone had a nearby patrol car so they locked the man in the backseat. Jeff's blood was boiling he was so angry. As Mickey opened the magazine of the suspect's pistol, showing the sergeant it was now empty of bullets, Jeff asked, "How's the cop?"

"Okay. He got shot in the arm. He's on his way to the ER."

Homicide detectives, media, television news helicopters, and spectators began to descend.

Traffic patrol was setting up to secure a large perimeter for the investigative team.

Sgt. Bryant walked right up to Jeff and stuck his nose in Jeff's face. "I don't know if you're brave or nuts. What the hell did they teach you in Seattle?"

"To hate fuckers that shoot cops," Jeff snarled.

"No. To run after cop shooters and get shot yourself." After a deep exhale, Sgt. Bryant grabbed Jeff around the neck. "Good work."

"Thanks, Sarge."

Once the sergeant walked away, Jeff found Mickey staring at him. A look of pure savage hunger in his blue eyes.

"What do you want, rookie?" Jeff teased.

"To fuck your brains out."

Jeff laughed.

As they walked back to the investigative team to hand over the suspect's gun and find out what they needed to do, Mickey wrapped his arm around Jeff's back, holding him tight.

Mickey tailed behind Jeff's car. When Jeff's headlights dipped and faced his garage, Mickey parked behind him.

Climbing out of his truck, Mickey met Jeff at the front door. He couldn't stop thinking about the way Jeff had handled himself today.

The minute they were inside Jeff's townhouse, Mickey dropped his backpack and body slammed Jeff into a wall. He grabbed Jeff's face and kissed him, sucking at his lips and tongue. Jeff dropped his off duty weapon that was inside his waist pack down on the floor next to Mickey's bag. He dragged Mickey's t-shirt out of his shorts and hiked it up his body.

Mickey paused from their kissing to jerk it over his head, doing the same to Jeff's. When their torsos were bare, they went back to kissing. Mickey gripped Jeff's hair, deepening their kiss to a penetrating, tongue sucking frenzy. Jeff used both his hands to dig into the back of Mickey's shorts, grabbing his ass cheeks and ramming his pelvis into Mickey's.

Mickey shoved Jeff back into the plasterboard and stripped his shorts and briefs down his legs as Jeff kicked off his tennis shoes.

Before Mickey could react to Jeff's naked body, Jeff spun them around and crashed Mickey against the wall. He ripped Mickey's shorts off, grabbing at his cock and balls when they were exposed.

Grunting, Mickey fucked Jeff's mouth with his tongue. They stumbled around the living room, trying to aim for the stairs without separating their mouths.

Jeff crushed Mickey against the wall at the bottom landing, setting their dicks upright side by side and humping him.

His head spinning, Mickey groaned and grabbed Jeff's hips, grinding against his cock and pubic hair. Jeff shoved him up the staircase. Step by step, they ascended, writhing against each other and sucking at each other's faces. When they made it to the top, he backed Jeff up roughly until they were standing next to his bed.

Jeff reacted violently and propelled Mickey back on the mattress with a strong shove. While Mickey's chest heaved, Jeff tore a condom off the strip and rolled it on. When he was sheathed, Jeff gave Mickey a vicious glare.

Mickey lay back, spreading his legs. "Fuck me, pig."

With the tube of gel in his hand, Jeff fell onto the bed between Mickey's knees and shoved two fingers into his ass.

Mickey gasped and tensed his back.

Jeff stared down at him, grinding his jaw as he penetrated Mickey with his fingers. "You want to get fucked, Stanton?"

The pleasure was so intense Mickey couldn't answer. His dick was throbbing and dripping and if he so much as touched it he'd come.

With one hand on Mickey's bent knee, Jeff fingerfucked him, rubbing on his prostate with each deep stroke.

Mickey opened his mouth to scream from the sensation, but only a thin stream of air came out. He was right on the verge and the friction was making him spin. He began grinding against Jeff's fingers in desperation.

When Jeff removed contact, Mickey blinked in agony. "Get in!"

Jeff mounted him, thrusting his hips where his hand had left off. With both his slick hands, Jeff gripped Mickey's cock and jerked at it like mad, pounding his hips into Mickey's.

As his climax welled up inside him, Mickey couldn't believe how intense it was. He rammed his ass upwards, taking Jeff deeper, clamping his hands around Jeff's to jack off with him, faster, harder.

"Fuck me! Fuck me, you nasty cop!"

Jeff wailed as his cock throbbed inside Mickey's hole. At the sound of Jeff's ecstasy, Mickey came, bucking his hips violently so Jeff's cock and his ass were deep and tight.

Mickey's cum splashed his jaw. Jeff kept thrusting for

the last few waves of pleasure, pressing their bodies so close together they were one.

Mickey opened his eyes to see an expression of bliss on Jeff's face. He grabbed the hair on both sides of Jeff's head and dragged Jeff down to his mouth while they were still connected. The moment their lips touched, Mickey felt Jeff's cock throb again inside him.

He locked his fingers behind Jeff's neck and sucked at his teeth and tongue, unwilling to allow them to part bodies.

Jeff lay limp against him, moaning as they kissed, trying to gasp air between sucking.

Finally having to breathe, Mickey collapsed on the mattress. Jeff drew back from him, dropping to his knees on the floor. As they panted, dripping with sweat, Jeff laid his head between Mickey's legs and rested on his spent cock.

Reaching down, Mickey massaged Jeff's head through his thick hair.

Jeff burrowed into Mickey's crotch, kissing his damp skin. Jeff's rough jaw made Mickey's crotch tingle and chills wash over his length.

When Jeff began licking at Mickey's balls, Mickey groaned in pleasure. Feeling Jeff's teeth, Mickey closed his eyes and his cock pulsated, coming to life. But he was shattered. It had been a long, draining day.

Jeff gnawed at his half-stiff cock, but it was just for affection. Mickey knew Jeff was beyond exhausted as well. After a moment, Jeff rested his cheek on Mickey's genitals. "I have to move but I can't."

Mickey laughed tiredly. Forcing himself to function, Mickey leaned up on his elbows. "A quick wash and sleep. I have to sleep."

Jeff sat back.

Making his way to his feet, Mickey reached down and hauled Jeff to his. They scuffed to the bathroom like zombies.

"One more day."

"One more day," Jeff echoed.

After they washed up, Mickey dropped into bed with Jeff in his arms. Wrapping him up in a tight embrace, Mickey fell into a deep sleep.

# Chapter 9

The buzzer sounded. Jeff cried, "No…no…" He hit the snooze button. Ten minutes later it went off again. Sobbing in agony, Jeff moaned, "I don't wanna get up, I don't wanna…"

Mickey rolled on top of him heavily. "Do we ever call in sick? Do we ever take a damn day off?"

"Huh?" Jeff cracked his eyelid open.

"How many days off you have accumulated, Jeff?"

"We can't ask the sarge from home. We should have asked him yesterday. We're always fucking short. He'll say no."

"You don't know that."

"Both of us?" Jeff asked. "Ask a day off for both of us, together?"

Mickey stared at him.

"That's a bit obvious, Stanton, don't you think?"

"Augh!" Mickey screamed, flopping to his back. "It's useless! Fucking useless dealing with you!"

"Not again," Jeff whined. "Mick, give it a fucking rest."

"So? Now we can't take a day off together? A new Chandler rule?"

"You want us out?" Jeff accused.

"People know we're friends. It doesn't mean we're gay just because two friends take a day off together. And they don't need to know it's to be together. When a couple of guys get used to working as partners, they never want to work a Lincoln car."

"Sarge wouldn't have us work one man Lincoln car, he'd stick me with Chris or Flo," Jeff complained. "If you want to take time off fine. But don't pull this on him, calling from home."

"Plenty of guys do it. It must be different in Seattle. If you can't call from home to get a day off, that's not LAPD's problem."

"Mickey…" Jeff moaned.

"Fuck you!" Mickey became defensive instantly. "What do you need your days off for if not for us to play together?"

"Well, I do need to visit the family once a year. They're all still up there."

"Whatever." Mickey threw up his hands dramatically.

Jeff tackled him before he was able to get out of the bed. "Fine. Call."

"You mean it?"

"But what will you do if only one of us can take the day off?"

"I won't do it then. All for two and two for all."

"Fine, d'Artagnan. But just remember, a cop got shot yesterday, so they're one down, right from the start." He kissed him.

When he parted to stare down at Mickey, Mickey pouted. "You're right. He'll never give us the day off."

"I know."

"Screw it. We have four off in a row after today."

"We do." Jeff kissed him again, getting horny.

"Will you plan time off with me? Put in our requests together?"

"You're so demanding!" Jeff put on a whiny woman's voice. "My husband is *so* demanding!"

"Shut up." Mickey laughed, wrestling with him.

Jeff kissed him again. Parting, looking down at Mickey's smile, his blue eyes and wavy blond hair, maybe…just maybe, Jeff did love him. "Shower," he announced, hopping off the bed.

As Mickey raced after him, Jeff felt him grab at his ass.

Laughing as they went, Jeff waited until they were in the bathroom before he spun around and held Mickey. Embracing him, chewing on his morning stubble, Jeff moaned, "I'd fuck you all day if I could."

"Tomorrow."

"Mm." Jeff kissed Mickey's neck, grinding their cocks together.

"Get in the shower. I love our alternating scrubbing ritual."

"Me too." Jeff pivoted around and turned on the water. As he waited for it to heat up, Mickey hugged him from behind. Savoring his embrace, Jeff wriggled against him.

"Me first," Mickey claimed as they stepped into the crashing spray.

"You first." Jeff waited until Mickey wet down before he began shampooing his hair for him.

❈

Again in uniform and at roll call, Mickey and Jeff sat shoulder to shoulder listening to the updated report on the injured officer.

"He was released from the hospital and is recovering at home. We're passing around a card for everyone to sign." The sergeant handed it to the first desk nearest his.

"And, the lieutenant has written up a commendation to Officers Mickey Stanton and Jeff Chandler, for capturing the suspect."

A small smattering of applause and cheers erupted around the room. Mickey winked at Jeff proudly.

"We'll put you in for officers of the month and cross our fingers." Sgt. Bryant smiled at them.

Mickey was so proud of Jeff he wanted to kiss him. Instead, he squeezed his thigh under the table.

When roll call adjourned, several officers walked by to pat them on the back and congratulate them. Flo crouched between them, hugging them around their necks. "I'm so excited! You're awesome."

"Thanks, Flo." Mickey smiled sweetly at her.

"You're so brave. You're my heroes."

"Golly gee, Officer Bower," Mickey teased, "you're embarrassing me."

Under her breath she whispered, "You two are so cute together. I'm so glad you found each other."

"Me too." Mickey reached for Jeff's hand.

Jeff looked around the room in paranoia. "I don't think so."

Flo acted surprised. "You're not out?"

"No. You know we're not, Flo," Jeff hissed, taking a paranoid look around.

"But I think everyone knows."

"What?" Jeff gasped. "No way."

"Why do you think everyone knows?" Mickey asked.

She took a quick glance at the few who lingered before going into service. "Chris said it looked like Jeff was giving you head in the church lot a couple of days ago."

Jeff choked, coughing in a fit as Mickey gaped at her.

She nodded. "He didn't spread it around or anything. I think he just told one or two people. I was there when he said it. I told him I thought it was cool."

"Agh!" Jeff cried. "Agh! No. Oh, God, Flo, no."

"Calm down." She giggled, whacking him.

Mickey glared at him. "What's the big deal, Jeff? So what if they know?"

"Mickey! We'll get into trouble and separated, fucking quick. Flo," Jeff whispered, "deny it. Okay? Don't confirm anyone's suspicions. We enjoy working together."

"Promise. I will." She left the room.

They were the last two sitting in the roll call area. Mickey stared at Jeff.

"We are so dead if Sgt. Bryant finds out." Jeff leaned his elbows on the table. "And now you want us to take time off together?"

Mickey tried to understand Jeff's point of view. Yes, if anyone confirmed they were sexual together they would probably be separated. But was it that horrible? People knowing? No, he didn't want to lose Jeff as his partner. He had to be sensible. *Am I too sensitive?* Mickey thought maybe he was. Insecure? It wasn't a pleasant feeling.

"You drive." Jeff nudged him.

"Bend over."

Jeff glanced back at him as he stood. "Ha ha." Holding Mickey back at the doorway, Jeff said, "We have to speak to Chris. He may be spreading that 'rumor' everywhere. I thought if he saw me sitting up that day at the church, he'd say something."

Mickey waited as Jeff picked up his kitbag from the hall to carry to the patrol car. "I would have thought so too."

"The minute we have a chance, meet up with him somewhere."

"Okay." Mickey tried to calm down. It was the right thing to do. He didn't want them pulled apart.

Mickey did the check on the car and shotgun as Jeff logged them into service on the computer. Once they were both ready, Jeff hit the button. Instantly, dispatch had them en route to a call.

"You okay, Jeff?" Mickey rubbed his thigh.

"A little freaked out, Mick. I don't want to come out. I don't want us separated."

"I know. It's fucked up."

"Let me send a message to Chris." Jeff leaned toward the computer screen and clicked the keyboard.

"What are you going to tell him?"

"That there's an ugly rumor going around that he's been saying nasty things about us. Something like that."

Mickey glanced over at Jeff, echoing, "Something like that."

"Yeah." Jeff bit his lip as he typed.

Mickey sighed tiredly. He just wanted to get through the day. He craved time off. He couldn't remember his last vacation.

∽∽

Late in their shift they finally got the opportunity to

meet up with Chris. As they pulled into a vacant lot, Mickey matched driver's windows with Chris.

From the passenger's side, Jeff leaned down to see him. "Hey."

"Hey. What's up?"

"Uh, Chris…Flo said you called us faggots."

Mickey choked. Jeff nudged him to shut up.

"Did I?"

"Don't get all coy. We're not queer, Chris." Jeff wanted to be very certain this rumor was squelched. "You told people I was giving Mick head? Are you fucking insane?"

The color of Chris's cheeks turned to crimson. "I…uh…"

"Chris!" Jeff shouted, "Why the fuck did you say that? I could kick your homo-loving ass!"

Mickey coughed. Jeff elbowed him in the ribs.

"Hey, man, you looked like you were sitting up from Mick's lap in the church lot. Okay?"

"No! It's not fucking okay! I dropped a goddamn pen on the floor and was reaching for it. I didn't have Mick's dick in my mouth, you disgusting moron! Who did you tell that to?" As Jeff leaned over Mickey's body to speak to Chris, he shoved his hand between Mickey's legs and massaged his crotch. Mickey stiffened and pressed back into the seat.

"No one!"

"Bullshit! Tell me who you told. Do you realize if you told one big mouth, everyone on the division will know? And if I find out I'm the topic of some fag rumors, I'll kill you, Chris Christian." Jeff rubbed and squeezed Mickey's hard cock enthusiastically.

"Man!" Chris held up his hands. "I swear, it's what it looked like. I'm sorry."

"You will be sorry when you're in the ER with your head up your anus." Jeff dug his fingers under Mickey's balls to his ass. "Why didn't you just say something that day? You could have asked and I would have told you what a fuck-up you are."

"Ask? Ask if you were sucking Stanton's cock?" Chris laughed.

"Yeah. Funny now, Chris. But how funny will it be when I kick your ass?" Jeff gripped Mickey balls, fondling them hotly.

"I'm sorry!"

"Who did you tell?" Jeff traced where Mickey had gone hard under his trousers.

"Uh, Bower…and I think just Fernandez. Unless they told someone else."

"You're fucking dead," Jeff snarled. "If you can't stop this from spreading, I will kill you, asshole."

"I will." Chris held up his hand. "I know you guys are straight. I'm sorry."

"If you know we're straight…" Jeff shouted, rubbing Mickey's rock hard cock with his palm. "Why the hell did you say I sucked Mickey's dick?" Jeff kneaded it in his hands.

"Look, Chandler, I will tell Bower and Fernandez I fucked up."

"I'll give you the rest of today before our weekend to fix this, asshole. Or I'll kick your homo-loving ass. You got that?"

"Yes. Sorry, man. Really. I'll take care of it."

"You'd better." Jeff watched him back out of the parking lot. He waited for him to disappear. "Thought he'd never leave." Jeff opened Mickey's pants and dove onto his lap.

"Christ! Jeff, you drove me insane."

"Shut up and come," Jeff replied with his mouth full. Closing his eyes, he drew hard on Mickey's cock, groping between his legs until Mickey was gasping and spurting into his mouth. Jeff moaned when cum filled him. Swallowing it down, Jeff sat up and shouted, "You homo-loving commie! You better straighten this out!" He shook his fist at the windshield, sitting back and laughing hysterically. "God, I love this job."

Fastening his gun belt, Mickey shook his head. "You're nuts."

"No. Your nuts." Jeff massaged them gently.

"We're out of here." Mickey put the car in drive and left the parking lot.

∽∾

Standing in a busy intersection in the late afternoon heat, Mickey directed traffic around an accident. No Hunter, no Blake, just some guys he didn't know manned the fire truck. A whistle in his teeth, Mickey looked back at Jeff who signaled it was his turn to allow traffic through. A half hour, standing on the boiling tarmac in rush hour traffic at a busy intersection, Mickey was dead on his feet and dying for the day to end.

Blasting his whistle, he held up his hand and waved the opposing side through. "Where's the fucking tow trucks?" he grumbled through the whistle and his clenched teeth. "Come on, you morons." He urged the slow drivers to pass through the snarl. Hearing Jeff's whistle, he stopped traffic and waited as Jeff waved his side through.

"I hate this. Christ, I'm hot!" Mickey pulled the whistle out of his mouth so he could frown. "I said stop you idiot!" he roared at a slow moving car trying to sneak past him. "What am I? A cone to veer around?" he argued with himself. "I'd give each of you a fucking ticket if I wasn't so hot."

He noticed Jeff stopped his side. Mickey popped the whistle back in his teeth, blasted it and waved the morons on.

After another half hour, the tow trucks dragged the two wrecked automobiles out of the way. He met Jeff at their patrol car, which was used to help detour traffic around the collision. Mickey sat down behind the wheel, shut off the overhead lights and left the intersection.

"I'm roasting." Jeff tried to pry his vest off his chest.

"Finally. Mr. Rain City complains about the heat."

"Shut up." As he aimed an air vent down his shirt, Jeff checked the clock on the dash. "Almost there. Get one last call and milk the sucker."

"You got it." Mickey drove around their sector looking

for something to give them an out for the day. "Hooker?"

"Where?" Jeff asked.

Mickey pointed.

"Here? A hooker in this neighborhood?"

"If she's not hooking, what the hell's she doing?"

"Wait a minute. That's that actress…uh…Angela Doppler."

"Oh God no." Mickey slowed down. "She's fucking drunk."

Jeff grabbed the radio. He cleared their traffic detail and gave the location of their contact. "Pull over," he told Mickey.

Mickey parked near her and they stepped out of the car.

"Ms. Doppler," Jeff called as he approached her.

She had an unlit cigarette hanging out of her lip, and her makeup was smeared down her face. "Huh?"

"Ms. Doppler, come here." Jeff held her elbow gently and steered her out of the busy street. "Are you okay?"

"I'm fine. Hey, handsome…"

Mickey stared at her sadly as Jeff dealt with her.

"Come here." Jeff allowed her to lean against the fender of the patrol car. "How much have you had to drink tonight?"

"Not enough. Hey, can you guys give me a ride? I have a party to go to." She dug into her purse, falling off the car.

Jeff hauled her back upright. "What are you doing?"

"Got a light?"

"No. Do you want us to take you home?"

"Home?" She snorted. "I have a party to go to. I just got ditched. Fucking boyfriend cheated on me, asshole."

Mickey sighed uncomfortably. Another cheating episode. Oh, goody.

"Let us drive you." Jeff took the cigarette out of her mouth.

"I need a cab. I can't be seen in a cop car. You nuts? Give me my fucking cigarette."

"Where do you need to go?"

Mickey was surprised at the patience Jeff was showing. He didn't have time for the Hollywood types. They annoyed him with their excessive behavior and the way they were pandered to by society even though they were a waste of space.

"I'm expected at Dean's place. You know, *Dean*." She stumbled off the fender again until Jeff caught her.

"We can take you."

"We cannot," Mickey sneered. "She's talking about Dean Smith. He's all the way up in Van Nuys."

"Van Nuys!" Angela pointed at him. "Van Nuys. Give me my cigarette."

"I'll get her a cab." Mickey was about to key his radio when he spotted one in traffic. He stepped out into the street and flagged it down. It veered his way and stopped.

"Get her in the fucking taxi, Jeff."

"Come on, Ms. Doppler. We got you a cab." Jeff held her arm, escorting her.

"You're cute." She tripped as she walked. "I want you."

"You can't have him," Mickey snarled. "He's mine."

Jeff shot him a reprimanding glance.

"Yours? Gay LA cops? Cool. I like you now."

As they approached the cab, Jeff opened the back door. "She needs to go to Van Nuys," he told the driver. "Can you do that?"

Mickey shook his head. "Pathetic."

"Gay cops," she laughed. "They should make a movie about you two."

"They have. *Hot Cops*, Centaur Films," Mickey shot back sarcastically. "Gay porn. Buy it."

"Gay porn," she giggled, climbing into the back seat. "I'll remember you, Officer gay-porn Chandler."

"God, I hope not." Jeff made sure she was in, closing the back door of the cab.

After it drove off, Jeff met Mickey on the sidewalk. "Why were you so mean to her?"

"I hate the Hollywood scene. A bunch of lowlifes drunk

or high all the time, thinking the law never applies to them. Most of them have no talent and wouldn't be in the business if their mommies and daddies weren't stars." Mickey headed back to the patrol car.

"Gee, Stanton, don't sugar-coat it. Tell me how you really feel." Jeff sat down beside him.

"We can't run her name." Mickey pulled back into traffic. "Some newshound will find it and screw with her."

"Aw, you do have a heart," Jeff teased.

"Now we need to find another call. Dumb woman." Mickey drove around looking for a traffic stop.

"That could be your sister."

Mickey shot Jeff a furious glare.

"Well? It's someone's sister."

"Shut up. Don't compare Aura to that slut."

Jeff held up his hands. "I'm just saying they're close to the same age, that's all. Poor thing."

"You want to fuck her too, Chandler?"

Jeff just laughed. "Yeah. I want to fuck a drunk, B-rated bimbo. You got me pegged, Stanton."

Mickey knew he was mad because he was exhausted, but something about Jeff always rubbed him the wrong way lately.

"There." Mickey flicked on his overhead red and blue lights. "Improper use of a signal. That's our ticket home. Tell radio we're clear of the suspicious person and out on a traffic stop."

"Yes, sir!" Jeff retorted sarcastically and picked up the mike.

*Fuck you.* Mickey waited for the driver to pull over and Jeff to give their location and the license plate before he approached the vehicle.

"Go." Jeff nudged him, climbing out of his side of the car.

Mickey approached the driver, leaning near the window as it descended. When he recognized another celebrity, he rolled his eyes at the folly.

~~

Jeff parked in his driveway. Again it was a struggle after they had changed in the locker room to get Mickey to come over. This hot and cold game was so exhausting Jeff never knew what was expected of him. Yet he knew when they were wiped out from thirty-six-plus, grueling, boiling hot, stressful hours on duty they tended to take it out on each other emotionally.

Once Mickey's headlights dimmed as he parked behind Jeff's car, Jeff waited for him. It seemed to take too long for Mickey to get out of his truck. About to go inside the townhouse and let Mickey sit there, Jeff exhaled in annoyance and marched over to the pickup and opened the driver's door. "What now?"

"Maybe I should just go home."

"Why do we play this game over and over again?"

"Because you piss me off."

All Jeff wanted to do was sleep. He grabbed Mickey's tee at the throat and jerked him forward. "Stop fucking with me," Jeff growled. "I'm too fucking tired for your shit."

Mickey's expression turned violent in an instant. He ripped Jeff's hands off his shirt and shoved him.

Catching himself from falling, Jeff grabbed Mickey around the neck and dragged him out of the truck. A deep, furious snarl erupted from Mickey. He gripped Jeff's shirt in both hands, clenching it in his fists, pinching Jeff's nipples in the process. A surge of passion raced to Jeff's cock. Roaring in rage, he body-slammed Mickey against the side of his truck and ground their cocks together. "Fuck you, you irritating son of a bitch. Go home. See if I care."

Under the glow of a streetlamp on the quiet lane, Mickey grabbed Jeff's jaw and forced it to his mouth.

As Mickey sucked on Jeff's tongue, Jeff shoved his hand down the front of Mickey's shorts. Dragging his fingers over Mickey's stiff length a few times, Jeff then pressed Mickey back painfully against the metal fender. With both his hands on Mickey's pectoral muscles, Jeff pushed off of

Mickey's chest to get away from him.

Hearing Mickey panting for air, Jeff took one step, looking back at him. "What are you going to do, asshole? Go cry in your pillow?"

"Fuck you, bitch," Mickey spat angrily.

Jeff grabbed his own cock in a tease. "You want it?"

Slamming his truck closed, Mickey went after him. Jeff was propelled violently toward his door.

"Stop pushing me, you motherfucker." Jeff shoved him back just as hard. When Jeff turned to put his key in his door, Mickey pinned him against it. Feeling Mickey's breath on his neck, Mickey's hand down the back of his shorts, Jeff's cock hardened and throbbed.

"You're the mother-fucking pig, bitch. Not me." Mickey pressed his index finger into Jeff's ass.

Jeff's dick pulsated against his door. A shiver raised the goose bumps on his skin. "Fuck you, Stanton! Fuck you!"

Mickey squirmed his finger in deeper. Jeff gasped, closing his eyes. He felt Mickey taking the keys from his hand and heard the lock turning.

The minute the door swung back, Mickey held Jeff around the waist, his finger still digging up Jeff's ass painfully.

Jeff clenched his muscles and tightened his jaw. Like hell he'd cry out. He wouldn't give Mickey the satisfaction.

Mickey kicked the front door closed with a bang behind them. As Mickey wormed his way in, Jeff felt the pain change to something more intense. He reached back, clutching Mickey's hips.

"You're a whore, Chandler." Mickey snorted. "You'll take anything up your ass."

Jeff broke out in a sweat. "Fuck you. Fuck you!" He flinched as Mickey probed deeper. "Get some fucking lube, asshole!"

"Why? Don't you like it?"

Jeff bellowed an angry yell and twisted out of Mickey's grip, spinning around to confront him. He lunged at him, clutching Mickey's shoulders and ramming him against the wall. A standing lamp fell in the dimness.

Pressed against Mickey's tall frame, Jeff inhaled him. His sweat, his musk. He sank his teeth into Mickey's neck, sucking his salty hot skin. Hearing Mickey's gasp, Jeff chewed on his muscular neck to his jaw, his earlobe, nipping it between his teeth.

Both Mickey's hands dug through Jeff's hair, hard, tight, strong fingers raked through his mane. Forcefully, Mickey urged Jeff's mouth closer to his, away from his jaw and ear. Resisting him, Jeff took the skin of Mickey's cheek between his teeth, snarling low and deep. Mickey's entire body trembled and he sucked in a hiss of air. His hands squeezed Jeff's head harder, forcing him to meet his lips. When Jeff was good and ready, he made for that hot mouth. On contact they both combusted. Jeff fucked Mickey's mouth with his tongue, pressing Mickey tightly to the wall behind him, shoving his t-shirt up his chest and pinching Mickey's nipples in his fingers painfully.

Mickey's hands dragged over Jeff's scalp, meeting and crossing behind his head until they lowered to hug Jeff's back. Jeff felt Mickey's tongue force its way into his lips. He sucked on it, swirling his tongue around it like it was Mickey's dick.

A low, tortured moan escaped Mickey's chest.

Jeff pushed back from him, catching his breath. "Slut… you want it, slut?"

"Fuck you. Fuck you, pig."

Jeff slid both his hands, palms facing forward, against Mickey's abs, gliding them down into his gym shorts until they came out the legs. Then he dragged the material down Mickey's huge thighs, exposing him.

Mickey panted, his arms limp at his sides, staring down at his naked cock.

Jeff gripped that engorged dick in his hand and used it to lead Mickey up the stairs to the bedroom.

The minute they stood near the bed, Mickey picked Jeff

up and threw him down on the mattress.

Before Jeff could scramble off, Mickey dropped all his weight on him.

"You dirty, dirty cop," Mickey sneered.

"Fuck you, Stanton. Fuck you!" Jeff shivered. He would beg if he had to.

With one hand on Jeff's chest, Mickey held Jeff down on the bed, stripping off Jeff's gym shorts with the other. When he was naked from the waist down, Mickey ran his fingers over Jeff's balls, and up his cock.

Jeff whimpered at the zinging sensation that rushed over him. Mickey grabbed one of Jeff's knees in each of his hands and pushed backward until Jeff was opened up for him.

Jeff couldn't catch his breath. His chest was rising and falling so quickly, he was dizzy.

Mickey burrowed his face between Jeff's thighs.

Reaching down, Jeff gripped Mickey's head to grind Mickey's coarse shadow into his crotch. It was so intense it made Jeff grind his teeth. He released another growl of desire. "Fuck me, you nasty bitch."

Mickey clamped his hands around the base of Jeff's cock and sucked it down to the root. Jeff howled and jerked his hips upwards at the act. Gripping the blond hair on both sides of Mickey's head, he thrust Mickey's head up and down his length, fucking Mickey's mouth. "You bitch! You dirty bitch!"

Mickey sucked hard, biting his lip-covered teeth down along Jeff's thick cock. When Mickey's finger dipped into Jeff's ass, Jeff was about to come. He cried, "That's it…"

Mickey jerked back, not allowing him to climax.

While Jeff cursed and screamed at him, Mickey sheathed his cock and coated himself with lubrication. After he knelt between Jeff's legs again, he slid two fingers into Jeff's ass. "Beg me, pig."

Jeff's hips raised to meet the penetration. But he bit his lip on pleading.

Mickey finger-fucked him deeper, hitting Jeff's magic spot. "Beg me, pig!"

Opening his lips to cry out, Jeff choked in agony when Mickey pulled his fingers away. "What are you doing to me?" Jeff shouted in fury.

Mickey lunged at him, pinning Jeff to the bed. Using his thumbs to deeply massage Jeff's hard nipples under his shirt, Mickey hissed. "You want it?"

Jeff humped Mickey's body frantically. Did he want it? Was Mickey insane?

Mickey started gnawing Jeff's neck, his cock finding its way to Jeff's slick hole, pushing against it.

Roaring in frustration, Jeff jerked his hips up, getting that hard prick in. He fucked Mickey, topping from the bottom, grabbing Mickey's back and jamming his own cock against Mickey's hot, sweaty skin as he pushed Mickey's dick inside him. His head swirling, Jeff opened his lips and howled as climax hit him. *"Ah! Ah! You fucking motherfucker!"*

Mickey went wild, thrusting his hips and choking on his gasps. Jeff felt Mickey's climax rush over him as Mickey sealed their crotches together so tightly Jeff was in pain. Mickey's prick throbbed as he came, deep inside Jeff's body. Jeff felt sweat dripping down on to his face and sealing their skin together. Mickey went limp on top of him, gasping for air.

Jeff wrapped his arms and legs around him, hugging Mickey so tight he knew he was crushing him. "Baby…my baby…" he crooned, "no one makes me feel this way…no one…"

After one last thrust of his hips, Mickey pulled out, allowing Jeff's legs to unfurl and drop to the bed. "I can't fucking move, Chandler."

Jeff let out a tired laugh. "Christ…I am so spent."

Oozing off the bed to the floor, Mickey rested his head on Jeff's leg. "Help me. I can't stand up."

With a supreme effort, Jeff managed to get to his feet

and hauled Mickey up with him. They held each other as they made it to the bathroom to wash up. Once they had done the bare minimum, they dropped on the bed, dead to the world.

# Chapter 10

Tuesday. A day off.

Mickey was dreaming something erotic. Jeff's balls and dick wrapped with duct tape. He opened his eyes and found Jeff on top his chest, sound asleep. Closing his eyes again, Mickey was so glad they were off duty for a few days, he could cry. Smoothing his hands down Jeff's muscular back, Mickey moaned as he remembered their sex. Hot, dirty, violent fucking. They were perfectly matched sexually. Of that, he would never complain.

Caressing Jeff's soft, feathery, brown hair, Mickey moaned happily. Time off with Chandler. Yes!

His cock was hard. The erotic dream had given him one hell of a morning erection. Add to that the memory of last night. Two wildcats, ripping and chewing at each other. Growl!

Mickey held onto Jeff and rolled over on top of him. As Jeff's eyes opened, Mickey smiled down at him wickedly.

"Weren't you just fucking me?" Jeff laughed.

Mickey folded the sheet back, exposing them. Admiring their overlapping bodies, Mickey smoothed his hands all over Jeff's skin amorously. "You get me so hot," Mickey purred.

"Mm…" Jeff wriggled under him.

"I want to fuck. Fuck. Fuck you." Mickey jammed his hips at Jeff with each expletive.

"Grrrr…" Jeff's eyes lit up wickedly.

Mickey inhaled Jeff's skin, running his hand down

Jeff's six-pack abs to his pubic hair. "I love you so much, you cocky motherfucker. You don't deserve it."

Jeff flipped them over roughly so he was on top. He cupped Mickey's face in his hands. "I deserve it."

Mickey felt slightly heartsick. There was never a return I love you.

Jeff slid his stiff cock between Mickey's legs. "But it's my turn to, fuck, fuck, fuck you." Jeff jammed his hips with each word the way Mickey had.

Mickey closed his eyes as Jeff ran his fingers all over his body, shivering from the chill.

"Want it now?" Jeff crooned.

Mickey grabbed Jeff's jaw. "Tell me you love me."

That surprised Jeff. "What?" He laughed uncomfortably.

Grinding his teeth, Mickey ordered, "Tell me you love me."

"Presumptuous bitch." Jeff laughed.

Mickey roared and shoved Jeff off him.

Ending up on the floor from Mickey's power, Jeff sat on his rump on the carpet with half the sheet still twisted around him. "Holy shit, Stanton! You trying to kill me?"

"I hate you, you asshole."

"Not again!" Jeff threw up his hands. "You're a broken fucking record."

Mickey whipped a pillow at him.

Deflecting it, Jeff gaped at him. "Can't you just be satisfied with what we have? Mickey, we have a great working relationship. And fucking mind-blowing sex. What the hell is all this love shit?"

Mickey was exasperated. There was no other word for it.

When Jeff began singing Tina Turner's *What's Love Got to Do With It*, Mickey stormed to the bathroom to shower.

❧

"This has to be a joke," Jeff muttered, still on his butt on the carpet. "How can a big, beefy, tough LAPD cop be so sappy?"

Standing, draping the sheets back on the bed, Jeff headed to the bathroom. As he stood at the toilet to pee, he shouted over the shower noise, "Hey, you started washing without me. We have a routine, Stanton."

"Fuck you."

"Okay." Jeff pushed back the door. "I never say no to you, good lookin'." He climbed in, soaping up his hands. "Come on. We have a routine here."

Giving in, Mickey turned his back to him, resting on the walls with his hands, bracing himself.

Jeff soaped up his body for him. "Mickey," he chided, "you keep asking me for something I'm not ready to give. This whole 'love' thing. Is it really that important to you?"

Mickey didn't answer.

After Jeff knelt down to wash both of Mickey's long powerful legs, he said, "Turn around."

When Mickey spun to face him, Jeff instantly took Mickey's cock into his mouth. Sucking until he was hard, Jeff backed up to look at it. "So nice. Mickey, the body on you…well…" Jeff shook his head and washed Mickey's legs. "It's superb."

"Shut up, Chandler."

"Why? You don't like me admiring your perfect ten physique?" Jeff soaped up Mickey's genitals, playing as he did. "Baby, why do we have to keep going around this merry-go-round? We're perfect as we are."

"I don't want to talk about it."

"But you do. You constantly throw it out there to create an obstacle in an otherwise perfect romance."

Mickey snorted and shook his head.

Rising up, Jeff continued to wash Mickey's chest. "It is perfect. You can't deny it. We fuck like demented wild animals."

"You are demented."

"Yes. I am. And I'm too demented for some kind of engagement to a man, followed by nuptials and marriage.

I thought by being gay I'd avoid that trap."

"I hope you realize you're pissing me off again."

Jeff held Mickey around his neck. "Why? Why can't we just be happy with what we have?"

Mickey took the soap and began washing Jeff. "Because it's not enough for me. I told you. I want exclusive rights to this body of yours."

Jeff shivered as Mickey ran his stiff cock through his fingers.

"I'd kill anyone who touched you."

At that powerful comment, Jeff opened his eyes. "Shut up."

Mickey shrugged.

"You'd literally kill someone I went with?" Jeff knew this had to be bravado. "You sound like the moron on that DV call we went to who left a message on his girlfriend's machine."

Mickey slammed Jeff into the tiled wall, snarling, "*I don't want anyone else touching you.*"

"You kissed Mark Richfield."

"Come on, Jeff. You really think that counts?"

"Where's the line, Mickey?" Jeff wouldn't mind kissing that gorgeous model one day.

"You do realize knowing you need other men drives me crazy, and hurts me."

"I don't know what I need. When will you realize I simply don't know what I want yet? I'm twenty-five years old, Mick. That's all. Twenty-five. I'm supposed to know what the hell I want?"

"I know what I want." Mickey pressed against him. The water beating down on them sent steam swirling like misty spirits in the air above them.

"That's you. I respect that it's what you need and want. Do you respect me?"

Mickey's chest pressed against Jeff's, his hand massaged Jeff's cock sensually. They kissed. Jeff closed his eyes. There was no question they were sexually compatible. That wasn't even up for debate.

As Jeff's body rose, Mickey clasped their dicks together, pulling on them as one while he licked Jeff's lips and chin. Jeff spread his legs. Squashing their cocks against one another in two hands, Mickey began to satisfy them.

Jeff was happy to receive. He relaxed his arms at his sides and savored the hand job. Opening his eyes, peeking down, Jeff loved the way their two heads looked up against each other. A rush of pleasure raced over him. "That's it, baby…yes…"

Mickey met his mouth, sucking at his tongue. Jeff wrapped his arms around him, holding Mickey tight as he began to rise. Parting from Mickey's lips, Jeff looked down again, he loved to watch. Mickey was jerking them off like he meant it. Squeezing tight, fast, rough, it was perfect.

"I'm there." Jeff gasped, his hips thrusting involuntarily.

Mickey moaned and Jeff could feel Mickey's cock throb with his. Cream sprayed out of both slits combining to run down Mickey's fingers with the water.

"Beautiful," Jeff hissed.

"I love you. I don't care if you never say it back."

Jeff pulled Mickey closer, his hand around his neck. "I will. Give me time."

Mickey kissed him softly, moaning into his lips.

❦

After he made a pot of coffee, Jeff dropped a few slices of bread into the toaster. "What's on the agenda, Mick?"

"We're supposed to call Blake." Mickey sipped his coffee, the delivered morning paper under his elbows open to the sports section.

"Right." Jeff set the butter on the table with some knives.

"I wanted to go to the range as well."

Jeff groaned. "No. Not today."

"Quals are coming. I need to shoot."

Smiling as he walked behind where Mickey was sitting, Jeff draped his arms around his neck and rubbed their scratchy cheeks together. "Shoot into me," he purred.

Mickey set his cup down, reaching over his head to hug Jeff close.

Inhaling Mickey's fragrant, shampooed hair, Jeff nestled his face into the blond waves and Mickey's neck, running his hands down Mickey's chest. After a deep moan, Mickey rose up, crushing Jeff against the refrigerator and sucking at his mouth. Closing his eyes, Jeff whimpered as the desire heightened. A day off to fuck, and fuck, and fuck…

The toast popped and was ignored.

When Mickey's hands dug into Jeff's gym shorts, Jeff shivered and ground his cock into Mickey's palm. "I need to be in you, Stanton…" he snarled in a deep voice.

He felt Mickey shiver and nail him into the refrigerator harder. It tipped and slid against the wall with a shuddering metallic noise. He grabbed the hair behind Mickey's head and tugged him back, staring at his face and the expression of longing on it. Those blue eyes of his lit something on fire inside of Jeff. A deep vibrating growl began in Jeff's chest as he forced Mickey out of the kitchen, backing him one step at a time, still holding his hair in a tight fist.

Mickey's teeth appeared under his top lip as the violence of their love-making commenced, that wicked dance of pain and pleasure they both loved so well. With one hand, Mickey grabbed Jeff's throat. "Let go."

Jeff tightened his grip on Mickey's hair, sneering at him.

The tips of Mickey's fingers dug deeper into the flesh of Jeff's neck. "I said, let go," Mickey ordered.

"Make me, asshole."

With a roar, Mickey slammed Jeff into the wall near the bottom of the stairs. It knocked the wind out of Jeff as he hit the plasterboard. He released his grip on Mickey's hair.

Mickey ran his crotch up and down Jeff's, rubbing two stiff mounds together. Jeff could see Mickey's jaw was grinding by the twitching muscles in his cheeks. With both hands, Jeff gripped the wrist of the hand Mickey still held around his neck and began removing it from his throat. Mickey slapped the wall next to Jeff's head with his free hand, making Jeff jump from the start it gave him.

They were both panting from the excitement and Jeff trembled as he forced Mickey's powerful grip off his skin. Once he had Mickey's wrist in both hands, Jeff twisted it, making Mickey wince from the pain. Slowly Jeff worked him into a police hold, a straight-arm-bar. Moving behind Mickey's back, Jeff kept pressure on Mickey's elbow as he held his right wrist in an iron grip. "Move, asshole." Jeff urged Mickey up the stairs. Resisting at first, Mickey flinched as Jeff tweaked his hand backward. One step at a time, they ascended to the bedroom.

When Jeff had Mickey facing the bed, he began using pain to lower him down on it. The muscles in Mickey's back and arm strained as he tried to defy him.

"Down," Jeff ordered in his police voice. "Now." Once he had Mickey where he wanted him, he released the pressure point hold, grabbed Mickey's gym shorts, and jerked them down his ass.

Mickey spun around and backed up on the bed, his knees held tightly together.

Laughing at him, Jeff dropped Mickey's shorts to the floor. "Going somewhere?"

"Fuck off, bitch."

Jeff loved that kind of talk. He flipped his cock out of his shorts and pumped it as he stared down at Mickey. "More like, you're going to get fucked, *bitch.*"

When Mickey started getting off the bed, Jeff tackled him. With his fingers, he dug between Mickey's tightly clenched knees and pried them apart. The sweat running down their faces from the effort, Jeff wedged Mickey's legs wide open, dropping down between them. The abruptness made Mickey gasp and flinch.

Jeff buried his face into Mickey's balls and felt his tightly wound posture relax. As Mickey's legs splay open,

Jeff licked his sack and inside his thighs in long wet laps. "Christ, you taste good."

Mickey laughed in amusement. "You going to spend all day there? Or fuck me, asshole?"

Jeff stood, took a rubber off the strip of condoms on the nightstand and slid it on. Stepping out of his own shorts, he held the lube and crawled over the bed to Mickey again. After squeezing some of the gel onto his fingers, he smoothed it around Mickey's hole. "Knock, knock…" Jeff teased wickedly. "I'm coming in…" With two fingers, Jeff slid inside, massaging Mickey and getting him to loosen up.

A hiss of passion escaped Mickey's lips. "Fuck you, Chandler."

"On the contrary, I'm going to fuck you, Officer Stanton." Jeff found the magic spot inside Mickey, causing Mickey's hips to elevate instantly. "Christ, you're fantastic." Jeff licked his lips at his handsome partner.

"What if I said no, you can't have it?"

"I'd laugh in your face." Jeff kept up the rhythm of his fingers, enjoying watching Mickey writhe. When Mickey jolted back and hopped off the bed, Jeff was furious.

"I said no."

"What?" Jeff crossed the room toward him. "Get on the bed, asshole!"

Mickey shoved Jeff back. "Say you love me, dickwad."

"You're being a jerk! Get on the stupid bed." Jeff lunged at him.

They grappled in the middle of the room. Jeff gripped Mickey's upper arms, and Mickey tried to remove that hold, twisting away. Finding some inner strength, Jeff wrapped around Mickey's waist and roared as he picked the big man up. He forced Mickey back on the bed, landing on top of him. The look on Mickey's face was pure shock. Jeff wondered if Mickey thought he wasn't strong enough to lift him. Before that moment, Jeff didn't think he was either. Using his knees, Jeff pried Mickey's thighs apart. With a forearm positioned on either side of Mickey's head, Jeff stared down at him. Through his panting breaths he asked, "Do you really not want me in?"

Mickey grabbed Jeff's face and kissed him, sucking at his tongue and whimpering in anguish.

When Jeff felt Mickey straddling his hips, he sighed with relief and aimed his dick between Mickey's legs. A sharp, quick thrust and he was inside his lover. As Mickey rocked beneath him, moaning against Jeff's lips, Jeff rammed his hips into this treat of male flesh and felt his passion rise. Under him, Mickey's cock, trapped between them, pulsated and came, ejaculating its load onto Mickey's stomach. The moment Jeff felt it, he roared and jammed his hips deep, coming and shivering from the intensity.

Catching his breath, Jeff dropped limply on top of Mickey. As their chests rose and fell in tandem, Jeff made it to his elbows to look down at Mickey's face. A glistening teardrop had made its way from the corner of Mickey's eye to his sideburn. Jeff's breath caught in his throat. He leaned up higher to get a better look into Mickey's face. He wouldn't meet Jeff's eyes, his head turned hard to one side, staring at the wall.

"Mick?" Jeff felt his chest pinch in pain. "Mick, what's going on?" Raising his hips, Jeff pulled out of Mickey's body. Using his hand Jeff tried to turn Mickey's jaw and make him meet his eyes. Mickey's teeth showed in that angry snarl of his.

Jeff stumbled off the bed, looking down at him in agony. "Don't do this again. No, Mickey. Come on."

Without a word or eye contact, Mickey climbed off the bed to the bathroom.

Jeff yanked off the condom and followed him. Seeing Mickey washing up, Jeff tossed out the rubber and propped himself against the doorframe. Seeing Mickey's deep hurt, Jeff felt a lump in his throat. "I do love you," he whimpered.

Mickey spun around, meeting his gaze instantly.

"But I'm scared, Mick." Jeff felt his heart constrict with panic.

As if he couldn't believe what he heard, Mickey opened his mouth to reply but didn't.

Jeff wiped at his eyes roughly, embarrassed by anything that made him look weak or soft. He was a tough motherfucking cop. No one made him cry. "I'm scared." Never had he thought he would tell that to a soul.

Immediately Mickey's hard stance melted. He held Jeff's waist. "Of what?"

"Of you. Of us." Jeff made another angry swipe at his eyes.

Mickey drew him against his skin.

The contact of their bodies from their chest to their knees, Mickey's scent and the strength of his embrace, made Jeff weak. "I don't want to put myself into a position of getting hurt."

"I won't hurt you."

"Everyone says that in the beginning." Jeff bit his lip hard to stop his emotions.

"Trust me."

"I tried that route. I got burned."

"Not with me you haven't."

When Mickey parted just enough to see Jeff's eyes, Jeff felt humiliated. "I can't, Mick. I'm too afraid."

"You never mentioned any of this to me." Mickey stroked Jeff's cheek gently.

"I wanted to forget it." Jeff felt another sharp pain in his chest. He never wanted to bring it up to a soul, and convinced himself he had forgotten it.

As gently as if he were assisting an injured child while on duty, Mickey escorted Jeff to the bed. They sat down together, and Mickey held Jeff's hand, kissing his cheek and nestling in his hair. "Talk to me."

"I can't." Jeff hated feeling emotional. Hated it.

"Is it the reason you left Seattle?"

Burning sensations raged through Jeff's stomach. He tilted his face away in shame. *Oh God, I can't go there.*

Mickey's coaxing hand turned Jeff's face toward his.

After Mickey pecked his lips, he whispered, "What'd the cocksucker do?"

"He…" Jeff clenched his jaw. "He knocked up a dispatcher and married her." Voicing that agony was like taking a shot to the chest.

Mickey folded Jeff into his arms and rocked him against his body.

"I loved him, Mick…" Jeff swallowed the anguish down his throat. "He fucking had me. Told me all the things you do." Jeff paused to breathe; he felt as if he couldn't get any air into his lungs his chest was so tight.

Mickey caressed Jeff's hair, rubbing his back in comfort.

"I found out from the rumor mill. He didn't even have the guts to tell me himself." Jeff wiped his wet eyes on Mickey's shoulder. "Some stupid note went up on the board about an engagement party."

"Oh, Christ." Mickey squeezed him.

"I almost shot him, Mick." Jeff rested his cheek against Mickey's. "I almost shot him."

Mickey sat back from him, cupping Jeff's face as he wiped his teary cheeks with his thumbs. "I get it. I get what's going on now."

Jeff looked away from Mickey's blue eyes. He felt spent.

"Let's finish our breakfast." Mickey rose up, reaching out for Jeff.

Feeling as if he were coming off another twelve-hour shift, and exhausted, Jeff allowed Mickey to wash him up in the bathroom, help him get dressed, and escort him back to the kitchen.

He never wanted to tell a soul what that man did to him. It was so painful, he promised himself he would forget it.

The realization that, that bastard was preventing him from loving again killed Jeff.

Mickey lowered the bread back into the toaster to warm. He refreshed their coffee cups and urged Jeff to his seat. After Mickey caressed the hair back from Jeff's forehead, Jeff whispered, "I'm sorry."

"Don't be."

Jeff urged Mickey to his lips, kissing him softly. When they parted, Mickey gave him a loving smile.

Feeling numb, Jeff watched as Mickey buttered the toast and joined him at the table. He ate, but he couldn't taste anything.

# Chapter 11

Mickey held a grocery bag with two six-packs of beer, limes, and a bottle of tequila. Jeff balanced a cheesecake in a white bakery box in one hand as he rang the doorbell.

When the door swung back, Mickey found Hunter's bright smile. "Hey!"

"Hello!" Jeff replied enthusiastically. "We finally managed to get together off duty. Believe it?"

"Come in. Hiya, Mickey."

"Hunter." Mickey shook his outstretched hand.

They followed Hunter to the kitchen. Mickey noticed Blake outside near the barbeque grill.

"Cheesecake." Jeff held up the box. "I hope you guys like it?"

"You kidding? Love the stuff." Hunter set it on the counter.

"And beer." Mickey removed two six-packs from the grocery bag. "And…"

When he exposed the bottle of Cuervo, Hunter laughed in amusement. "Party!" Hunter took the bottle from him. "You guys are great."

The sliding door opened. Mickey turned to see Blake's handsome face as he entered. "Hey, guys."

"Blake." Mickey greeted him, checking out his outfit. "Wow."

Jeff pointed to Blake's football jersey shorts. "Where did you get those? I love them."

Blake toyed with the white exterior laces that crisscrossed his crotch. "Sexy, huh."

"Hell yeah." Mickey laughed.

"Hunt loves them." Blake winked at him.

"They brought tequila, Blake." Hunter displayed the bottle.

"Uh oh. Drunk cops?" Blake teased. "What are we in for, Hunt?"

"Who knows?" Hunter stuck his tongue in his cheek. "Want some now?"

"Sure." Jeff winked at Mickey.

As Hunter opened a cabinet and began setting shot glasses on the counter, the doorbell rang.

Mickey asked, "Oh? Are we expecting more guests?"

"Yeah. A surprise." Blake grinned at him as he passed by on his way to the door.

Jeff mouthed to Mickey, "Surprise?"

Mickey shrugged.

Hearing Blake greeting more men at the door, Mickey and Jeff moved to the hall to see. With Jeff crushed against his back, Mickey recognized Tanner and Josh. "Uh oh, here comes trouble," Mickey muttered.

Jeff jammed his cock into Mickey's ass playfully. "Josh Elliot. My, oh my."

"Here."

They spun around to Hunter who was holding out two shots. Mickey took one as Jeff took the other. Remembering something, Mickey set his glass down on the counter. "Wait. Hang on." He dug a couple of limes out of the grocery bags.

"Great." Hunter took them to the sink to rinse.

"Hello!" Josh's light green eyes gleamed as he approached. "I'm in heaven! Cops? Firemen? Yes!"

Mickey choked on his laugh as Josh rubbed his own hard cock through his gym shorts seductively.

When Tanner stood behind Josh, he announced, "I'm not even going to tell him to behave or apologize for him. I'd be doing it all afternoon." Tanner reached out his hand. "Hello, Mickey, Jeff. Great to see you guys again."

"Ditto," Jeff said, as they each shook Tanner's hand in greeting.

After Hunter sliced up the lime wedges, he announced, "We're about to begin getting wasted. You guys game?"

"Yes!" Josh stepped deeper into the kitchen. "Tequila. My favorite." After Josh eyed both Mickey and Jeff, he crooned, "Where's your guns, fellas?"

Jeff shot back his tequila before he replied, coughing on the burn, "That's better than asking if we have a gun in our pocket."

"No," Josh teased, "I already know you're happy to see me."

"Christ, Tanner." Hunter shook his head, handing out more shots. "How can you bear it? I'd never leave the bed."

Blake scolded his lover, "Hey. I'm standing right here, Hunt."

"Shut up and take a shot." Hunter handed Blake a glass.

Mickey picked up a lime wedge and threw the booze back into his mouth, chewing on the tart fruit right after. "Damn that's nice." He shivered from the heat.

"Let's sit outside. It's gorgeous out." Blake gestured to the back patio.

Hunter took the tequila with him, as Jeff carried out the plate of limes.

"Nice lawn, Blake," Mickey teased, pointing to the dead grass.

"Hey. I don't have to mow it, and it's a waste of water." Blake poked at the coals in the grill with a metal tong.

Relaxing in a chair near a round table, complete with an umbrella for shade, Mickey began pouring more shots into the empty glasses. As he handed them off, he noticed Josh sitting on Tanner's lap. Meeting Jeff's gaze, Mickey exchanged grins with him.

After Jeff took his full glass from Mickey he said, "Christ, what a cutie he is."

It didn't even make Mickey flinch. After their conversation that morning, Mickey felt confident in their relationship for the first time. "No kidding."

"Who's a cutie?" Josh asked, thanking Mickey for his refill.

"You." Mickey handed out the limes next.

Tanner snaked his arm around Josh's waist, giving him a hug. "My cutie."

"Mm." Josh wriggled against Tanner.

Jeff laughed. "Insta-wood."

Hunter broke up with laughter. When Blake had a glass of booze in his hand, Hunter made a toast. "To Josh Elliot, today's eye candy."

They echoed it and threw back the tequila.

"Wow. Nice." Josh blushed. "I'm embarrassed. Surrounded by handsome macho studs and they're all admiring me? How amazing is that?"

Tanner kissed his cheek in adoration.

Hunter relaxed in a lounge chair across from Tanner and Josh. "I'm surprised at you, Tanner. I thought you were straight."

"I was. He corrupted me."

Mickey laughed, giving Jeff a smile.

"Sucked his cock." Josh rested his head on Tanner's shoulder.

"Yipes." Jeff shivered. "That'd convert any straight guy."

"Not any," Hunter snorted. "I know one, now dead, who would have resisted."

"Hunt," Blake found a seat next to Hunter's lounge chair, "forget the Nazi."

Josh looked around in confusion. "Nazi? What am I missing?"

Jeff offered to tip more booze into everyone's glass. "Tom Young. Didn't you hear about what he did to Hunter? Or what he wanted to do?"

"No…" Josh answered timidly as he steadied his glass and Jeff poured.

Mickey said, "Jeff, Blake and Hunter may not want to

talk about that."

Once Jeff finished off the bottle, setting it back on the table, he asked Hunter, "You want us to drop it?"

"No. I don't." Hunter shot the last glassful of booze down his throat. "I think Blake and I both need to know what he was going to do to me. I'm just curious and Blake needs to get over the fucking guilt."

"Wow." Josh looked back at Tanner. "Are you as lost as I am?"

"Yes," Tanner said sternly. "Who the hell was this guy, Blake?"

"Beer?" Blake said, standing up.

"I'll get it." Mickey waved Blake back to his seat. As he stood, Mickey heard Hunter say, "Blake, shut up, sit down, and let Jeff talk." Mickey took a six-pack out of the fridge and dug though the drawers for a bottle opener. When he returned to the patio, Jeff was explaining to Josh and Tanner what had happened.

"He used to work with Hunter in San Diego. The bastard hated gays with a passion."

Mickey pried open the tops before he handed them around the circle of men.

Jeff took a swig off the neck of the bottle. "He started harassing Hunter again in LA."

"Sick." Josh cringed, drinking his beer.

"Then I played a practical joke on him to get even." Blake looked defeated as he spoke, rolling the beer bottle in his hand. "I asked a friend of mine who worked for the ambulance corps to find a pretty drag queen."

"Man, did he." Hunter shook his head.

"The guy was very convincing." Blake leaned over his lap to speak more softly. "I told Tom there was a young woman who needed his help. He fell for it."

Mickey studied Blake. He knew how hard this part of the story was for him.

"She was on her knees in front of Tom in minutes." Blake took another swig of beer.

Hunter waited, continuing the story for Blake when he stopped. "The second before he's ready to spurt, she stops. Yanks off her wig."

"Shit." Tanner laughed nervously.

"Tom freaked," Blake whispered. "But before the queen even left the station, a fully involved apartment fire was reported over dispatch."

Mickey watched Blake's face carefully. He remembered that day too well.

Hunter's eyes circled the group. "He ran into the burning blaze. Killed himself."

"No!" Josh choked.

"Jesus." Tanner rubbed his face.

Jeff wiped his mouth after a drink from the beer bottle. "Poor Blake blamed himself for that asshole's death."

"Blake." Tanner reached out his hand to him. Blake took it for a quick squeeze.

"That's not the end of the story." Jeff's eyes were gleaming.

Mickey knew that look. Fury.

"Oh?" Tanner gave Jeff his full attention.

"Tom's parents went to his apartment to clean it out." Jeff's expression became bitter.

Mickey held his breath though he knew the whole tale.

"They found Mr. Tom Young's collection of Nazi paraphernalia."

"Sick!" Josh cringed.

"It gets worse." Jeff sneered, "That asshole made plans to kidnap Hunter, torture, and kill him."

Mickey waited for it to sink in. Josh was gaping in terror at Hunter as Tanner rubbed his eyes in agony. Blake cringed and took a deep drink of beer while Hunter's eyes glazed over.

"Jeff…" Mickey shook his head. "We don't need the gory details."

"Don't we?" he scoffed. "Blake? You still feel guilty for that bastard?"

Hunter turned to see Blake's expression. "You do. Don't lie."

Blake shifted in his chair.

"Jeff. No." Mickey knew the horror he was about to reveal and he didn't think Hunter needed to know.

Josh wrapped his arms around Tanner's neck and shivered. "That's nasty. I'll have nightmares for a week."

"Jeff. Please." Mickey reached out his hand to him. He could see Jeff's rage clearly. "Babe."

Mickey knew Jeff's mind was working on going through the step by step plan the detectives had found on Tom's computer.

"Babe." Mickey stood up and knelt next to Jeff. "Enough."

Finally Jeff met his eyes. It seemed to calm him down.

Mickey stroked Jeff's hair back from his forehead to comfort him. Jeff grabbed Mickey's hand and kissed it. He turned to Blake with his teeth bared at the hatred for the dead man and snarled, "Just be glad he was killed, Blake. You wouldn't want what he was planning on doing to Hunter wished on your worst fucking enemy."

Hunter slumped over, covering his face. Blake rushed to his side, rubbing his back. "Hunt. It's done. He's dead."

"Stop feeling guilty!" Hunter roared at his lover. "They don't even want to tell me what he was going to do it was so bad. Do you get it?"

"Yes. Yes." Blake ran kissed all over Hunter's face.

Josh hummed, "Oh yes, two firemen at it. Yum."

Mickey turned to see Josh's impish eyes. It was just what they needed to break the tension. Everyone laughed and relaxed back in their chairs.

"Can I tell you how I seduced Tanner to the dark side?" Josh suggested. "It'll change the mood out here, I promise."

Adoring Josh for his levity, Mickey smiled at him, making himself comfortable on the patio at Jeff's feet, leaning back on his legs. Jeff caressed Mickey's hair lovingly. "Yes, Josh. Do tell." Mickey egged him on.

"Told him I swallowed." Josh grinned. "And he didn't have to even call me the next day…unless he wanted more."

A chorus of lustful moans soon followed as Tanner laughed at everyone's reaction. "He was so bad. I had no choice."

Mickey felt Jeff hug him from behind as he groaned, "Torture."

"Which one of you cops is the top?" Josh hissed, squirming on Tanner's lap.

"We share." Mickey grinned at him.

"I'm a bottom. Love it." Josh closed his eyes and made his face into a swoon of passion.

Hunter whimpered loudly. "I hate you, Tanner."

"Hunt! I'm right here!" Blake whacked him playfully.

Mickey turned over his shoulder to see Jeff's expression. "Looks like Blake has his hands full as well."

"No law against looking, copper." Jeff smiled.

"Any law against watching two cops do it?"

"Joshua," Tanner chided. "Behave."

"I thought you weren't going to bother telling him that," Hunter laughed, finishing his beer.

"Can't help it, Tanner. I'm drunk." Josh pulled his shirt over his head.

"Oh God," Jeff moaned at the sight of Josh's tanned skin.

Blake looked over in the direction of his neighbor. "Hope like hell Charlie Filmore is out for the day."

Josh threw his shirt at Jeff and reclined on Tanner's lap in a more seductive pose.

Jeff inhaled Josh's shirt deeply until Mickey tugged it out of his hands. "Officer Chandler. I'm going to have to discipline you." As Mickey tossed the shirt over a chair, he found Josh massaging his cock as he stared at him. "Don't look at me when you do that." Mickey laughed nervously.

"Why not?" Josh purred.

Behind him Tanner was rubbing his forehead in restrained amusement. "I can't do a thing about him, boys.

He's incorrigible."

"Who's asking you to stop him?" Hunter took off his own shirt.

Mickey felt Jeff's body shifting behind him. When he twisted around, Jeff was topless as well, and raising Mickey's shirt over his head. "Jesus." Mickey elevated his arms as Jeff stripped him.

"Yes!" Josh dug his hands into his own shorts, obviously pumping his cock.

The sight of Josh giving a solo performance had everyone enraptured. When the tip of Josh's cock flashed out of his gym shorts, Mickey's dick throbbed hungrily. "Holy fuck."

Jeff reached down Mickey's chest, massaging his pectoral muscles and nipples.

Licking his lips, Mickey surveyed the crowd. Hunter had his hand down Blake's shorts as Blake stared at Josh.

Finally, even Tanner's attention was focused on the little show.

Josh opened his lips and closed his eyes.

Mickey was in heat.

With one hand Josh, lowered his shorts, exposing all of his cock. With the other, he pumped, slowly.

Mickey's entire body stiffened and pressed back into Jeff's legs. Behind him, Jeff licked his ear and face, Jeff's hands still running up and down his torso.

Josh tucked his shorts under his balls, using one hand to stroke between his legs and the other to fist his cock. Tanner began nuzzling into Josh's hair sensually.

"Jeff," Mickey hissed. "Jesus Christ…" His heart was beating behind his ribs like mad. Jeff moaned a deep heaving breath into Mickey's ear, reaching to stroke Mickey's erection through his shorts.

As Josh gave an exemplary performance, Mickey took another quick look at Blake and Hunter. They were mutually masturbating as they stared at the lovely Josh Elliot working magic on them all.

Mickey felt Jeff's hand press against his back. He realized, Jeff was reaching into his own shorts now as well.

"*Ahh,*" Josh moaned softly, his hips moving in a hypnotic rhythm, his leg spread wide.

Jeff's hand encircled Mickey's cock inside his shorts. At the same time, Jeff was fisting himself.

Tanner finally succumbed to his lover's erotic seduction, digging his hand into his own shorts.

Josh wriggled out of his clothes. Naked, he writhed on Tanner's lap, running one hand all over his own chest and nipples, the other pumping his fantastic dick.

Mickey felt like he was holding his breath waiting for Josh to come. As Josh's hand quickened on his own prick, Mickey felt Jeff's keeping time. "Holy fuck…" Mickey seriously couldn't believe his eyes.

"Ah! Ah!" Josh spurt cum all over his own chest, milking his cock and massaging his own balls.

Mickey closed his eyes and came, feeling Jeff's cock shuddering behind him. A noise of gasping sounded from the two firemen. Mickey was so stunned he didn't even turn to look. Forcing his eyes open, he found Tanner had come as well, and rested his head back on the chair to recover while Josh toyed with the white blobs of semen on his own tanned skin.

"Josh Elliot," Mickey hissed, "you naughty fucking boy."

"Mm, just like Steve Rambo in *Right Hand Man*…" Josh sighed.

Hunter laughed, addressing Blake, "A solo act in a porn movie, Blake. Something you'd know nothing about."

"Holy shit. Did that just happen?" Blake gawked at his sticky hand.

"Put on your shorts, Josh." Tanner kissed his cheek.

"No. I feel sexy." Josh squirmed around on Tanner's lap.

"You're drunk." Tanner laughed, cupping his hand over Josh's crotch.

Mickey was about to combust all over again. He knew

they were all a sticky mess. Jeff breathed in his ear. "Is this cheating?"

"No. It's insane." Mickey glanced down at Jeff's hand, which was still massaging his cock gently. When Josh's bedroom green eyes opened, he was gazing at Mickey. Mickey's breath caught in his throat.

"Hey, copper. You like the show?"

"Hell yeah," Mickey panted.

Josh used Tanner's hand to massage his package.

"Uh…were we going to eat, Blake?" Mickey couldn't tear his eyes away from what Josh was doing.

"Food? Who needs food?" Hunter moaned.

"I told you I'd never get him to behave," Tanner warned.

"Motherfucker," Blake whimpered. "He'll have me going again in a minute."

Mickey peeked up at Jeff. He was glued to Josh, his hands still inside both their shorts. "Someone do something," Mickey pleaded.

"Why?" Jeff sighed.

"You want him to stop, Mick?" Hunter laughed.

Meeting Josh's wicked grin, Mickey bit his lip. "Isn't this insane?"

Staring at Mickey, Josh began sucking Tanner's right index finger while simultaneously rubbing Tanner's left hand up and down his cock.

Another throbbing pulse of pleasure washed up Mickey's prick. Jeff chewed on Mickey's neck and jaw, stroking his sticky cock as he did.

"Am I the only one who thinks this is nuts?" Mickey scanned the tight circle again.

"Yes." Jeff licked Mickey's face.

"Blake?" Mickey asked in agony at seeing Josh revving up for act two. When Blake didn't answer Mickey turned to look. He and Hunter were lip locked. "Jeff? Why am I the only one who's a nervous wreck at the moment?"

"Because you're thinking about us getting caught doing

something lewd and getting in trouble."

"Duh."

"No one can see us, Mick. The patio is recessed against the back of the house. You'd need a helicopter to get a view."

"But…" Mickey's attention was on Tanner's hand, wrapped around Josh's cock while Josh used it to pleasure himself. "Stanton."

"Shh…enjoy it. This way we can both witness Josh's dirty deed and talk about it while we fuck each other later."

"Christ…" Mickey blinked, not wanting to miss a trick. And Josh was one wicked trick.

"Wouldn't you love to see Tanner top him?" Jeff hissed devilishly in Mickey's ear. "See him pump hard into Josh's ass?"

"Jeff…" Mickey felt his prick throb in Jeff's palm. Mickey's throat went dry. "Hell yeah…"

"Imagine them doing it, Mick…" Jeff licked Mickey's earlobe. "Tanner fucking Josh's tight hole."

Josh slid Tanner's finger out of his mouth, still connected to Mickey's eyes, and seductively touched the tip of his tongue to his top lip. It was subtle, but very effective. "What do you want me to do, Mick?"

Mickey tensed up. "Did you hear what Jeff just said to me?"

"No. What did he say?" Josh spread his legs giving Mickey and Jeff a grand view.

"Nothing." Mickey shivered.

Josh whispered something into Tanner's ear. Tanner's low reprimanding voice replied but it was too soft for Mickey to hear it. Josh pleaded again, working Tanner's hand on his cock faster.

It appeared to Mickey that Tanner was going just as crazy as the rest of them over his lover's uninhibited actions. The expression on Tanner's face was a cross between resolve and agony. "Blake," Josh breathed, "get the lube."

"Oh God…" Blake moaned.

Before anyone could change their minds, Hunter bolted

into the house.

Mickey's heart stopped. Josh softened his lover up by kissing him, running his tongue over Tanner's teeth.

Trying to calm down, still sitting on the patio between Jeff's legs, Mickey closed his eyes and rested his head on Jeff's lap. "Tell me this isn't happening. I feel like this is my drunken hallucination."

Jeff laughed softly. "You're the one who thought bringing tequila was a good idea." He leaned over to kiss Mickey's lips.

A breathless Hunter tossed rubbers and lube at Josh as he dashed back to his seat with Blake.

"Here we go." Jeff nudged Mickey to watch.

Josh rolled a condom on Tanner's enormous erection, preparing it with lube. When Josh eased himself down on it, on top of Tanner's lap, Mickey was about to pass out, and it appeared so was Tanner. The big, brawny lifeguard closed his eyes and opened his lips, shivering visibly.

"Holy fuck!" Blake choked.

Jeff wrapped his arms around Mickey from behind, rubbing his face into the back of his hair sending tingles down Mickey's spine. He reached up to loop his arm around Jeff's neck, holding him tight as Jeff dug into Mickey's shorts.

As Josh slid up and down on Tanner's cock, his own bobbed and seeped pre-cum. Mickey gulped audibly as Josh grasped each of Tanner's massive thighs, bracing himself and began impaling himself on Tanner's length.

"Jeff," Mickey groaned pathetically. "Jesus Christ, Jeff…"

"Bet you wanna suck his cock."

Mickey imagined it, but wouldn't. He tightened his grip on Jeff's neck. "Faster."

Jeff pumped his fist quicker on Mickey's cock.

When Tanner came, Mickey heard Blake and Hunter gasp with him. He didn't even look at them because he knew what he'd find.

As Tanner recovered, Josh sank down on Tanner's lap, wedging that big cock deeper, and grabbed his own dick in both hands.

"Shit." Mickey was a goner. He closed his eyes and came a second time, his body tightening up from the intensity. Behind him, Jeff did the same to himself, grunting in Mickey's ear.

"Ah, ah!" Josh's cum sprang out of him like a fountain.

Mickey gazed at the sensual scene with exhausted eyes. It was too surreal to be happening.

Finally spent, Josh splayed out on Tanner's lap, panting.

Tanner wrapped both his muscular arms around that prize and hid his face in Josh's brown mop of hair.

Hunter led Blake into the house. Mickey assumed it was to clean up. They were all a mess at the moment.

"You think they have more than one bathroom?" Mickey asked Jeff.

"Let's find out."

Mickey stood stiffly, reaching for Jeff's hand. "You are unreal, Josh Elliot. Un-fucking-real."

Josh gave them a contented smile.

Entering the kitchen, Mickey nosed around the bottom floor and found a bathroom with just a toilet and sink. He turned on the light and dragged his shorts down to wash up as Jeff did the same. "This was too weird, Jeff."

"But enjoyable." Jeff laughed.

"I suppose now we'll be able to relax." Mickey dried off with the small hand towel, handing it to Jeff.

"For an hour. Until Josh decides intermission is over."

"Why did Tanner let him do that?" Mickey draped the towel over the sink.

"I don't think Tanner has much control over that one. Besides, he didn't cheat, did he?" Jeff smiled ironically.

"No."

Jeff encircled his arm around Mickey's waist. "What a cool thing to have shared with you."

That lit Mickey up. "Yeah?"

"Hell yeah. I wouldn't want to have witnessed that and told you about it afterwards."

"Me neither. I'd have been very jealous."

"I know." Jeff kissed him. "I'm starved."

"That grill must be ready by now." Mickey opened the bathroom door and met up with Blake and Hunter in the hall.

"Jesus, Blake." Mickey met his gaze.

Holding up his hands, Blake replied, "I had no idea, fellas."

"Put the food on the grill," Jeff complained, "A man needs more than two orgasms and three shots of tequila to survive."

"Coming right up." Blake headed to the kitchen.

As the four of them entered, Tanner and Josh were coming in. "Hi," Josh flirted.

"Go." Tanner nudged him from behind.

"Oops! Be back!" Josh waved.

All four men stared at Josh's ass as he walked by. Shaking themselves out of it, Blake began delegating, handing out salads, plates, and the meat to grill.

~

Jeff sipped his second beer, watching Blake flip burgers on the fire. Tanner and Josh were tossing a football across the yard and Hunter was making sure the table had enough paper plates and plastic-ware to go around. When Mickey returned from a bathroom break, Jeff reached out for him and drew him to his lap.

"Am I up for the next performance?" Mickey laughed.

"No. I just want you close." Jeff sniffed Mickey's armpit.

"What's up, babe?" Mickey ran his hand through Jeff's hair.

After inhaling him and rubbing his face against Mickey's skin, Jeff gazed at Mickey's eyes. "You…uh…"

"Me, uh?" Mickey took the beer out of Jeff's hand and sipped it.

Jeff struggled terribly with what he wanted to ask him.

The nightmare relationship he'd had in Seattle was like a fire breathing dragon and Jeff didn't know if Mickey was the knight to kill it off for him.

Shifting off Jeff's lap, Mickey slid a chair up to Jeff's knees and sat facing him. "Talk to me."

Blake announced, "Almost there, guys."

Pausing in his thoughts, Jeff watched Hunter as he held a plate for Blake to fill with the cooked hamburgers. He knew Blake and Hunter were very happy cohabitating, and through an earlier conversation, he found out so were Josh and Tanner.

He wanted Mickey with him, full time. He was just petrified.

"Jeff?" Mickey rubbed his knuckle over Jeff's cheek.

"Nothing." Jeff wondered if maybe now wasn't a good time to talk about it.

"Tanner!" Blake shouted. "Food's ready."

Josh caught the ball like a running back and raced toward the patio. "Smells great. I'm starved."

Hunter set the platter on the table. "Dig in, guys."

Jeff tried not to upset himself with his own doubts about living with Mickey as he watched the men load their plates with hamburgers, coleslaw, potato salad, and pickles.

Waiting as Mickey made up a plate, Jeff was surprised when Mickey set it down in front of him. "What are you doing?"

"For you." Mickey smiled at him.

"Thanks." Jeff knew Mickey was different from his first bad experience. That other man was not as kind, or nearly as thoughtful as Mickey was. He had to convince himself Mickey and Lance were different people. He could trust Mickey. It was the truth. He knew this relationship with Mickey made the one he had with Lance look like an adolescent crush.

Had Lance been there for him emotionally the way Mickey had been? No. The answer to that question was no.

And staring at Mickey, his thick, wavy, blond mane

and sea blue eyes, Jeff was getting the feeling he *could* love again, take that plunge off the cliff and freefall. He trusted Mickey with his life on the job, maybe it was time to trust him with his heart in the bedroom.

"Good one, Blake!" Josh nodded his head as he chewed. "What'd you do to the burgers?"

"Secret ingredient." Blake relaxed at the table next to Hunter.

Hunter boasted, "Blake's the best damn chef around."

"I know." Mickey sipped Jeff's beer. "I tasted his food at the station. Damn good."

"I cook." Josh continued to consume the burger. "Come on, Blake, what'd you put in it?"

"It's just a little soy sauce and garlic." Blake wiped his lips on a napkin.

"Nice." Josh devoured the food hungrily.

Jeff caught Mickey's eye. "Neither of us can cook."

"We can learn." Mickey took another forkful of coleslaw.

Tanner asked, "What do you guys do? Order out?"

"Pretty much." Jeff took a drink of the beer he and Mickey were sharing.

Hunter shook his head. "That gets old. And fattening."

"My sister's a decent cook," Mickey said. "I could get her to show me some recipes or something."

"Where does your sister live?" Blake asked.

"We share an apartment in Cerritos."

Josh stopped eating to stare at him. "You mean you guys don't live together?"

Jeff flinched and didn't meet anyone's eyes. He knew he was nuts. Maybe it was time to let go of the fear and just do it.

"Why the hell not?" Josh exclaimed. "Mickey, tell me you don't want Jeff in your bed every night?"

"Joshua," Tanner warned, "why don't you shut up and eat?"

Jeff suddenly wasn't hungry. He set the rest of his

burger down and pushed his plate aside, finishing the beer.

An awkward silence prevailed.

"I just don't get it, that's all." Josh wiped his hands on a napkin. "I'd go nuts if I couldn't live with you, Tanner."

*Fuck!* Jeff rose up to toss his plate in the trash. Once he had, he entered the kitchen through the sliding door, having a feeling everyone was going to whisper behind his back. He headed to the bathroom to wash his hands and relieve himself, staring at his reflection in the mirror. He looked tired. He felt exhausted. Recovering from the twelve-hour shifts took time. After taking a minute to adjust his mood, he stepped out of the bathroom. Blake was in the kitchen.

But these men could see it was right. This relationship with Mickey, it was the one, wasn't it?

Hunter had taken a chance on Blake, Tanner on the wild and crazy Josh, wasn't it his turn to take one more chance at love?

"You okay?"

Jeff looked outside. Everyone was joking and laughing again.

When Blake rested his hand on Jeff's shoulder, he met Blake's eyes.

"Don't listen to Josh. You guys go at your own pace."

"I feel guilty, Blake. Mickey's been asking to move in. And I want him to…"

"But?"

"I just had a crappy experience before him. And I dread the pain of another break up. I don't know if I can do it yet."

"If it's right, you will eventually."

Jeff looked out the sliding door. Mickey was staring his way. Jeff didn't know if he could see in or if there were reflecting glares preventing it.

"I was going to slice up the cheesecake," Blake changed the subject. "Should I? Or should we wait and digest a little?"

Since Jeff wanted to go home, he said, "Let's do it now." Blake opened the refrigerator to retrieve it.

"You want me to help clean up, bring the salads in or something?"

"Hunter can do that. Just go and relax."

"Thanks, Blake."

"No problem."

When Jeff pushed back the glass door, Hunter was indeed clearing up the remaining salads to take back inside while Mickey tossed the garbage into a plastic bag. As Jeff stepped out, Mickey paused to look up at him. They caught eyes but said nothing.

Jeff shifted aside as Hunter passed into the kitchen. "You need help, Hunt?"

"No. I got it. Thanks, Jeff."

Josh entered the house next. As he did he whispered, "Sorry, Jeff. I didn't mean to stir things up."

"It's okay."

Josh gave him a light caress on his side as he continued on.

When Tanner made a move into the house that looked a lot like an effort to give him and Mickey alone time, Jeff felt like total shit. He had no idea what had been said in his absence.

Mickey tossed out the last of the dirty paper plates and brushed off his hands. "You want to go?"

"Blake's cutting up the cheesecake."

"So?"

"Mickey…" Jeff sighed, walking closer to him. He held his waist and kissed him. "I am tired. To be honest, I'm dead on my feet from the booze, the heat, the long week we just had…"

"Let's go." Mickey shrugged.

"We'll stay for the cake and then go."

"Up to you."

Jeff hugged him, closing his eyes and resting on Mickey's shoulder. The feel of Mickey embracing him was so comforting and secure, Jeff knew he could trust him. He just had to let go of his own fear.

Hearing noise behind him, Jeff released Mickey and turned around. Blake had sliced up the cheesecake and set it out on the table. "We better eat it quick. It'll melt in this heat."

The rest of the crowd soon followed and were enjoying the sweet treat.

Mickey and Jeff shared a slice since Jeff had completely lost his appetite.

"Blake, you mind if me and Mick head out after this? The long week is catching up to me."

"No. Of course not. I know what you mean. After Hunt and I go through our two twenty-fours we tend to sleep the whole next day."

"Augh," Mickey cringed. "And I thought twelve hours was bad."

"It's different, Mickey," Hunter replied. "We're not at it all day in a patrol car."

"We are." Mickey grinned wickedly.

"No!" Josh gasped. "You do it on duty?"

"Mick!" Jeff chided, but laughed as he did.

"Tell me!" Josh revved up, fidgeting in his chair.

Mickey glanced at Jeff sheepishly.

Jeff had to smile at Josh's enthusiasm. "I'll give you one tidbit, Josh. I know you, you'll be stripping off your shorts again."

"Duh!" Josh dug his hand down them.

A big smile on his face, Jeff said, "We went on a residential alarm recently. It was false but we had to search the house since the back slider was unlocked." Jeff noticed Mickey covering his smile. "Well, we're checking it out, you know, making sure there's no sign of a burglary or property damage." Jeff watched Josh's hand shift under his shorts. "Anyway," he continued through that distracting sight, "ends up we're in a gay couples' house. They had some photos around, you know, of the two of them together. One of the guys is a model. Mark Richfield. You know him?" Jeff looked around the perimeter of their tight circle.

"Yes…" Josh crooned. "I do."

"Why am I not surprised." Tanner laughed.

"Then you know what the guy looks like," Jeff replied, grinning. "Anyway, we find some photos of him in a book of male nudes, and by the time we got to the kitchen…" Jeff grinned at Mickey demonically.

Mickey hissed, "Jeff was on his knees in front of me."

"Agh!" Josh whimpered, pumping his cock.

"And the guys that owned the house came home." Jeff chuckled. "Found us in a rather compromising position."

"Shit!" Hunter laughed. "Were you dead?"

Mickey added, "Mark's partner is an ex-LAPD cop."

Blake gasped, "Fuck!"

"He was totally cool," Jeff replied. "They were awesome. Really." He smiled at Mickey. "Mick kissed Mark Richfield."

Josh groaned. "I love that guy. I am so jealous!"

"How do you even know him?" Tanner asked.

"Are you crazy? He's been on *Forever Young*. He did a scene with Keith O'Leary and Carl Bronson. A threesome. It was absolutely to die for." Josh addressed Mickey, "So, you just grabbed the guy and planted one on his lips? In front of his ex-LAPD lover? How the hell did you manage that without getting shot?"

"We were out on patrol and caught up to the two of them jogging," Mickey explained. "When we pulled up, Mark practically dove into the front seat to get at the air conditioning. And, well, he was right fucking there."

Josh groaned pathetically and his hand began moving in his shorts frantically. "Oh, please…I can't believe it. Do you guys know them well enough to get together with them?"

Jeff gaped at Josh's actions. "Jesus, Josh! You'll have us all coming in our shorts again. Stop it!"

Controlling his laughter, Mickey said, "Yes, Josh, Mark gave us his phone number and told us to call him."

Josh feigned agony, reaching out for Tanner who was sitting next to him. "Unfair! Make them share Mark Richfield, Tanner."

Jeff shook his head. "Are you kidding? You and Mark in the same room? Josh, I don't think I can handle that."

"You're mean!" Josh accused. "I worship that guy. I cut out every ad he's ever done."

"You do?" Tanner smiled in amusement. "I've never even heard of him."

Blake stood. "Hang on." He entered the house.

Jeff said, "Look, I'm not even sure me and Mick will meet with them. I think they were just being nice. What the hell would those guys want with us? You should have seen their house. We're not in their league."

Blake returned with a magazine opened to an advertisement. "That's him, right?" He pointed to the ad.

Jeff reached for it but Josh beat him to it. "Yup," Josh confirmed. "Isn't he dreamy?"

Hunter asked, "How the hell did you know who the guy is, Blake?"

"I read an article about him ages ago. He was voted LA's most eligible bachelor."

They all got a good chuckle out of that.

The magazine made the rounds. When Jeff had it on his lap, he admired Mark and a handsome black male model wearing nothing but Ralph Lauren jeans. "He is very pretty." He passed it to Mickey.

"Well," Josh warned, "if you guys ever get on friendly terms with him, I want to meet him."

"What will you do when you meet him?" Tanner asked warily. "There's no way you're going to play with yourself in front of that guy. Uh uh." Tanner wagged his finger.

Josh pouted his lip in exaggeration. "Killjoy."

"I may look stupid," Tanner laughed, "but I'm not letting you and this male model play together. You have to be kidding me."

"On that note." Jeff rose up. "Blake, it's been…uh…an experience."

"No shit." Blake stood up to shake his hand. "Thanks

for coming."

Hunter got to his feet as well. "We really do need to make this a regular occurrence."

"Yes!" Josh hopped up.

"I meant the gathering, not the sideshow," Blake admonished.

"That's up for debate," Hunter teased.

"Bye guys." Jeff waved at Tanner and Josh.

When Josh gave both he and Mickey a peck on the cheek, Jeff smiled sweetly at him. "And you behave, pretty boy. Don't give Tanner a heart attack."

"Well, I'll try." Josh played modest.

With Mickey behind him, Jeff walked to the truck. Jeff waited as Mickey unlocked it and climbed into the driver's seat.

"Christ, Mick, I'm dead on my feet." Jeff slouched low.

"Me too."

Jeff checked the time, it was nearing six. "You still want to go shooting tomorrow?"

"We have to practice, Jeff. Qualifications are coming."

"Okay." Jeff closed his eyes as Mickey drove them back to his townhouse.

∽∾

They walked through the front door, dragging their feet. Mickey tossed his keys aside and began stripping for a shower. He felt hot and dirty from the afternoon's events.

Standing outside the shower door, his hand under the water, he didn't wait for it to heat up, just stepped under the cool spray. A flesh colored blur appeared outside the glass. Jeff was urinating at the toilet, then he pushed back the door. "Mind if I rinse?"

"Not at all."

Jeff stepped in and moaned under the cool water. "Yes. Oh man, I was so hot in that backyard."

"In more ways than one." Mickey chuckled rubbing soap on Jeff's chest.

"I still can't believe Josh did that."

"I felt bad for Tanner. I mean, shit, Jeff, I wouldn't want you to do that."

"He must realize that's Josh's nature." Jeff shrugged tiredly.

"I suppose." Mickey couldn't handle a man like that. "I'm done, babe. I need to lie down."

"Me too. Shut it off."

Mickey closed the faucets as Jeff grabbed two towels. Rubbing one over his head, Mickey did a quick wipe down and stepped out of the tub. After he draped the towel over the rack, he walked into the bedroom and dropped down on the bed with a deep sigh.

Jeff flopped heavily next to him.

Coiling around him, Mickey nuzzled into his neck and closed his eyes. It didn't take long before both men were fast asleep.

# Chapter 12

The ringing telephone woke Jeff. Groggy from a deep sleep, he looked over at the clock in confusion. It read eight-thirty. Mickey stirred next to him. Rubbing his face, Jeff picked the extension up off his nightstand and said, "Hello?"

"Jeff."

At the sound of that voice, Jeff bolted upright.

"Ya there?"

"What the hell do you want?"

Mickey propped himself up on a pillow, looking at him in concern.

"I just wanted to hear your voice, Jeff."

"How did you get my number?" Jeff's pulse raced and his breathing became quick and sharp.

"I called your mom."

"My mother? You fucking called my mother?" Jeff glanced at Mickey who was sitting up, staring with more than concern. He somehow knew who it was.

"Yes."

"What do you want?" Jeff shouted. "I don't want to hear *your* voice, you fuckhead!"

"I divorced her, Jeff."

"So?" He was furious. "What the hell does that have to do with me?" Mickey rubbed Jeff's leg gently. In reflex, Jeff brushed it off. He didn't want anyone touching him at the moment.

"I just thought we could talk."

http://www.youtube.com/watch?v=kkshHySfRD8time for justifiable homicide. No problem. You get that?"

"You don't mean that, Jeff."

"Don't I?" Jeff laughed at the insanity. "I won't even give you a chance. I'll fucking gun you down in cold blood. Believe me. Never call here again. You got that, dipshit?"

"Jeff!"

He hung up, threw the phone, and raced down the stairs to his car. Something in Jeff broke. Yes, maybe the sound of Lance's voice was a reminder of what they had, but it was also a reminder of what an asshole Lance was. And his Mickey was not that asshole.

Suddenly, like a light had turned on in Jeff, he knew Mickey was his man. What the hell had he been waiting for?

"I finally got pushed off the cliff, Stanton." He grabbed his keys. "I love you, you son of bitch. I hope you can forgive me for being such an ass."

༺༻

"Mouse?"

"Hi, Aura." Mickey tossed his gun pack and keys on the table.

Aura emerged from her bedroom and stared at him. "Not another fight."

Mickey dropped on the sofa. "His ex called."

"Ex-wife?" She sat next to him.

"No, his ex-boyfriend."

"So?"

"I can hear they still feel something for each other. Christ, Jeff was so enthralled he didn't even see me leave."

"Why did you leave? Why didn't you wait to talk to him?"

Mickey laughed sadly. "I didn't want to hear how much they miss each other and want to get back together. Believe me."

"Oh, Mouse." She hugged him. "I guess gay relationships are just as hard as straight ones."

He hugged her back, closing his eyes, trying not to

believe he could lose Jeff. "It was the reason he's kept me an arm's length, Aura. He was really in love with this other guy. He told me how hard it is for him to let go and feel deeply for another man again."

"I sort of don't blame him. That sounds like a really painful break up."

Mickey sat back to see her eyes. "It was. The guy got a woman pregnant and married her."

"Ouch! Poor Jeff!"

"I just hate to think he's still hung up on a man who can do that to him."

Loud pounding rattled their door.

Aura smiled. "Guess who?"

"Mick!" Jeff shouted through the wood.

"Go!" Aura nudged him.

Mickey stood off the couch and turned the knob. Jeff burst in and landed in his arms. "Why did you leave?"

Gripping him tight, Mickey replied, "I couldn't bear hearing your attachment to that guy."

Jeff gripped Mickey's face and stared into his eyes. "I told that piece of shit if he comes down to LA I'll gun him down in cold blood."

Mickey shivered at the seriousness of the threat.

"And I will, Mick. I wouldn't mind going to jail if it meant getting that nasty skank off the planet."

"Wow," Aura said.

As if they remembered she was there, Mickey pulled away from Jeff's grip.

"No! Don't do that on my account. I'm outta here." She jumped to her feet and raced to her bedroom, closing the door.

Mickey held Jeff's hand and urged him to sit on the sofa with him. "I just couldn't believe the passion in your voice."

"Passion?" Jeff choked in disbelief. "Come on, Mick."

"I suppose I'd have preferred apathy."

Jeff threw up his hands in defeat.

"You act like it's nothing, but because of that relationship you won't commit to me."

"I will."

"When?"

"Now." Jeff forced him to lie back on the couch.

"Now?" Mickey asked between kisses.

"Now." Jeff ground his crotch against Mickey's underneath him.

Mickey gripped Jeff's jaw to make their eyes meet. "How?"

"Will you marry me?"

"Be serious, Chandler," Mickey growled.

"I am."

"What are you talking about?" Mickey hated to think this reaction was purely from a phone call from the Great Northwest when he'd been trying to get Jeff to commit to him for months.

"Be my bitch." Jeff jammed his hips into Mickey's.

"I am your bitch." Mickey was confused.

"Are you stupid? I'm proposing!"

"I don't see you on your hands and knees with a ring, asshole."

Jeff exhaled in exasperation. Sliding off the couch to the floor, he got on one knee and opened the waist pack that was sitting behind him.

When he produced Mickey's firearm, Mickey flinched back.

"Mick Stanton," Jeff declared formally, "will you marry me?" He slid the loop of the gun's trigger over Mickey's finger.

"Jeff…" Mickey didn't know what to say or do. He set the gun down on the table and smiled sweetly at his lover. "Is this some knee-jerk reaction from that stupid phone call?"

"Jesus, Mick!" Jeff rose up. "I can't do anything fucking right."

Getting to his feet quickly, Mickey gripped Jeff's arms. "I just want to know your motivation. I've been begging you for ages to live together, to commit to me, and one ugly phone call from your ex and suddenly you're hot on marrying me."

"Get the fuck away from me!" Jeff shoved him back. "I knew this would happen. You think I want to put my heart out there again? I knew it."

As Jeff stormed to the door, Mickey grabbed him.

Immediately, Jeff roared in fury and shoved him against a wall with a thud. "Get away from me!"

"Jeff! Calm down."

"Don't tell me to calm down, Stanton, after what I just did. You're the same as Lance! A fucking lying cunt!"

Mickey grabbed Jeff's face by his jaw and nailed him back against the closed front door with a thundering thud that shook the apartment. "I'm nothing like that prick you were crazy in love with. Don't even try to compare us. You think I'd knock up a woman and leave you? Is that how well you know me?"

"Get off me, asshole!" Jeff roared and body slammed Mickey away from him.

It sent Mickey flailing backward into the coffee table, throwing the gun onto the floor. The minute he regained his balance, Mickey lunged for Jeff who had begun opening the front door. The force of Mickey's advance slammed the door shut with another loud bang and sent Jeff flying against it.

Mickey gripped Jeff's jaw in an iron hold and pressed their lips together. It made Jeff growl deeply, a sound that sent Mickey's toes curling in desire.

"Fuck you, Stanton!" Jeff sneered. "You can't have it all! You can't use me!"

"Like fucking hell I can't," Mickey snarled, digging his hand into Jeff's shorts.

Jeff held Mickey by the shoulders and heaved him back. Mickey had clamped onto Jeff's waist causing them both to go flying backward. They landed on the coffee table with a crash, flipping it into the air and on its side. Mickey pressed Jeff into the carpet as Jeff snarled like a wildcat. When Jeff's eyes darted to the gun, which lay on the floor nearby, Mickey reached for it, shoving it so hard it spun and hit the linoleum in the kitchen. Straddling Jeff's hips, Mickey ground into them, a deep, rumbling growl escaping his clenched teeth.

"What do you want from me, Stanton?" Jeff cried, pushing at Mickey's shoulders to get him off. "I love you so much. I'm trying to tell you what you mean to me. I finally get it, Mick. I'm ready to be just yours. What the hell else do you want from me?"

"To fuck you…make you my whore." Mickey tore Jeff's shorts down his hips.

"You think I use you, ya prick?"

"You know fucking well you do." Mickey chewed at Jeff's neck, pushing Jeff's shirt up his chest.

"Leave me alone." Jeff struggled to get out from under Mickey's weight.

"Never." Mickey found Jeff's erection and pumped it.

Jeff let loose a sensual moan, causing the chills to race up Mickey's spine.

Lowering to hiss in Jeff's ear, Mickey whispered, "Josh Elliot's cock."

"Ahhh, no…you're too cruel…"

"Tanner's thick cock up Josh's ass…" Mickey fisted Jeff's dick faster. "Josh's gasps as he climaxed. Jeff, can you hear it in your ears now? *Ah, ah*?" Mickey sucked a deep stream of air through his teeth. "Get a good look at Josh's balls, Jeff?"

A low grunting preceded Jeff jerking his hips up into Mick's hands. As Jeff came, Mickey fisted him harder, making Jeff buck with the intensity. Before Jeff had even finished ejaculating, Mickey had him by the shirt and dragged him to his bedroom. Throwing him on the bed, Mickey stripped off both their shorts and sheathed his cock in latex. As Jeff moaned and rocked side to side, Mickey pressed Jeff's thighs back and wide. Sliding in, Mickey thrust against him, closing his eyes as the sensations began to intensify.

Under him, a breathy whisper urged him on. "Tanner's

dick up Josh's hole."

Mickey smiled and looked down at Jeff's demonic expression. Bracing his arms on either side of Jeff, Mickey drove in deeper.

"Josh Elliot and Mark Richfield doing sixty-nine," Jeff breathed, "sucking each other's cocks."

"Oh, fuck!" Mickey came, ramming his hips into Jeff's body. It churned so deeply in his balls, Mickey whimpered in agony. Catching his breath, Mickey dropped his weight on top of Jeff heavily.

Once they took a moment to recuperate, Mickey leaned up on his elbows. Jeff's bright green eyes seemed to glow in the dim room. "Yes."

"Yes, what? Josh and Mark together?"

"No. You and me together."

"Yeah?" Jeff's expression perked. "You mean, yes, you'll marry me?"

"But I'm not wearing a fucking Glock as a ring."

"Mickey!" Jeff wrapped his arms around him.

"I love you, babe." Mickey crushed him against him.

"You said yes! Mick, I know I was a jerk to put you off. But I trust you on the damn job with my life. Christ, I have to be able to trust you with my feelings. And I do, Mick, so much."

As they kissed, a small rap was heard at the door.

"Uh, guys?"

They parted lips and panted as they stared at the closed door.

"What, Aura?" Mickey asked.

"There's a loaded gun on the kitchen floor."

Mickey pulled out of Jeff quickly, tugging the condom from his spent cock.

"I'll go. You wash up." Jeff drew his shorts up his legs.

"Thanks."

⁓⁓

Jeff tucked his shirt in and left the bedroom, closing the door behind him. "We keep forgetting you're here,

Aura. I'm sorry."

"Man. Did you guys fight? The table was on its side and there was a lot of noise. I thought a neighbor would call the cops." She laughed. "Talk about irony!"

Jeff picked up the gun from the floor and carried it back to the vinyl waist pack it was usually hidden in. "Christ, that would be just our luck." He concealed the pistol and zipped up the pouch, setting it back on the table.

"Did you fight and have make-up sex?" Her eyes gleamed.

"I asked him to marry me, Aura." Jeff couldn't believe how good it felt to say that.

She squealed in delight and jumped on him for a hug.

As he rocked her, she whispered, "Man, did you guys just have sex? You smell delicious!"

Jolting in embarrassment, Jeff nudged her back from him. "Shit. I keep forgetting how hot you are about it."

"Yum." She leaned close and inhaled.

"It's your bother we're talking about, Aura." Jeff felt like she was as bad as Josh. Well, not quite.

"Uh, you're not my brother, hot stuff."

When Mickey appeared, Jeff sighed with relief.

"Mouse!" She raced to him and jumped up to hold him. "You told her?"

"Is that okay?" Jeff's heart sunk.

"More than okay," Mickey replied, smiling at him.

She backed up and asked, "So? Official? Like I can tell Mom and Dad? And we'll hire a wedding planner?"

"Jesus!" Jeff held his heart as he panicked.

"Why don't you let us handle all the details, Aura." Mickey smiled sweetly at her.

"I'm so excited." She jumped up and down.

"You need a life," Jeff advised. "Mick, she needs a life."

"I've got one." She held Mickey's hand and brought him across the room to Jeff. "Seeing my brother so madly in love that he's getting married."

"Were you serious, Jeff?" Mickey asked.

"Hell yeah. As a heart attack. Why? You getting cold feet already?"

"No way." He embraced Jeff.

"Mm!" Aura giggled.

"What would she have done if she was at Blake's earlier?" Jeff laughed.

"She'd think she'd died and gone to heaven." Mickey chuckled with him.

"Huh? Who? Blake? Is he cute?" she asked anxiously.

"You'll meet all our friends at the wedding, missy," Mickey informed her.

When Jeff met his eyes, Mickey kissed him softly.

"I love you guys," Aura sighed.

"We love you too, Aura." Jeff winked at her.

# Chapter 13

Jeff carried his box of ammo and his gun pack to a bench at the harbor range. Sitting down, he placed a pair of goggles on his eyes and the bulky ear protection over his head. Shots were going off around him in the echoing room.

As Mickey sat next to him, Jeff leaned his shoulder on him warmly. Waiting for their turn, Jeff checked that his magazines were loaded and stuffed them back into his gun belt. Though they were in jeans and LAPD t-shirts, they had their duty belt around their waists so they could practice drawing from their holsters.

Two side-by-side spots opened up. They jumped up to claim them. Bringing the target forward by pressing a button, Jeff clipped the fresh image of a torso onto the machine, sending it out to the end of the range. A fresh box of bullets on the ledge in front of him, Jeff took up a correct stance for the practice and waited until Mickey was ready. Mickey nodded.

Jeff held his hands in front of him and counted to three in his head. Like lightning, he unsnapped the holster with his thumb, drew, aimed, and fired off three rounds; two to the body, one to the head. Stuffing the gun back in his holster, snapping it, again he waited for Mickey, eying him from behind the divider. As if they were in direct competition for speed and accuracy, the minute Mickey moved, Jeff reached for his gun, drew, and fired.

When they neared the end of their first clip, Jeff noticed Mickey pausing, watching him. In the silence of the ear protection, Mickey mouthed, "Go."

Smiling, knowing Mickey wanted to witness him shooting, Jeff loved the attention. Getting back into his macho gun stance, Jeff peered back at Mickey. Mickey held up one finger, two, then three. Jeff drew and fired his last three shots. After he holstered his gun, he gazed at Mickey. Once Mickey glanced around, he smiled demonically and rubbed his own zipper flap under his gun belt.

Jeff knew Mickey had wood. So did he.

They reloaded fresh magazines and chambered a round. Jeff nudged Mickey this time. "Go," Jeff mouthed. As Jeff watched, Mickey waited for the signal. Jeff held up his fingers, one, two, three.

The speed in which Mickey unholstered and fired six rounds off blew Jeff away. He couldn't wait to see Mickey's target.

When Mickey spun back for Jeff's approval, Jeff hung his jaw in exaggeration and cupped his crotch for emphasis.

It made Mickey crack up with laughter.

They finished all their practice rounds. Before they headed to the outer table to clean and oil the guns and fill the magazines back up with bullets, they brought the targets forward to inspect.

Jeff was very proud of his tightly packed spread. Only one bullet went out of the center mass, not including the perfectly placed headshots. He leaned around the divider to inspect Mickey's. "Son of a bitch!" he shouted, though no one could hear in the noise and ear covers. Jeff nudged him and shook his head. The cluster of rounds was so perfect, it was a single hole in the center ring. *Christ, I adore him.* Jeff moaned, completely lovesick.

When they left the room, Jeff lowered the ear protection so it hung around his neck. "You are so fucked. I'm horny as hell. I had no idea you shot so well. Son of a bitch, Mick."

"I figured shooting together would do that. You think I'm stupid?" Mickey pulled the slide off his gun and dropped the spring and barrel onto the counter. As they cleaned and oiled the weapons efficiently, they exchanged heated glances.

Once the guns were assembled and tucked inside their vinyl packs, and they had taken off their duty belts, Jeff pointed to the bathroom to wash the gun oil from their hands.

The heavy gun belt over his shoulder, the off duty waist bag around his hips, Jeff scrubbed the black gunpowder and grime from his hands.

"Hey!"

He spun around and found Sgt. Bryant in his civilian clothing. "Sarge. Were you out there?" Jeff laughed.

"Yeah. Damn quals are coming." He stood at the sink next to them. "I have some good news for you guys."

"Yeah?" Mickey dried his hands on paper towels.

"I wasn't going to mention it until roll call on our next day on."

"What?" Jeff tugged paper towels from the dispenser.

"You both got officer of the month for that arrest you did of Officer Sanchez's shooter."

"Cool!" Mickey raised his palm for a high five. Jeff slapped it happily.

"Well done, boys. I'm really pleased."

"Thanks, Sarge." Jeff shook his hand.

"My pleasure, Jeff. You two were awesome. See you in a couple of days. Have fun on your time off."

After Sgt. Bryant left, Jeff watched Mickey gather his things. They walked out together. Jeff smiled brightly as they left the range and locked their on-duty belts in the trunk of his car.

Once they were sitting in the front seat of the Mustang, Mickey asked, "Think we should invite him to the wedding?"

"You are joking, right?" Jeff started the car and drove out of the lot.

Mickey shrugged.

"If we let anyone at work know, we'll be separated."

"What about rings?" Mickey asked. "We'll both suddenly be wearing wedding rings."

"I won't wear it at work. Just off duty."

When Mickey went silent, Jeff reached for his hand. "Mick. I can't not be your partner at work. Please. If I can't watch your back and you can't watch mine, I'll quit."

Mickey laughed softly. "Okay. I get it."

"Good." Jeff smiled contentedly. "Just our families and gay friends."

"Okay."

"God," Jeff shouted, "I love you. You're so fucking easy."

Mickey sidled closer on the bucket seat, reaching over the console. "You have no idea how easy I am at the moment. Watching you shoot…mm…you hot fucking cop…I wanted to screw you right on the floor of the range."

"Grrrr…" Jeff wriggled against the leather upholstery.

Mickey's fingers began massaging Jeff's crotch under the heavily armed pack around his waist.

"Fuck. Mick. I'll have to pull over I'm so hot."

"Pull over…" Mickey crooned, kneading Jeff harder as he grew an erection.

The scent of gun oil and testosterone wafting up Jeff's nostrils, he was about to burst.

"Josh Elliot's cock."

"Unfair!" Jeff whined. "Don't play dirty. I'm driving."

"Josh jacking off in front of firefighters and cops…" Mickey cranked up the passion.

"Fuck, Stanton!" Jeff knew they were still a few miles away from either of their abodes. His zipper opened and Mickey reached inside it. On the contact of Mickey's fingers to his skin, Jeff went insane. "Fuck!" He pulled into a parking lot of a multistory office building. Backing into the farthest corner of the fenced lot, Jeff threw the car into park and lunged at Mickey.

Once unclipped, their waist packs dropped to the passenger's side floor with two heavy clunks.

Jeff connected to Mickey's lips, tearing open Mickey's tight jeans in the process. The minute he had Mickey exposed he dropped down to Mickey's lap, enveloping Mickey's cock with his mouth. Mickey gasped and his legs tensed, causing his feet to kick the interior of the car. With Mickey's fingers digging into his hair, Jeff closed his eyes, inhaled Mickey's musky scent and sucked fast and furious with so many erotic images in his head he could spurt.

"I'm there…I'm there, Chandler…" Mickey moaned, his cock pulsating in Jeff's mouth.

Jeff squirmed as Mickey's cum filled him, sucking down to his root, not wanting to stop. Sitting up, gasping to catch his breath, Jeff ripped open his own jeans. "Do me."

Instantly, Mickey was face down on Jeff's lap, Jeff's cock deep inside his throat and his hand kneading Jeff's balls through the denim fabric. Jeff bucked his hips up, fucking Mickey's mouth, holding his head in place as he did. "Oh, Stanton… Oh!" Jeff closed his eyes and tensed up, pushing back into the bucket seat as he came.

Mickey continued sucking him, moaning as he did.

"I love you, you wicked, dirty cop." Jeff gasped for air.

When Mickey sat up, he was smiling devilishly. "I love it when you tell me you love me."

Jeff wrapped his arms around Mickey's neck and brought him to his lips. As they kissed, Mickey fondled Jeff's spent cock gently.

Tasting his cum on Mickey's tongue, Jeff moaned. He was so in love he knew, just knew, this was stronger than the last failed relationship. It felt so fucking right.

A rap on the window gave both of them heart failure.

They sprang apart and Jeff covered his crotch, his breath stopping at his panic.

Wearing a slick silk business suit, Mark Richfield was smiling through the glass at them.

"Oh my God." Jeff lowered the window.

"Naughty, naughty." Mark wagged his finger as he

chided them.

Jeff tucked his cock in his pants and zipped up. "Do you work here?"

"No. This is where Adam Lewis works. He's an agent and a dear friend. Do you know him?"

"No." Mickey laughed, but it sounded like he was nervous.

"Oh? Just parked here for some afternoon delight?" Mark's green eyes shimmered in the sunlight.

"Yes!" Jeff chuckled, his cheek heating up.

"We do need to stop meeting like this. Steve will think we're planning it." Mark leaned into the window. He inhaled deeply. "You two…wow…I could roll on your scent like a dog in heat."

Jeff cracked up. "You are so fucking adorable."

"Can't help it. I love gorgeous men. And cops? Bloody hell. I have a soft spot for those, I can assure you."

"Tell him," Mickey urged.

Jeff smiled proudly. "Mick and I are getting hitched."

"No!" Mark's light eyes widened. "I'm thrilled!"

"Can you come to the wedding?" Mickey drew closer to the driver's window where Mark was leaning in.

"Yes, of course. When is it?"

"Oh." Jeff looked over at Mickey. "We haven't gotten that far."

"The minute you know. Call. I assume you mean me and Steve."

"Yes," Mickey answered quickly.

"Good. He'd be cross if I came alone and he wasn't there to watch over me." Mark winked.

"With Josh there, you'll need watching," Mickey muttered.

"Sorry?" Mark leaned in closer.

"Nothing." Jeff brushed it off. "I'm really glad we bumped into you again, Mark."

"Me too. Seems I must have blowjob radar to keep finding you two giving head. Either that, or you're always at it."

"Always at it," Jeff replied, laughing.

"I don't blame you." Mark leaned back inside the window. "You're both smashing. Can I kiss the bride?"

"Oh, baby!" Jeff grabbed Mark's face and planted one on him. When it became passionate, Mickey punched Jeff in the shoulder to get his attention.

"Wow." Mark blinked.

Panting for breath, Jeff sighed, "Wow, is right."

"I better go before I get in big trouble. Bye, boys. Just ring and let Steve and I know the date." He waved as he walked off.

Salivating at Mark's delicious strut, not to mention his taste, Jeff was brought back to reality by another jab to his shoulder.

"What?" he whined.

"What?" Mickey asked in disbelief.

"You kissed him." Jeff put the car in drive.

"Not like that."

"Come on. Think of it as my bachelor party. One last smooch."

After a deep exhale, Mickey sighed, "What the fuck will Josh do when he finally meets Mr. Richfield?"

"Strip and beg him?" Jeff chuckled at the image. "That is one meeting I would love to witness."

"Fuck." Mickey giggled. "We better have a pre-wedding party, because I don't want my parents to witness that."

Jeff clasped Mickey's hand and kissed it.

෴

They stopped at the station to drop off their gun belts at their lockers. Jeff tugged open the steel door and hung the heavy leather belt with all its gear onto an internal hook. Slamming it closed with a metallic bang, he paused, looking back at Mickey as he did the same.

"Let's get out of here. I get enough of this place on duty."

Mickey nodded, meeting him to walk together down the narrow corridor.

Jeff paused to greet one of their supervisors. "Lieutenant."

"Chandler, Stanton…what brings you two in on your day off?"

Mickey replied, "We just got back from the range to practice for qualifications."

"Oh. Good. I'm glad you're keeping up on it." He was about to walk away when he turned back to say, "I almost forgot. You made officers of the month for September."

"We met Sgt. Bryant at the range, and he told us." Jeff smiled.

"Come here." Lt. Stryker tapped Jeff's arm for them to follow him.

They waited outside his office patiently. The lieutenant appeared with two engraved plaques. "We should wait until we present them to you in roll call, but have a look."

They each took one of the awards. Jeff read their names side by side on the brass plate. He met Mickey's gaze and grinned at him. "I like the way that looks."

"Me too." Mickey's eyes shined.

"Act surprised in roll call. Think you can do that?" The lieutenant took back the awards.

"Sure, Lieutenant." Mickey laughed.

"Now get out of here and enjoy the sunshine."

Waving as they went, Mickey put his arm around Jeff's waist. At his touch, Jeff looked around the area at the few uniformed officers milling around.

"You mind?" Mickey asked.

"No." Jeff curled his arm around Mickey's and they walked out of the station together to Jeff's car. *What the hell. We're engaged.* Jeff grinned happily. And he could always say that the lieutenant had just given them some good news if anyone asked.

Once they were seated in the car with the air conditioning running, Jeff asked, "Yours or mine?"

"Mine. Let me call my parents and tell them."

"We need to shop for rings." Jeff started them moving

out of the area.

"Where do you want to do this? A church?"

"Uh, no." Jeff shook his head. "No religion. Hate the shit."

"Pick a restaurant. I'm good with anything."

"Wow, there's a lot I haven't thought about. Maybe Aura can help us after all."

"Do you want a big wedding?" Mickey held Jeff's hand.

"Do you?"

"Not necessarily."

"Good." Jeff was relieved. "I don't care if you just want to have a justice of the peace at the beach and a couple of our closest friends for the ceremony, and a big party bash with everyone else."

"My parents will want to be at the ceremony. I think we should do all of it in one place so no one feels left out."

"Anything's fine, babe." Jeff kissed Mickey's hand.

"Tell me you love me again," Mickey purred.

Peeking over at him as he drove, Jeff crooned sensually, "I love you, Mickey Stanton."

"I will never get tired of hearing you say that."

"Good." Jeff relaxed in the seat. He wanted them at his place where they could snuggle in bed. Their bed.

# Chapter 14

On the Friday night before the big day, Mickey was already very drunk, slouched in a seat at the East/West Lounge in West Hollywood. Their bachelor party was in full swing and Mickey's favorite men were with him. That was all that mattered.

"Another?" Blake asked Mickey when he noticed his glass was empty.

"I'm toast. Do you want me to pass out?" Mickey laughed but it came out as a cough.

"No. Then you won't be able to get it up." Jeff leaned against Mickey's side, rubbing his thigh hungrily. "Pace yourself, copper."

"That's no fun," Josh announced, obviously well inebriated.

"Don't flip your pretty dick out in this place, Josh," Hunter warned. "You'll get tossed out."

"They can toss me." Josh made a hand gesture for jerking off.

Tanner leaned over to say to Mickey, "The wedding at the Ritz-Carlton? I never knew police made so much money."

"Blame Jeff. His parents are paying for it. After all, they are the mother and father of the bride."

"Ha. Ha." Jeff shook his head. "They offered," he answered, shrugging his shoulders. "What else has my dad got to do with his money?"

They were seated on a brown leather sectional sofa,

which curved in an arc against the corner of the room. There was no loud music so the group could talk easily and the lighting was bright enough to see one another without needing a flashlight, like some clubs. The waiter made his way over to their party. Josh's smirk appeared as he eyed him. Tanner whacked Josh playfully and Josh cuddled up against Tanner in response.

"Can I get anyone another round?"

"Yes," Hunter replied. "All of us."

"You are trouble," Jeff chided. "If you make Mickey puke and feel hung over for tomorrow, I'll beat you."

After the handsome waiter smiled and left, Blake continued the previous vein of conversation. "What's your dad do for a living, Jeff?"

"Executive at Boeing." Jeff finished his drink, setting it on the tiny black table in front of him.

"Ooh!" Josh reacted, "Rich? Mickey, you did good."

"Yeah, Josh, it was Jeff's money I was attracted to." Mickey kissed Jeff's cheek. "Not his sex appeal."

"Uh oh." Jeff nudged Mickey. "Look who made it."

Mickey raised his chin up to the direction of the door. "Well, at least Josh can embarrass himself here instead of tomorrow at the wedding."

"Hullo, boys."

"Hey, Mark. Steve. Glad you guys could make it." Jeff stood off the couch to shake their hands and make introductions. As he went around the group, Jeff finally got to Josh, who was gaping at Mark with his jaw hanging open. "Yes, Josh, that's Mark Richfield." Jeff shook his head. "I would warn you about him, Mark, but it'll be useless."

"Oh?" Mark thanked one of the lounge employees as he brought him and Steve chairs for them to join the large group.

"Another Mark Antonious admirer?" Steve relaxed and tugged on Mark's slacks to get him to sit down.

Tanner peered over at Josh. "Aren't you even going to say hello?"

"I'm too stunned." Josh didn't blink.

"Hullo, cutie." Mark winked at him. "Sorry we're late, chaps. Are we well behind on the alcoholic beverages?"

Mickey held up his empty glass. "The bride and groom to be are drunk. But I suppose that was the point of the gathering."

Steve shuddered. "I hate to think of the last wedding I was at."

"It was Keith and Carl." Mark nudged him. "Not the one you're thinking about."

"Oh. Good." Steve turned to watch a waiter bringing a tray over to hand out fresh drinks. After the waiter had doled out the liquor, Steve ordered a beer and Mark asked for a martini.

"So? Are you excited?" Mark wriggled in his chair.

"Yes." Mickey glanced over at Josh. His stare was glued to Mark. "Very." He got Jeff's attention and gestured to Josh.

Jeff laughed. "Joshua. Wake up out of your fantasy."

"Huh?" Josh spun around, his cheeks going crimson.

Blake chuckled. "I thought you'd be naked and in the midst of a climax by now. I'm disappointed, Josh."

That comment made Hunter break up with laughter.

"Did we miss something?" Steve took his beer from the waiter and thanked him.

"Either he's behaving himself," Tanner announced, "or he's in shock."

"Sorry?" Mark tilted his head curiously.

Jeff revealed, "Josh gave our group a one man performance at Blake's place a few weeks back."

"I'm sorry I missed it." Steve smiled.

Mark gave Josh his attention. "Are you that naughty, pretty boy?"

"You have no idea," Tanner breathed in reply.

Jeff exchanged glances with Mickey. "He's star struck."

"He must be." Mickey grinned, looking back at Josh. "Mr. Elliot, say something."

"Can I come on you, Mr. Richfield?" Josh's lips curled

into a demonic grin.

"Right to the point!" Mark blinked as he laughed.

Steve chuckled, sipping his beer. "Come on one of his naked photos."

"Been there. Done that." Josh licked his lip.

"Uh, where were we?" Mark gave his attention back to Mickey. "Yes. The wedding. Your families are supportive?"

"Yes." Jeff set his full drink down on the table in front of them. "Both sides. Cool, huh?"

"Miraculous." Mark reached out to stroke Steve's leg. "We don't have that luck, I'm afraid."

Josh stood abruptly.

Tanner asked, "Going somewhere?"

"Yes. Be back."

When he darted off, Mickey stared at Mark. "I think you finally got to him."

"I am flattered. He's adorable." Mark's green eyes sparkled.

"I better make sure he's okay," Tanner said as he stood.

Blake stated, "Sure, Tanner. That would be my reason for checking him out too."

Mickey waited as Tanner left the group. "Where were we?"

"Families?" Hunter suggested.

"Families," Mickey laughed.

※

The rented limousine dropped Mickey and Jeff off at Jeff's townhouse. Holding each other tight, they walked to the front door, still giggling and very drunk. Jeff held out the key to the front door but it circled the lock a few times before making contact.

Once Jeff managed to get them inside, he heard Mickey go into a laughing fit. "I knew Josh would crack."

Jeff tossed the keys on the coffee table and collapsed on the sofa, kicking off his shoes. "When he did a lap dance on Mark, I thought was going to piss my pants."

Mickey snorted as he inhaled air, his hilarity making

him gasp for breath. "He…he almost got us all kicked out, the perv."

Dabbing at his tears as he laughed, Jeff replied, "Thank fuck Steve has a sense of humor." Jeff rolled on the couch, holding his stomach as he roared.

"Steve? Thank fuck Tanner does. I couldn't believe Josh, pivoting around and humping Mark's leg." Mickey fell down on the couch and couldn't contain his laughter. "I'm dying…help me…" He wiped at his eyes and dropped like a heap on top of Jeff.

Jeff was choking he was laughing so hard. "Fucking Richfield just gaped at him in shock…did you see his face?"

"Oh, fuck…I'm dying…" Mickey rolled on Jeff's side, crushing him underneath.

"And when they kissed, holy fuck…" Jeff whimpered, wiping his eyes with the back of his hand. "I thought the whole room would combust. Everyone in the place stopped moving to gawk."

Mickey gasped for oxygen, moaning like he was in agony. "When they dueled tongues, I thought Steve was going to lose it."

"Tanner picking Josh up like that, almost over his head…oh, it was priceless, Mick."

"I wish I had a video camera. Honest…I would love to relive that moment." Mickey started gaining some control of his hilarity.

Jeff sighed deeply, feeling spent from all the laughing. "Mick, it was great. I'm thrilled we got those two face to face."

"It made Josh's year, believe me." Mickey sat up, dragging Jeff with him. When they were upright on the cushions, Mickey asked seriously, "Any doubts about tomorrow?"

"No."

"Now's the time, Jeff."

Jeff's smile faded. "You having second thoughts?"

"Not on your life."

"Good."

"Come closer. You're too far away." Mickey wrapped his arm around Jeff and dragged him on top of him.

Jeff held Mickey around the back of his neck, pressing their crotches together as he sat on top of Mickey's lap, straddling him. They kissed softly. The touch of their tongues made Jeff's heart race.

"I want to be naked like this." Jeff sighed. "There are too many layers between us, Mick."

"Let's go upstairs."

Backing up to get to his feet, Jeff reached out and held Mickey's hand as they climbed the stairs to the bedroom. A gentle caress brushed over his bottom as he went. Jeff smiled at Mickey's teasing contact.

Once they were standing beside the bed, Jeff began opening Mickey's shirt buttons. They were both dressed in smart casual, cotton shirts and dress slacks. He peeled the material back from Mickey's chest, admiring the wall of muscle and sparse chest hair. Sliding the shirt down Mickey's arms, Jeff tossed it aside and waited as Mickey reciprocated.

Soon they were both naked from the waist up. Jeff opened Mickey's black slacks, dropping them and his briefs down his legs. He kissed Mickey's cock on his way, helping him step out of the trouser legs and his socks.

When they were undressed, Jeff urged Mickey to his lips. Swaying softly as they kissed, Jeff was more used to them ripping, tearing, and snarling. It was rare for them to be slow and unhurried. Combing his fingers back through Mickey's hair, he sighed against his lips, "I love you."

"What? I didn't hear you." Mickey giggled.

"I love you." Jeff humored him.

"Still didn't catch it."

Grabbing Mickey around his waist and diving with him onto the bed, Jeff pinned him underneath, with a leg on each side of Mickey's hips and staring down at him. "I said…read my lips, Stanton…I love you!"

"Grrr!" Mickey reached up to tug Jeff down to his

chest. "Get over here, future Mrs. Stanton."

"Oh? Am I playing the Mrs.?"

Mickey ground his hard cock against Jeff's. "Which would you prefer, top dog?"

"My turn to fuck you, Mrs. Chandler." Jeff reached back to the nightstand. As he prepared, Mickey held his knees, opening up his body for Jeff. "I love it when you do that." Jeff grinned wickedly.

"Come and get it, handsome." Mickey tilted his hips up.

Before he dove in, Jeff rubbed his face into Mickey's balls, inhaling his scent and tasting the sweat off his skin. When he licked Mickey's rim, Mickey inhaled and whimpered. Smiling contentedly, Jeff teased it with his tongue, making Mickey squirm under him.

"Oh, fuck me…Chandler…ah…"

Jeff tickled the tip of his tongue against Mickey's ass, lapping up to his root and the base of his balls. When he arrived at Mickey's stiff cock, Jeff sucked it down to the bottom. A deep, rumbling growl vibrated through Mickey's body. It made him smile, even with his mouth full. He pumped up and down on Mickey's erection a few times, tasting his pre-cum and feeling him quiver. When Mickey was rising to an orgasm, Jeff knelt up and slid his slick dick inside him with a hiss of a breath. Once he had penetrated up to his balls, Jeff stayed still, savoring the connection. Under him, Mickey began bucking, obviously too pent up to wait. After watching Josh Elliot and Mark Richfield cock tease the crowd, it was torture waiting another minute.

Jeff began thrusting, thrilling in the erotic, whimpering moans of his lover. Aiming his hips to hit the right spot for Mickey, Jeff knew he had struck gold when his lover howled with delight and grabbed his own cock. Mickey fisted himself like mad. Just watching his pleasure lit Jeff up. "Oh, babe. I'm there." He jammed his hips tightly to Mickey and grunted as his came, forcing himself to open his eyes and see Mickey as he climaxed.

White cream sprayed Mickey's chest as he slowed down

his fisting and bared his teeth from the intensity.

Filling his gaze with Mickey's beauty, Jeff knew he'd love him forever, and always love him the most.

"Chandler…" Mickey exhaled deeply. "Fuck…"

Giving one last thrust in, Jeff pulled out and caught his breath. "I'd love to sit here and ogle you all night, but we have to wash up. I need to drop dead, Mick."

"Ditto, babe." Mickey managed to stand.

They walked to the bathroom to clean up and brush their teeth.

Once they were side by side on the bed in the dark room, Jeff cuddled around Mickey, sealing him against his body. "Goodnight, future Mrs. Chandler."

"Goodnight, future Mrs. Stanton." Mickey laughed wearily.

Smiling contentedly, Jeff closed his eyes and fell asleep.

# Epilogue

Displayed on the wall of awards in the West Bureau Division, a brass and wooden plaque hung with dozens of others. For the month of September, two men's names would forever be engraved together. *Officer Mickey Stanton and Officer Jeff Chandler, Officers of the Month.*

Sneaking a touch of Jeff's hand as they passed it, Mickey smiled at the badge of honor. And in a small, carved rosewood box in their home were two solid gold wedding bands, overlapping.

*The End*